R0202253498

06/2021

D0929648

DISCARD

An
UNOFFICIAL
MARRIAGE

An
UNOFFICIAL
MARRIAGE

A Novel about
Pauline Viardot and
Ivan Turgenev

JOIE DAVIDOW

Arcade Publishing · New York

Arcade Publishing books may be purchased in bulk at special discounts for sales promotion, corporate gifts, fund-raising, or educational purposes. Special editions can also be created to specifications. For details, contact the Special Sales Department, Arcade Publishing, 307 West 36th Street, 11th Floor, New York, NY 10018 or arcade@skyhorsepublishing.com.

Arcade Publishing® is a registered trademark of Skyhorse Publishing, Inc.®, a Delaware corporation.

Visit our website at www.arcadepub.com.

10 9 8 7 6 5 4 3 2 1

Library of Congress Cataloging-in-Publication Data is available on file.

ISBN: 978-1-950691-78-4
Ebook ISBN: 978-1-950691-82-1

Printed in the United States of America

AUTHOR'S NOTE

Edmond de Goncourt wrote, "History is a novel that happened. A novel is history that might have happened." Certainly, that can be said of this novel, based though it is on history. I have, in some cases, condensed events to improve the pace of the story. The dates, places, people, and letters quoted are real where they are known but I have invented a great deal that is unknown. Throughout this book, I have borrowed from Ivan Turgenev, George Sand, Frédéric Chopin, Pauline Viardot-Garcia, and Louis Viardot, sometimes putting their written words into their mouths.

PART ONE

ON THE EVE

Only hear the word love! What an intense, glowing sound it has!

Saint Petersburg, 1843

WINTER FALLS ON SAINT PETERSBURG LIKE a white curtain. One day an ice floe appears on the Neva. The waters roil and a mist arises, hovering over the city. The next morning the river is firmly frozen, with ice so thick the wooden bridges are removed, and carriages roll across wherever they like. Overnight, the colors all disappear, obliterated by the winter snows, leaving only the wind moaning at the edges of the windows.

Everywhere, there is snow. It covers the houses, the streets. The ice on the frozen canals is blanketed in powdery white. Day and night snow falls, while the wind, wailing down the wide boulevards, sweeps it into hills and valleys. In early November, Saint Petersburg is cold, harsh, and glorious.

But in the uppermost gallery of the Imperial Theatre, high above the stage, the heat rising from thousands of enraptured bodies renders the air stifling. Here, where the environs are unsuitable for ladies, only men are permitted. They roost in narrow rows, mercilessly squeezed onto hard wooden benches, delighted to be there. They understand not a word being sung, and have only the vaguest notion of what sort of entertainment an opera is meant to be, but every perch is enthusiastically occupied.

Ivan Sergeyevich Turgenev, unaccustomed to such claustrophobic conditions, is much too expensively dressed for such a cheap seat. His long legs are bent at an excruciating angle, knees to chest, and he hunches his broad shoulders to avoid the men on either side of him. When he arrived, he found the situation so untenable, he thought of escaping at the first interval. But then she appeared onstage, a tiny figure so far below him that through his opera glasses, she appears both real and imaginary.

Her voice though, her voice is so close beside him, she might be singing softly into his ears, a voice so beautiful, he wants to die listening to it. The sound that pours so smoothly into his ears flows down through his body, reverberating in his chest and belly, pulsating between his legs. And he stays, although he is unable even to adjust his feet without treading on his neighbor.

At the final curtain, he scans row upon row of red and gold boxes, watching the aristocrats, the intelligentsia, the merchants, even the wealthy Jews of Saint Petersburg; the audience is in a frenzy. Women dressed in white gowns and covered in gems frantically tap gloved hands against folded fans, and men in a splendor of uniforms applaud wildly. Young dandies in the stalls throw their top hats into the air, calling "Viardot! Viardot!"

The curtains part, and she steps into the spotlight. Pauline Viardot-Garcia, so small yet so majestic, sinks into a deep curtsy, lifts her head, and crosses her hands over her chest. Through his opera glasses, he can see that her strange, dark face is covered with bewildered tears, and he weeps with her.

Then she is gone, and the enormous chandelier is lit, illuminating the hall.

High above in the gallery, men climb over Ivan's knees, thrust elbows into his back as they push and shove one another toward the interminable stairway that leads down to the street. For three-quarters of an hour, he is unable to move, oblivious to the rough *valenkis* that trample his calfskin boots. He imagines her reclining in a dressing room filled with flowers, a gossamer robe revealing the contours of her body, soft black hair flowing over her shoulders.

Until an old usher leans over him, breath sour with the remnants of cabbage and onions. Ivan Sergeyevich raises damp eyes and hurries off.

* * *

It is his habit to read the newspapers, and the newspapers are filled with Pauline Viardot-Garcia, only twenty-two years old, young heiress to a family of deities, sister of the immortal soprano Maria Malibran, and daughter of the great Spanish tenor and composer Manuel del Populo Garcia, who took his family from Spain to Paris to further his career, dropping the accented "í" in his name at the border. Saint Petersburg has not had a season of Italian opera in twenty years and has gone mad for it. In the salons, he hears no one speak of anything else. Performances are always sold out, which is why even a wealthy young lion like Ivan Sergeyevich has had to settle for the cheapest seat.

In the newspapers, he reads that before every performance, crowds brave the punishing cold to wait for la Garcia to emerge from her apartments at Demidov House. They surround her carriage, climbing onto the driver's bench, clinging to the door handles. The emperor has sent his own guards to protect her.

Ivan Sergeyevich has seen drawings of her gowns, her dressing room—and her husband, a slight man with an impeccable arc of pomaded hair and an insipid moustache. He has read that this husband has a penchant for art and a passion for hunting, and that he is old enough to be his wife's father. And Ivan Sergeyevich suffers at the thought that that man awakens to find the head of a goddess on the pillow beside his.

Ivan is desperate be near her, to speak with her, and he is not altogether without hope. His mother is one of the richest women in Russia, and his late father could trace his noble lineage to the fifteenth century. Ivan Sergeyevich is a spoiled Russian aristocrat like so many others, with German university degrees and spurious ministerial positions or military commissions. But he has written a verse-romance, *Parasha*, which has won the approbation of Vissarion Grigoryevich Belinsky, chief critic of *Notes of the Fatherland,* and has gained him entrance to the most exclusive salons in the city.

* * *

He is riding in a wide sledge, frozen, not with cold—he is covered in layers of fur—but with apprehension. Lips dry and motionless, he says nothing as he watches the city streets glide by. Pedestrians trudge across the snow, bent over against the wind, their cloaks flapping behind them like wings. Sparrows and pigeons pick through frozen horse droppings in the hope of finding undigested kernels of grain. A cloud of smoke rises as a door is opened, then quickly shut.

Ivan Sergeyevich is rarely silent. He hides a deep-seated insecurity in a superfluity of words. He has even been guilty of lying—never at the expense of another person, but merely to improve an anecdote—and sometimes, for the shameful purpose of self-aggrandizement. His friends rarely object to his excesses because he is such an entertaining conversationalist. But this morning he has hardly uttered a sound. His companion, fat little Major Komarov, shifts under a pile of furs. "Are you unwell, my boy? Your brow is damp."

Ivan makes no reply. In a few moments, he will meet her, Pauline Viardot-Garcia.

As the sledge turns into the porte cochere on the Nevsky Prospekt, the driver pulls leather reins, light as strings, bringing two prodigious horses to a stop. Under the critical gaze of the czar's guards, he struggles to maintain his dignity as he leaps from his box and leans into the sledge to unbuckle his passengers from under their fur blankets.

Ivan Sergeyevich emerges and stomps on the hard snow as he shakes his garments into order. The morning sky is still a dull silver. In early November, the pale copper sun makes only a brief daily appearance before resuming its winter hibernation. Ivan looks up, scanning the long rows of windows, wondering which ones are hers.

He is a big man, tall and built like a bear, with a broad chest and shoulders, but his face betrays such a guileless spirit that he might give the impression of a simple, sturdy laborer, if it weren't for the fact that everything about him exudes the softness and the near-effeminacy of Russian nobility.

Louis Viardot is waiting to greet them in the entrance hall. He is not the sort to kiss another man three times like a Russian, or even twice, as is the custom in his native France. Instead, he offers his hand to be shaken in the English manner. Ivan Sergeyevich is so agitated, he fears that his customary charm will fail him, and he won't know what to do or say.

As he follows Viardot and the major down a corridor toward a closed door, the sense of her nearness grows. The major's chatter, the elaborately inlaid wooden floors, the silk-covered walls, the embossed ceiling, all disappear and he is suspended in air, floating.

Viardot knocks, then opens the door without waiting for an answer, astounding Ivan with this husband's sense of entitlement.

And there she is, seated at a table. The prima donna who brought thousands of Russians to their feet at the Imperial Theatre is no more than a slender young woman in a dark woolen gown, her shoulders wrapped in an embroidered shawl. Yet she exudes an aura of restless energy, like a bird alight on a branch, about to take flight.

Major Komarov marches into the room, moving stiffly, weighed down by his overabundance of medals and the rows of large brass buttons that form a curving path over his plump belly. Ivan Sergeyevich, in a blue swallowtail coat and checked trousers, follows timidly behind.

"Ma chère," Louis says, gesturing toward the two men. "You remember Major Komarov." The major bows from the waist and snaps back upright, then rushes to bend his head over Pauline's outstretched hand. "Madame, permettez-moi. I had the pleasure of being in the audience to hear you in the *Barbiere*. I was stunned, Madame. Please allow me to add my humble words of praise to the storm of compliments you have already received."

She nods, smiling, displaying a mouthful of startlingly white teeth. "The warmth and affection I have received from the Russian audiences have been extraordinary." Even when she speaks, she sings.

Louis Viardot says, "And this is the gentleman I mentioned to you yesterday. Ivan Sergeyevich Turgenev has offered to teach you a little of the Russian language."

For an instant, Ivan fails to realize that Viardot is referring to him, and then he panics, fearing that all the words he has rehearsed in his mind will escape him.

"Madame, hearing you sing has been the greatest privilege of my life." His normally mellifluous voice is strangled, high-pitched, like an old woman's. It's an embarrassment that afflicts him in moments of great stress or even moderate mirth. Dear God, he thinks, she'll take me for a eunuch.

Viardot nods at the major. "If you'll excuse us, we'll leave you for a moment. We have plans to discuss. Major Komarov has graciously invited me to visit his hunting lodge on the Finnish border." He ushers Komarov through the door, leaving it open.

And Ivan Turgenev is alone with Pauline Viardot.

She gestures to a chair opposite her own. "*Je vous en prie, Monsieur*, please sit down. It's kind of you to call on us this morning," she sings. "I have so many questions to ask you. I'm hoping you will be willing to help me a little. I very much want to be able to perform something in Russian."

She is even more magnificent than he imagined, at once as natural as a schoolgirl and as noble as a queen. A soft smile never leaves her lips. She tells him that she learned Spanish, French, and Italian at home with her family, where the three languages were spoken interchangeably and often in combination. She knows German and very much enjoys reading Goethe.

She learned English as a small child, when her father performed in London and New York. Now, she hopes Monsieur Turgenev will help her to learn Russian so that she can communicate with her Saint Petersburg audiences directly. She understands that French is the language of their drawing rooms, but surely, Russian must be the language of their souls. *N'est-ce pas?*

She tilts her head to one side, and he is enchanted. She looks at him, her eyes still asking the question, as though his response will be the most interesting thing she will hear that day, and he is so terrified of disappointing her, he is unable to speak.

She is so unlike any other woman he has ever seen that he is unable to force his gaze from her strange face, the face of an exotic, alien being. Her eyes—so large, so black, encased by thick lids that give her an almost amphibian aspect—might be petrifying. But she looks at him so gently, smiles so softly, he feels as though he has been given some special dispensation, as though in her great wisdom, she has not failed to recognize the kindness of his heart, and so has decided to spare him. Her face, though hardly pretty, is so intelligent she is even more enchanting at close proximity than she had been through the barrier of opera glasses. It occurs to him that ugly women who please men must ignite more furious passions than earth's most perfect beauties.

He is still silent, so she reaches across the table to find a piece of music. She says, "*Eh bien*, Mikhail Glinka had the kindness to bring me this aria from his new opera, *Ruslan and Ludmila*. I would like to sing it, but I would need to pronounce the language perfectly, and I am incapable of even reading it. Would you be willing to begin by teaching me your Cyrillic alphabet?"

Her eyes flash in his face like sunlight, and again she smiles softly. He stares at her without moving, without breathing. She asks, "Why are you looking at me like that?"

He goes red. "Forgive me, Madame." He clears his throat, attempting to lower his voice. Their conversation reminds him of a duet between a cello and a piccolo, and he, alas, is the piccolo.

"This . . . this is the first time I have had the honor of being in the presence of a great singer." He is trying to imitate a bassoon. "Shall we begin at once?"

"Oh yes, please!" She claps her hands and the whole world is smiling. Her delight, her enthusiasm are so infectious, so genuine.

Eagerly, she picks up a sketchbook. "I have been studying the alphabet, trying to decipher the letters." She points with the tip of her pencil. "This 'A,' is it like our French letter?"

"Yes, it indicates more or less the same sound."

"More or less will never do. I will need to be precise." She notes the sound of the letter in her sketchbook then, one by one, points to all the letters she recognizes. The "E"? The "O"?

"Yes, they are the same."

"The 'P'?"

"No, that has the sound of a hard French "R."

"Ah, in that case, what is this backward 'R'?" She draws it with her pencil: Я.

"That is pronounced 'ya,' meaning 'I.'" He points to his chest.

"Ya." She points to her own chest, and he imagines small, round breasts beneath the embroidered shawl, the dark bodice. Then, with her pencil, she embellishes the Russian letter, giving it a nose, a chignon, an eye with a heavy black brow. She has made the backward R a caricature of her own profile. She turns the sketchbook toward him, giggling, her head inclined, shoulders rising, covering her mouth with one hand, and it's as though the universe is laughing with her, the stars dancing to the music of her laughter.

He feels he has known her for years, and yet has known nothing, never lived until he saw her. He would gladly kiss every crease and seam in her dress, would kneel before the embroidered slippers that peep out under her hem. He could spend the rest of his life in this room, never leave this place.

Within an hour, she has placed all the letters of the Cyrillic alphabet in a neat grid on a page of her sketchbook with their sounds annotated. She consults her agenda, suggesting times for future lessons. He will see her again tomorrow.

But happiness has no tomorrow. It has no yesterday. It neither remembers the past nor thinks of the future. It has only the present—not an entire day, but an instant. And for an instant, Ivan Sergeyevich is ecstatic. He knows that he will see her again, and again. He will sit, as he is sitting now, near her, gazing at her, but what he does not know is that he will never again feel as he does in this instant, when all his sensations are so new and so sweet. He shivers inwardly, thinking that this is it, that he is in love.

Back in the sledge, he is motionless, afraid that if he moves, he will spill the feelings that fill him to the brim—sadness and joy, the desire and dread of life.

The major leans toward him. "How did you find Madame Viardot? Is she not remarkably ugly?"

In a squeaky voice, Ivan replies, "She has been called ugly, but how are we to define beauty? By the regularity of facial features alone, or by the grace of gesture, the subtle choice of dress, the gently modulated speaking voice, the brightness of dark eyes that seem always to be intrigued, like the eyes of a curious little animal? There is a frankness and good nature in her manner, a modesty. She is poetry. She is music. I bow down before her."

* * *

He thinks of her constantly. Only through the greatest effort is he able to think of anything else. He is sure that he is going mad, that falling in love with this woman will end all hope of finding happiness, and he tells himself that there is nothing he can do to prevent it.

When he awakes in the morning, his first thought is of Pauline. If it is the morning of a day when he knows he will see her, his whole being fills with happiness. His toilette, his hair, his clothing are always impeccable, but on those mornings, he torments his valet, checking again and again to be sure that no errant crumb, no stray hair has been overlooked.

His wealthy mother controls him with a grudging allowance she withholds whenever he displeases her. But he always manages to bring some small surprise along to his meetings with Pauline. He cannot afford to give her gifts of jewelry or even flowers, but he brings her a book, a copy of a Russian song, a poem.

His friends know him as a man who is always late, notorious for completely forgetting dinner engagements. But he is punctual for his lessons with Pauline. So eager is he to be near her, he leaves his rooms early, growing light-headed as he draws closer and closer to her, stopping the droshky before he arrives at her hotel, then stomping nervously up and down Nevsky Prospekt, too excited to notice the glacial cold, until it's time to approach the czar's guards at the porte cochere.

Often, when he is admitted to the Viardot apartments, Pauline is busy with other visitors, and he waits, nervously chatting with Louis Viardot until he hears the blessed sound of her voice calling his name. Even if he has seen her the day before, at his first sight of her he is astounded that this woman, whom he has thought of every moment, is really standing in front of him.

They speak in French, peppered with Italian and German. They begin to speak a little in Russian. They speak of the tales of Homer, which Pauline adores, of Goethe, of his *Sorrows of Young Werther*, which has touched them both deeply.

When his questions become personal, she tells him that if he wishes to know her, he has only to read George Sand's novel *Consuelo*. She says that having in some small way inspired the protagonist of that book is the greatest thing she has done in the world, and he is astonished at her humility. George Sand, she says, is her dearest friend, her "Ninoune," her mentor.

While he speaks to her of Pushkin, she sketches him, a lock of chestnut hair hanging over his forehead, and he tells her she has captured him perfectly. He sketches her in return, round eyes in an oval face, and she insists that he has flattered her. And then she smiles her wide smile and tells him how much she will look forward to their next lesson, and he knows that he has been dismissed.

* * *

The Imperial Theatre, a shameless imitation of a Greek temple, seems to have been sculpted from the ice and snow that surround it. On either side of the great white marble façade, mountains of wood burn under wrought iron pavilions where coachmen and their horses gather to keep from freezing while they wait for their masters.

Ivan Sergeyevich Turgenev arrives early. Several anterooms prevent the cold from penetrating the theater itself. In the first, a butler takes his sable-lined overcoat and his overshoes. In the second, he is asked for his ticket, but he has no ticket. He cannot afford to buy a respectable seat, and there are no seats available at all, in any case. He mentions the Panayev box, saying that he is expected, that he is a guest. The usher is wary, but it's risky for a lowly doorkeeper to refuse the request of an impeccably dressed aristocrat, and when he feels a five-kopek piece pressed into his hand, he escorts the young gentleman through the third anteroom and unlocks the empty box. Ivan Sergeyevich takes a seat at the front.

Ivan Sergeyevich is a frequent visitor at the Panayev Sunday evening salon, though he finds Avdotya Yakovlevna irritating. She is one of the most beautiful women in Saint Petersburg, her hair the color of champagne, her complexion pale as the inner petals of a camellia. She traded on her looks to marry a man above her station, a wealthy dandy with literary pretensions. Although she has never set foot in a kitchen, she is called a great "cook," so adept is she at organizing charming dinners and receptions. As her parents were actors, she detests the theater but attends every performance, never missing an opportunity to show off her gowns and jewels.

He has counted on the Panayevs arriving late. By the time they enter the box, the second act of *Il Barbiere di Siviglia* is about to begin. Madame Panayeva notes his presence with a nod, maintaining her public smile, then retires to the red velvet divan at the back of the box with her husband.

The curtain rises on the lesson scene, a place in Rossini's score where the singer is expected to interpolate an aria to show off her voice. Ivan Sergeyevich is leaning so far over the edge of the box he is in danger of falling, and his huge back and buttocks are the only view on offer to those seated behind him. But neither problem concerns him. Pauline Viardot is standing downstage. The orchestra plays the opening bars of "Oh, my Ratmir" from Glinka's *Ruslan and Ludmila,* and the audience, recognizing it at once, erupts in cheers. Ivan mouths each word, each perfectly pronounced syllable as she sings it. They have been rehearsing it together for weeks. Her Russian is flawless.

The audience is on its feet. The ladies dab their eyes with their handkerchiefs whether they are tearful or not. Ivan does not drop his opera glasses, even to applaud. He remains firmly focused on Pauline's expression, on her eyes, while, frantic with joy, he expresses the full measure of his enthusiasm with shouts of "brava!"

* * *

In the desolation of a Russian winter, the richest young men in Saint Petersburg have filled Pauline's dressing room with hothouse roses, camellias, violets. Bottles of Veuve Clicquot chill in ice buckets on a sideboard. Elegantly dressed women arrange themselves on green leather sofas. Men, brandishing medaled sashes, hold crystal champagne glasses in kid-gloved hands.

The floor is covered with a rug fashioned from the skin of a bear shot by one of Pauline's admirers. She has had the animal's four paws covered with small golden stools, and assigned each of these cherished seats—one to Colonel Igor Zinoviev, the hunter in question; one to Count Mateusz Wielhorski, a gifted amateur cellist; one to Stepan Gedeonov, the son of the theater's *directeur générale*; and one to Ivan Turgenev, who, at the moment, has absented his assigned stool and joined Louis Viardot beside an immense porcelain stove.

He is nodding in agreement with whatever it is Viardot is saying, but he is too distracted to pay much attention, much too aware of Pauline's precise location as she nears him, then moves away, greeting guests, squeezing hands. He is careful not to let her catch him looking at her too often, but there is nothing else in the world worth seeing. She is wearing a simple, white lace dressing gown, and a single lily adorns her chignon, yet every elaborately coifed and jeweled woman in the room is invisible beside her.

From the corner of an eye, he catches Avdotya Panayeva kissing the prima donna three times on the cheeks, then flipping open her fan and leaning in so close that only the extravagance of her coiffure separates her head from Pauline's. He strains to hear what she is saying. Avdotya Yakovlevna finds it amusing to cause trouble.

Pauline is laughing, glancing at Ivan.

Louis Viardot, who has mistaken his wife's glance as a signal directed at him, nods to Turgenev. "Perhaps it's time I began to graciously show our guests to the door."

Ivan Sergeyevich watches them retrieve their hats and walking sticks, cloaks and gloves, all of them aristocrats, superfluous people who exist for no reason, happy and satisfied with themselves. When they arrive at wherever it is they are going next, they will boast that they have just come from the dressing room of Pauline Viardot.

Stepan Aleksandrovich Gedeonov remains seated, his slender bottom stubbornly perched over the golden paw. The very eligible son of the theater's manager, he arranged this dressing room under the stage for Pauline and furnished it handsomely, makes sure that it is kept warm, and that all Saint Petersburg knows that it is he whom she can thank for it. Ivan has no intention of allowing Stepan to outlast him.

Louis Viardot spreads his arms to encompass the two young men. "You are both joining us for supper, we hope? Pauline? Shall I wait for you to dress?"

"No, I won't keep you. Our other guests will have already arrived at the restaurant. You had better go on ahead with Stepan Aleksandrovich. Ivan Sergeyevich will escort me. Will you send the sledge back for us? I won't be long." She tosses a reassuring smile at Stepan.

When offered a chance at joy, an older man approaches it with trepidation, knowing that it has its consequences. He examines it, turns it over, looks for flaws, asks for guarantees. At twenty-five, Ivan simply seizes it. He is alive in a way he never thought possible. Every sensation is overwhelming, every sound, every smell, the perfume of the flowers that fill the room, the restless shadows that dance against the walls behind the oil lamps.

As the door closes behind Viardot and Gedeonov, Pauline disappears behind a screen with her hearty Alsatian *femme de chambre*. Ivan is desperate to look, to catch a glimpse of a naked arm, a shoulder, but he dares not risk it.

Moments later, she reappears in a green velvet gown, relaxes onto one of the leather sofas, kicks off her slippers, leans back, and folds her legs under her skirts. Her huge black eyes fall on Ivan, landing gently.

"I have heard nothing but compliments. You are the only person I can trust to be truthful. Tell me honestly, how was my Russian pronunciation? Is there still some champagne? I think I can allow myself a sip."

Her eyes have paralyzed him. What was it she said? Champagne. Yes, champagne. And she asked him something else. Her Russian.

"Your pronunciation was perfect, like a true Muscovite!"

His hand shakes as he fills her glass.

She asks, "What's the matter? Your face has gone completely white. You are ill."

"It's just a headache. I . . . suffer from headaches."

"Geneviève! Bring my cologne and a handkerchief. Ivan Sergeyevich, come sit here beside me. Close your eyes."

She dabs his temples. "This always helps me. How do you feel?"

How can he describe to her how he feels? He is being carried on the wings of an angel. She touched him. With her own hands, she cooled his brow.

"Better. I feel better."

"Better? Are you sure? Because I ought to say something you may find a little unpleasant."

Surely, nothing could be unpleasant, not tonight.

"Madame Panayeva is annoyed with you. She told me that you stole into her box, and that during the ovations you screamed so loudly there were complaints."

He giggles with relief. "Avdotya Yakovlevna is absurd."

Pauline inclines her head, laughing, her shoulders rising. She is more beautiful than any woman he has ever seen. They are laughing together, looking at one another. Laughter fills his body, lifts him like a balloon. He is wafting beside her, weightless.

Until she looks away.

"Madame Panayeva told me something else. I will tell you precisely what she said. She said that if my name is mentioned in conversation, you begin to tremble, that you tell everyone that you are in love with me, that you proclaim it in every drawing room to anyone who is willing to listen and even to those who are unwilling. She said it would be difficult to find a man more desperately in love."

Time stops. The lamplight ceases flickering. She knows. But why shouldn't she know? He wants her to know. She asked him to stay behind. She asked him to sit beside her. Her magnificent hands cooled his brow.

"I *am* in love with you. That is the misfortune that has befallen me."

She gets up and crosses the room, stands with her arms folded across her chest. He thinks she looks as though she is covering her heart to protect it.

"Is it true? Are you seriously in love with me?"

"Yes . . . yes. I love you, stupidly, madly." He speaks with the voice of a man who has been diagnosed with a terrible illness and is asking whether the disease will be fatal. His hands are shaking again, not with fear or boyish shyness, but with sweet horror at the realization that he has confessed.

Her voice is a melodious murmur. "You are certain you are not exaggerating? You are absolutely sure?"

"Oh yes. I have no doubt at all."

"Ivan Sergeyevich, I am so sorry. I hope that I am not at fault, although I suppose that I must be. Truly, I could not have known. A married woman, a mother, presumes, perhaps unfairly . . . Our talks have been . . . lovely, truly, but they have been conversations between friends, have they not? Nothing more has passed between us. You must promise that you will never speak of this again. Not to me. Not to anyone."

He has lost her. He is tempted to fall to his knees, to beg.

"Forgive me," he says. "Forgive me."

She calls her *femme de chambre* who has been discreetly lurking behind the screen. "Geneviève, have you gathered my things?"

He looks up to find her smiling a little sadly at him. Smiling! Nothing has changed. He has not been banished.

"Ivan Sergeyevich, come, help me with my cloak. Louis will have sent the sledge back for us."

* * *

The Panayev's rooms have been transformed into a garden. Potted magnolia trees in full bloom greet guests on the land-ings. Windowsills are blanketed in fragrant herbs. Orchids hover like butterflies around crystal lampshades. Tables overflow with blossoms. None of the luxuries of English or French civilization are lacking. Women in thin muslin gowns, creamy shoulders left bare to show off their jewels, are seated around the edge of the room, gossiping behind their fans.

Outside, a frozen splinter of moon does little to relieve the aching blackness of the night sky. The streets are silent and white, white. Wherever the eye travels, it finds only white.

Inside, the rooms are a kaleidoscope of light and color—the myriad greens of leaves, the violet, crimson, and fuchsia of flowers.

Outside, there is silence. Sleighs glide noiselessly over packed snow.

Inside, the rooms are filled with music and the percussive buzz of voices, accented now and then by a woman's fluty laugh.

A long table is laden with elaborate platters of sturgeon, salmon, juniper-scented grouse, lashes of caviar, cherries in liqueur, borscht, pickled vegetables. Waiters in black jackets and white gloves offer champagne or vodka. In the kitchen, a French chef is putting the final touches on supper.

Russia still clings to the Julian calendar, which puts the new year thirteen days behind the Gregorian date. But on the thirty-first of December 1843, Saint Petersburg's upper classes are ready to celebrate a western New Year's Eve. The jewelers at Gostiny Dvor bazaar have been busily cleaning and resetting the stones on dozens of tiaras. Color plates from the latest editions of *Le Bon Ton, Journal des Modes* have been studied and copied, passed from hand to hand, from dressmaker to dressmaker. No Parisian salon is more fashionable than this Saint Petersburg gathering.

Ivan Sergeyevich is dancing. He is a superb dancer, and he loves to dance, but he has never before danced the way he is dancing tonight. Pauline has danced with him four times—a quadrille, a mazurka, a polonaise, and now, a waltz, a breathless, whirling waltz. They are turning, spinning, gliding. Beneath his hand, he feels her slender waist, only slightly restrained with light stays. Her skirts swirl around his legs. Their bodies move together, deliciously, ecstatically. He is laughing, laughing louder and louder as her laughter echoes his. He holds her gloved hand, squeezing it just enough to be reassuring. And every now and then, when he catches her eye, he gives her hand an extra little squeeze, as though sharing a secret.

Everything is in confusion. His nerves are tight as harp strings, his whole being is filled with one sensation, one idea, one desire. She looks up at him, her head thrown back. What a noble face, what wide eyes, bright, a little wild, nostrils open, breathing eagerly.

And the music stops. Supper is announced.

She drops his hand. They stand together without speaking, both of them panting softly. She looks around. "The others have all gone in."

He is about to offer her his arm. But she reaches up, takes his face in two gloved hands, and kisses his mouth. He is almost too shocked to feel her lips against his and has to convince himself that this is really happening, that she is kissing him.

"There," she says. "Now everything is as it should be!" And she hurries off in search of her husband.

Even at the young age of twenty-five, Ivan is sophisticated enough to know that there are infinite gradations between the status of a woman's friend and that of her lover, and a man is seldom simply one or the other. Pauline has offered him her friendship. Her playful kiss, he knows, was not a promise of love, but he is flying on the hope that it was a hint love might be possible.

That she spends the rest of the evening at her husband's side, returning steadfastly to a man she never left, does not dash his hopes or even discourage him. He can be patient. He knows he will love her for the rest of his life.

After supper, as the guests mingle in the salon where pastries and chocolates have replaced coulibiac and caviar, Avdotya Panayeva accosts him as though he owes her something, trapping him in conversation while following his eyes across the room to Pauline.

"Do you think you are a shallow man, Ivan Sergeyevich?" she

teases. "You are very amusing, but you must know that you are accused of being shallow. Your friend, Vissarion Belinsky, defends you. I have heard him say that 'Turgenev wrote *Parasha* and shallow people do not write that sort of thing.'"

"I assure you, Madame, from the depths of my heart, that I am the shallowest of men, but I know how to love good people."

* * *

The artist draws back the curtains and places a chair beside the window. The languid December sun, he says, will complement Madame Viardot's features.

Prince Volkonski, director of the Imperial Theatres, has demanded a portrait of his prima donna, but no such portrait is painted in Russia without written authorization from the czar himself. Pyotr Fyodorovich Sokolov was the only possible choice. He is the court favorite, commissioned to portray the czarina, the princes, and princesses, the grand dukes and duchesses of the Romanov family.

Pauline had seen enough of Sokolov's work to realize that he became fashionable by brazenly flattering his subjects. Even so, most of them optimize their appearances with elaborate hats, intricate coiffeurs, fur pieces, important jewelry.

She will have none of that. She is wearing a plain day dress with a lace collar, her hair sleeked back in her usual chignon.

Seated on a straight-backed chair, her hands folded in her lap, she faces Sokolov squarely without smiling, watching him assess her with his artist's eyes. The expression on his face tells her that he objects to her lack of ostentation. He, himself, is expensively dressed, although he keeps his beard unshaped and his hair long to reassure his aristocratic clients of his creativity.

As a cloud slides slowly across the sun, Sokolov moves around the room, lighting lamps, repositioning them. He circles Pauline, searching for the most attractive angle.

"If you would be so kind as to turn your heard toward me."

She has already begun to feel bored. "You will not object if my pianist accompanies your work?"

To sit still doing nothing all afternoon would drive her mad, so she has arranged to review her next role. The rehearsal pianist the theater management has sent her is a myopic conservatory student whose thick spectacles torment him by sliding down his long greasy nose. He pushes them back up with one finger, bends his head close to the music, then attacks the keys as though he is afraid they might attack him first.

Pauline continues to stare at Sokolov but she is with Mozart now, with Zerlina, a country girl, swept away by the advances of the handsome nobleman Don Giovanni. *Là ci darem la mano, e mi direi di si.* Give me your hand and say "yes." Perhaps she should turn to Don Giovanni and then turn away as she sings her reply. *Vorrei e non vorrei. I would like to and I wouldn't . . .* No, Zerlina is no silly flirt. She is a child of the South, like Pauline herself, a young Spanish woman, born with an ardent nature. Don Giovanni must fascinate her, the way a serpent fascinates a bird. She should be bold, spirited, yet too weak to resist him. Yes. No. She would like to, but she had better not. Tempted, not tempted. Turgenev, not Turgenev.

Turgenev! His face, helpless but unashamed, his eyes, soft and affectionate. Many admirers stare at her. But Turgenev isn't curiously gazing at a prima donna. He sees a woman. When he looks at her, she sometimes feels she is in danger. God knows where that would lead. Peace of mind is the best thing in the world.

Vieni mio bel diletto! Don Giovanni sings. Come my beautiful darling. Then Zerlina's reply. *Mi fa pietà Masetto.* But I pity my husband. *Presto, non son più forte.* Soon I won't be strong enough to resist. *Non son più forte, non son più forte.* Not strong enough, not strong enough.

Sokolov steps back for a long look at his subject. "Your face has taken on a lovely softness, Madame, something liquid in your eyes. Perhaps the reflection of a pleasant thought? I will try to capture it."

Pauline pinches the back of her hand hard.

"One moment! Forgive me, Monsieur Sokolov." She turns to the pianist. "Please move on to the second act. The duet with the husband, with Masetto."

March 1844

L ENT HAS BEGUN, AND THE OPERA season has ended. With
the noise of rehearsals, performances, and receptions stilled,
Pauline is becoming restless. In the silence, she has begun to
think of those closest to her. Her two-year-old daughter Louisette
has been billeted for months at Nohant in the south of France,
watched over by George Sand and Frédéric Chopin, aided by a
nurse and a nanny. George sends cheerful reports on Louisette's
progress, each paragraph a knife thrust into Pauline's belly. The
child is walking, now; the child is losing her baby teeth; the child
chatters like a chaffinch.

Alone at a table by the window in her study at Demidov House
where she has so often met with Turgenev, she is trying to draw
her little daughter's portrait from memory, and it is not going
well. Already this morning she has completed pencil portraits of
her beloved *ninoune* George Sand (with braids wound round her
ears, not sparing her double chin), her dear Chip-Chip, Frédéric
Chopin (only slightly exaggerating his long nose), her older
brother Manuel, a singing teacher at the Conservatoire de Paris
(elegant, with a fine mustache), and her sweet mother, Joaquina
Garcia-Sitchès (matronly, in a demure lace cap). She hopes that
by drawing them, she will manage to bring them closer to her,
and she has given them all mouths that smile at her, eyes that
gaze at her affectionately. She plans to have the portraits copied
and sent to France, more convincing versions of those perfunc-
tory little notes designed to assure loved ones they haven't been
forgotten.

Louisette's portrait is proving to be difficult. What must she look like now? Pauline hasn't seen her daughter in months, and children of that age change almost daily. Is it possible she would no longer recognize her own child? She sketches a round baby face, a halo of curls, pauses, lost, her pencil hovering over the paper. Outside her window, the snow shivers in the wind as it falls, and she pulls her shawl closer around her throat.

* * *

Spring comes slowly to Russia. In early March, there is not the slightest sign that it will ever arrive. But at noon, there is no wind, and the sun, feigning warmth, has tricked Pauline and Ivan into leaving the sledge and walking part of the way back along the Nevsky Prospekt to Demidov House. Ivan Sergeyevich had been lying when he told her that he knew an excellent lithographer who could copy her drawings, but this morning when he appeared to fetch her, the address of the best printer in Saint Petersburg was in his pocket. He has found yet another reason to be with her, to be useful to her, to serve as her guide and interpreter, to be important in her eyes.

In a few days, the Viardots will begin the long journey to Vienna where Pauline has been engaged, traveling overland while the dirt roads are still packed hard with frozen snow, but at the moment, Ivan Sergeyevich is thinking only of Pauline's hand, resting on his arm. Beneath the bulk of warm clothing, he feels her body brushing his. He is trying to memorize the color of the sky, a blue that threatens to turn gray; the color of her cheeks, flushed from the cold; the smell of her cloak, of wool, of fur and lavender, and he is struggling to lock those precious details into a gilded chest from which they can never escape.

The broad avenue opens onto an immense square as they approach the monumental Kazan Cathedral. Ivan has prepared a little speech. The words are trembling on his lips, desperate to escape, and he finds it so painful to hold them in that his mouth forms an agonized grimace, until he becomes powerless to stop them and they tumble out in a great rush.

"You will be leaving soon." His voice is squeaking. *Why must it always squeak at the moments when he needs to sound the most serious, the most masculine?* He pauses, clears his throat. Now that he has begun, he must find the courage to continue. "Forgive me for asking this, but allow me to open my heart to you once more. When I told you that . . . I told you that I loved you . . ." He hadn't meant to beg. *Oh, he sounds so pathetic.*

Pauline steps away from him, distancing herself. He would like to snatch that word "love" back. Perhaps he should have said, "care" or "affection" or even "esteem," but those words would have been false. He had to say "love," and having said it, he has no choice but to continue, to try to reel her back to him. He goes on talking like a fool. *Dear God, he feels the fool.*

"You asked me to promise never to say those words again and . . ." *What's happened to his breath?* He can't finish the sentence and has to stop, to breathe in and out before he can go on. "and I have not said them. But I have felt them. I will never stop feeling them." *Why, why, did he say that?* "Perhaps I had no right to speak."

Pauline has lowered her head, so that all he can see is the top of her bonnet. If only she would look at him, he could see what she is hiding. He could read her face.

She begins to ask questions to which he has already told her the answers. What will he do in Petersburg for the remainder of the season? Where will he spend the summer? He may never see her again, yet in these last moments, she chatters.

He has braced himself for scolding, even anger and rejection, but he never imagined that she might reply to a second declaration of his love by merely changing the subject. She has smiled at him, laughed with him; her eyes have held his. She impulsively kissed him. And he . . . *What had his foolish imagination, his blind hope allowed him to suppose?*

He answers her questions simply, politely, but he goes on trying to see her face, bending his head down, turning it this way and that, peeking under the brim of her bonnet. *Let there be a smile for me lurking there, something to relieve this torture. Let her turn to me, oh please.*

Having exhausted her supply of questions, she looks up, but not at him. She looks off into the distance, speaking in that full ringing voice of hers, so resonant he could swear the sledge horses waiting in the square have lifted their heads and pricked up their ears.

"You speak of love. But I am a married woman."

Yes, he knows that. She is married to a fine fellow. Louis Viardot has treated him with nothing but kindness.

Ivan has dared to say "Your wife is the greatest singer, no, she is the *only* singer in the world." Or "Your wife is the most extraordinary woman I have ever known," always referring to the woman he loves as "your wife." If Viardot suspects his feelings for Pauline, he would never be so indelicate as to mention it.

She is shaking her head now, as though trying to shake her thoughts back into place. "I am even more married to music. I must go wherever I am engaged. I came to Russia because I had so little chance elsewhere. The thrones of the opera houses of Europe are all very firmly occupied. I have rivals everywhere. My contract in Paris was not renewed because Giulia Grisi, who is no more than a stupid goose with a beautiful voice, hired claques to cheer for her and to jeer at me. She bribes the critics with lavish gifts, and my notices, which were glowing when I made my début, turned disastrous. Even when I return to Vienna, where I had such success last season, I will have a rival in Eugenia Tadolini."

She is not looking at him. Her face is lifted toward the sky, toward the sun. "But I'd go mad if I could not sing. I understand music in some deeply instinctive way. I can snatch the notes from the page and send them spinning into the souls of those who hear me. I need the opera stage. In creating a role, I give birth to another human being, almost as surely as I birthed my little daughter Louisette."

He watches her walking slowly away from him along the cathedral colonnades. Hands thrust into her sable muff, she moves with the haughty grace of a queen. Her head, held high, appears to float weightlessly on her long neck.

He calls after her. "You must surely know that you are the greatest singer in the world."

She continues walking, speaking without turning to him. "I may be the greatest singer in Russia this season, but I know very well what I would have to do to please the audiences in Paris, to win their applause and their support. It would mean flattering their bad taste. I would have to sing bad music prettily, and I detest prettiness in art. I prefer that they should come to me."

And then she stops. He has caught up to her now. "Each time I open my mouth to sing in public, I risk everything. No matter how loud the applause, no matter how prolonged the ovations, no matter how enthusiastic the reviews, my success is only temporary. It takes all my energy, all my concentration to survive each performance. An artist who truly cares about her art had better not care very much for anything else."

She turns to look at him, and he is sure he sees it. She was able to hide it in her voice, but he finds it in her eyes. She touches his arm, and he feels as if she is embracing him, pulling him close to her with a gloved hand resting on the sleeve of his heavy coat.

He tries to imagine that this moment will last forever, that he will always be at her side, watching her face, her body close to his.

They are approaching Demidov House, where he will say goodbye to her. He assures himself that he will see her again. It's unthinkable that these moments will be the last he will ever spend with her. But time will drag. At first, he will savor the ephemeral joy of his memories. Later, when he begins to feel the enormity of the distance between them, the longing will become excruciating.

At last, when he knows the day, the hour of their next meeting, he will begin counting the interminable minutes.

"I may write to you?"

"You will not write anything my husband may not read?"

"I will swear to be discreet if you will promise to read the words I am not permitted to put on paper."

"Jean." She has never before called him "Jean." He has been Monsieur Turgenev, then Ivan Sergeyevich, never Jean. "I am not free to love."

His eyes close in rapture and a kind of dread that he will be unable to bear such bliss. That he can never ask her to leave her husband, that she will leave Russia, that he will suffer the cold alone—all the thoughts that will torment him when she's gone—are far from him now. She said that she was not free to love him, but all he heard was the single word, "love."

In the entrance hall of Demidov House, she places a gloved hand on the polished brass railing of the grand staircase, a foot on the carpeted bottom step, and then she turns. "Give my regards to the good Major Komarov, and to our dear friend Madame Panayeva." Then she bends her knees in a deep curtsy and looks over her shoulder, laughing.

And she hurries up the steps. At the landing she leans over the railing. He is still there, looking up at her.

She calls down. "Write to us. Love us always."

Us.

Hotel König von Ungarn, Vienna, April 1844

I T'S AS THOUGH SHE'S FALLEN INTO something dark, and emerged to find herself covered in a gray film of sorrow and guilt. She needs to float in the misty channel between sleeping and waking until she can find its source. *Maria.* She dreamed of her sister again.

Pauline opens her eyes. Sunlight has crept under the hem of the closed curtains like a message slipped discreetly under the door. It must be morning. It must be late. She wants to cling to the darkness. She rolls away, pulls the eiderdown up over her head. Oh, Maria, the greatest soprano in the world. Maria had the genius to die when she was only twenty-eight years old, before her halo had lost a single ray. She has been gone now, how long? Pauline counts back through the years. Eight. Gone eight years, and still her sister haunts her.

And if she had lived? Pauline would have been a great pianist, as great as her friend Clara Schumann. No, greater. Clara herself says so. Even Maître Liszt said as much. Liszt, her teacher, a man so beautiful that even now she trembles beneath the soft Viennese sheets at the thought of him. He told Maman he would launch a career for her. And Maman? Maman said, "You can close the piano now, Pauline. You have your father's voice, your sister's voice, my voice. You were born to sing." Pauline wept. She wept, but she became a singer.

She was fifteen years old that year. Her voice had begun to reach its maturity, but it was no more than a wild animal, a roaring, untamed force trapped in her skinny little body. Every day, her mother trained her, building muscles to control the breath.

29

She permitted her to sing nothing but scales and intervals, scales and intervals, while with all her heart, she longed for Schubert piano sonatas.

What had been difficult became easy. A leap of an octave was no longer a strain. Pauline sang two five-note scales in one breath, then five, six, seven. Within six months she could sing ten. Within a year, she was strong enough to set the voice free, and it became her slave.

She faced her first audience eclipsed by her sister's enormous shadow, terrified that Maria's voice would float out of her mouth the moment she opened it. And it did. It was as though Maria Malibran had flown back from the dead and nested in her little sister's throat. Women fainted when they heard her.

Now if the public arrives at the theater curious to hear the sister of Maria Malibran, they leave crying, "Viardot! Viardot!" It's time Maria's ghost left her in peace.

Last night at the Royal Court Theatre, the Viennese called her back twelve times after the final curtain of *Roberto il Diavolo*. In Saint Petersburg, after *Il Barbiere*, they called her back sixteen times. How many times did they call Maria back when she sang the role at the Teatro Valle in Rome? No more than that, surely.

Pauline settles onto a mound of goose-down pillows. She looks about the hotel bedroom. How the Austrians love to adorn things! Every inch tufted, tasseled, gilded and carved. Cherubs perch on the headboard and footboard of the bed. The mantel is crowded with porcelain figurines, miniature paintings in elaborate gilt frames, an ornate enameled clock.

Louis has gone back to France ahead of her. She is alone, without enough work to fill her days, without enough performances, enough music. Few acquaintances, fewer friends. If only Ivan Sergeyevich were here to shake her out of this tedious gloom! He is no more than a memory suspended in the glistening ice of the Neva, but he knew how to make her laugh.

Perhaps it had been unfair of her to kiss him. Perhaps she'd been so deafened by applause, she'd begun to think that there was nothing she couldn't do, that anything she wanted was hers.

A letter had been waiting when they arrived at the hotel in Vienna. "From Turgenev!" Louis said, in his oh-how-delightful tone of voice. She held the envelope for a moment before opening it, examining Ivan's familiar penmanship as though she might get a glimpse of his face in the long, slanted strokes.

He wrote that he'd tried to visit "our dear little room," but that somebody else was living there. He apologized for burdening her with his words. *Why was he always apologizing?* "I'm sorry to be telling you this," he wrote. "We unfortunate victims of starvation must feed on our memories."

Louis insisted on answering the letter himself for both of them. He wrote pages and pages in reply to Ivan's meager paragraphs, pages of hunting deer and wild boar, pages of *cher ami*, ending at last with *a vous de coeur.*

Pauline stood behind the chair, her arms around her husband's neck, leaning over to read what Ivan had written. Shouldn't she add a few little lines of her own, she asked, a *petit bonjour* before sealing it? Perhaps she'd been reckless; at the very least, she'd been naughty. She wrote that hearing of his memories gave her the greatest pleasure, that she was eager to see him again. She signed it in the language of Goethe, *eine wahren Freundin*, a true friend.

She is well aware that her marriage to Louis Viardot is irrevocable. He is twenty years too old for her, but she likes him very much, and he adores her. What would she do without Loulou to make all her arrangements, negotiate her contracts? Why in the world would she long for the company of a handsome Russian who has never done anything important? Whatever is the matter with that young man, behaving as though she were the one great love of his life?

She tells herself it must be nearly midday. *Get out of bed! Walk about in the bright optimism of the Viennese spring. Take Geneviève with you to the Prater gardens.*

She rings the little bell on the table beside her bed, and Geneviève is there in a moment, brusque as a nurse, trailing starched apron strings. She pulls back the heavy damask drapes with strong, round arms, and the sun dashes in as though it has been waiting all morning for permission to enter the room.

Château de Nohant, La Chârtre, May 1844

THE LITTLE GIRL IS LEARNING TO talk now, although she still pees wherever she likes. Louisette Viardot runs around Nohant, chasing George Sand's poodle, Pistolet, to whom she speaks in a made-up language that George identifies as Sanskrit. The child has another language for Chopin, whom she calls "*petit Chopin.*" George identifies this language as Polish, although it's more in the order of a French baby-talk imitation of Chopin's accent.

They are taking their afternoon meal at the round table in George's small salon, and Chopin, who is more in love with Louisette than anyone, has caught her and pulled her onto his lap. "Have you very many teeth?" he asks.

She makes a sad face. "Only four!"

"Four!" He kisses her hands. "Let me see!"

Louisette leans across the table to steal a chop from the platter, then resumes running around the room, pursued by Pistolet, who believes that the chop rightly belongs to him.

George is going through her mail, absently tearing a piece of bread into bits.

"A letter from Pauline in Vienna! Shall I read it to you?" She unfolds the pages, leaning both elbows on the table.

"*Dearest Ninoune,*

You have probably heard that my success here in Vienna has been colossal. I can be so bold as to say so, because everyone says it.

33

*The newspapers report it and the public demonstrate it. You can
imagine how happy I am to sing for such an audience . . ."*

George falls silent, scanning the page. "Ah, here is the real news.
Louis is in France and longs to see his daughter.

*"'I envy Loulou his happiness because he will see you before I do.
I have charged him to kiss you and embrace you for me. He will
have some news, which I hope will give you pleasure. I beg you
to write me, to comfort me here in my widowhood. My favorite
occupation is thinking of you and reading your letters. And I have
plenty of time to do that, because I am not singing often and I
have no new roles to learn. A thousand caresses from your most
passionately devoted poodle. (And in that capacity, I send my
regards to Pistolet.)'"*

"We are to tell the little angel that Mamita will be here soon."
    George looks around for Louisette. "Who is as sweet as a lamb?"
    "*Moi!*" A squeal from beneath the table.
    "And where is your Maman?"
    The little girl crawls out on all fours, stands up and points
to George. "*La voilà!*" She is laughing, scrambling back under
the table, where Pistolet is eating more than his share of the
mutton chop.
    George's mouth forms an O. "How can we bear to return her to
Pauline and Louis? I will tell them their little one is not here, that
she has gone off on a pleasure trip to the Marquesas Islands or that
a young swain has abducted her. Loulou will be jealous when he
sees how the child has become attached to us. But then, Louisette
will realize that he is her father, Chip-Chip, and it will be our turn
to be jealous."

Château Courtavenel,
près Vaudoy-en-Brie, France, June 1844

In the flaming light of summer, the barouche rolls along the Fontenay-Vaudoy road. Its passengers, two middle-aged men in shirtsleeves, are using their straw hats to fan the sweat from the faces.

Louis Viardot chews his upper lip as though he is attempting to swallow his moustache. He is not accustomed to being without his wife, and he worries that she is not getting on well alone in Vienna, but he is much more afraid that the château will disappoint her. On the basis of drawings sent to them in Saint Petersburg, Pauline's mother bought it on her behalf at auction. For this first viewing, Louis has brought along the painter Ary Scheffer. If the château is a disaster, he will need his friend's support, and if it is wonderful, he will need to show it off.

At forty-seven, Scheffer's clear, Dutch-blue eyes are already half-hidden by drooping lids, and his modest little beard fails to disguise his sagging chin. He has the soft-spoken manner of a man without a trace of malice in his character, and the wisdom of a man who has seen and suffered a great deal.

As the barouche rolls through the open country toward a horizon so unobstructed, it's easy to imagine that the earth ends there, Scheffer is fixated on the deep blue of the midday sky, the wide ribbons of poppies that border the fields, the wheat's feathery brushstrokes. He feels his friend's anxiety but knows better than to acknowledge it. Instead, he attempts to distract him.

"How do you explain this landscape," he asks, "the harmony of color, the balance, the symmetry? We mortals strive in vain to imitate God's genius, excusing our sorry efforts by calling them 'art.'"

Scheffer is a fervent Lutheran with a god who is always available to be thanked or blamed, and he pities Louis Viardot's obstinate atheism. As young men, they had both gravitated to the circle that had formed around Général de Lafayette, where they met George Sand and Maria Malibran. Their long friendship has been anchored in a commonality of political opinion, unshakable trust, and the tolerance both men consider a fundamental measure of good character.

"No, Ary," Louis says, "art is more than an inadequate imitation of nature. It raises us above our human baseness, our innate cruelty and amorality. It is the antidote to war, misery, and injustice. And artists, who are born with the godlike ability to create, are beings of a higher order."

"Is art so powerful, Viardot? You worship artists as I worship God. You worship your wife."

Viardot strokes his moustache, unsure how to respond. "I astonished myself by falling in love with her." he says. "Do you remember?"

"You astonished everyone. Nothing in your carefully controlled life led me to believe you were capable of such a chaos of emotions."

"My feelings for her were perfectly rational. She had the genius of an artist, and conversed easily on many subjects. I only worried that she was neither old enough nor sufficiently disillusioned to accept such a rational match."

And so he enlisted the help of George Sand, who worships Pauline almost as much as he does. She thought the girl needed a protector, a man capable of negotiating her contracts, making her arrangements. Louis Viardot seemed suitable enough. He was an old bachelor without hope of marrying, as he was burdened with the care of two spinster sisters. And he held the improbable position of *directeur général* of the Théâtre-Italien, a responsibility he undertook without the slightest idea how an opera house should be managed.

To sell tickets, he engaged an eighteen-year old girl who had made an impressive début at Her Majesty's Theatre in London, wagering that the Parisians, still mourning the death of the divine Maria Malibran, would flock to hear her younger sister. And he took the enormous risk of casting her in the opening performance of the season—Rossini's *Otello*—knowing full well that Desdemona had been Maria Malibran's signature role.

The girl was a sensation. Reports of her success appeared in every newspaper and Viardot congratulated himself on his own brilliance. The *Revue de Paris* crowed that the hopes of all lovers of art rested on Mademoiselle Garcia. In the *Revue de deux Mondes*, George Sand wrote that this new Garcia was superior to all the young singers in France for the beauty of her voice and the perfection of her singing, that she entered into the spirit of the composers, that she was alone with them in her thoughts. The poet Alfred de Musset wrote that she sang as she breathed, that she felt what she expressed, that it was not her voice she listened to, but her heart.

On the Vaudoy-Fountenoy road, Louis sees the small wooden sign that marks the turnoff for Courtavenel, and calls to the driver, who guides the horses into a shadow-dappled lane lined with ancient acacias.

* * *

"You know, Ary," he says quietly, "I had no illusion that Pauline returned my feelings, even after the wedding. I hoped that if I were unfailingly kind, she might learn to love me, at least a little. But since her huge successes in Saint Petersburg and Vienna, she has been surrounded by young admirers. I will spend the rest of my life fighting to keep her. The château must be her refuge, a home she will never be persuaded to leave."

A breeze ruffles the leaves in the acacia trees, disturbing the birds who have been napping in the heat. They pass merino sheep grazing on a little rise, willow-lined canals, stables, a poultry yard, a glass-roofed orangery, and Louis thinks the place will please his wife.

"This is all ours," he says, standing up in the carriage for a better look, steadying himself with a hand against the back of the driver's seat. "We have thirty-nine hectares."

As the carriage approaches the château from the south, they pass a lawn edged with rosebushes badly in need of pruning, circle a stagnant, slime-filled moat from which a constellation of insects arises, but he is not discouraged. When they pull up at the wooden drawbridge, he leaps out of the carriage and dashes across it, trailed by his friend.

Pauline's mother, who has been overseeing the repairs, appears in the shadows of the entrance, leading a little parade—two-year-old Louisette, her nanny Jeannette, Louis's hunting dog Sultan.

The spaniel reaches him first, leaping, ears flying. Then little Louisette tugs on his trousers, and he scoops her up. "Kiss your papa," he says.

Workmen are swarming over the slate roof. Around the edge of the moat, farmers swing scythes, cutting down weedy rushes. *His* slate roof, *his* weedy moat. He feels himself transformed into a country gentleman, taller, stronger, cleverer than he has ever been. It's almost too wonderful.

He kisses the air above his mother-in-law's hand. She retrieves it before Ary Scheffer can take his turn at this nonsense, and kisses both men on both cheeks, mouth to flesh.

"Come, let me show you what you have purchased," she says. "Come, Ary."

The entry hall is dominated on one side by a staircase. On the other, a wide archway opens onto a grand salon, two stories high, with a monumental gray marble fireplace. Louis traces the perimeter of the room, while the dog dances circles ahead of him, and little Louisette scurries behind him, eluding the outstretched arms of the nanny.

Ary stands quite still, looking up at the balcony that encircles the space, at the tall windows that frame a view of the park, dense with maple and chestnut trees. "Marvelous," he murmurs. "Marvelous."

Viardot grins ecstatically.

Maman says she worries that the house is hardly habitable, that the builder's estimate is much higher than she expected. ". . . and then there's the matter of the gardens, and the furnishings, which cannot be purchased until Pauline returns from Vienna to make her own selections. You will need draperies, rugs, beds . . ."

Louis is listening, but he won't allow her to dampen his joy. He is thinking of how much Pauline will adore the château, how delighted with him she will be, how she will laugh and embrace him when she sees it.

By the time the repairs are completed and the furnishings bought, he reckons they will have spent almost every last *sou* his wife has managed to earn in her entire career. But she will be a *châtelaine* with a refuge where she can regain the part of herself she gives to her audiences. And he will have his own forests, where he can hunt as much as he likes.

"We will have the place in order by August," he says.

His mother-in-law crosses her arms. "You are an optimist, Viardot."

They inspect the cloakrooms and waiting room, the dining room, the breakfast room, the summer room, the kitchens, storage rooms, staff quarters, and scullery. On the floor above, they wander down a long hall, lined on both sides with doors. Louis chooses a room for his billiard table, assigns rooms to his daughter, his sisters, to his mother-in-law, to aunts and uncles, to the inevitable guests.

Winding staircases lead to twin turrets, the château towers. The two men climb the steps to a circular room where spiders scurry over stone walls undisturbed, weaving lacy curtains. Louis struggles to open a dust-grayed window, leans out over the flat fields of Brie, over an old cart track flanked by gnarled apple trees.

"This will be Pauline's sanctuary, a place to be alone, to create, to avoid her tedious old husband."

Ary, joining him at the window, scratches an eyebrow. "How you love her!"

Louis nods. He imagines Pauline standing where he is standing, marveling at the view, at the boundless expanse of sky.

"She tries so hard to love me. I believe she truly wants to love me. I have that. I never expected more."

37 Ulitsa Ostozhenka, Moscow, January 1845

Varvara Petrovna Turgeneva considers herself a monarch. Her vast estates encompass twenty villages and six thousand serfs. In a country where fortunes are measured not in money, but in the number of souls one owns, she is indecently rich.

At her manor house in Spasskoye, she sits on a throne, ringing bells and giving orders. She calls her chief housekeeper her "chamberlain," and her personal maid, Agata, is her "lady-in-waiting." She never permits her maids to have children. If one of them inconveniently gives birth, she sends the baby away to be cared for in a distant village. Her butler, who has been given the title "Minister of the Court," is charged with announcing anyone who approaches her—including her son, Ivan Sergeyevich.

Varvara Petrovna is an elegant woman who has all her dresses sent from Paris, but no one has ever called her beautiful or even pretty. Her face is as round as the moon and her skin as pocked as its surface.

She was disliked by her mother, loathed by her stepfather, and barely tolerated by the uncle who died intestate, unwittingly leaving her everything. When she came into her fortune, she was a twenty-eight-year-old spinster, well past the age of marrying, but she wanted a husband and she could afford to buy one. A handsome cavalry officer, Sergei Nikolayevich Turgenev, had the misfortune to ride onto her estate one day, hoping to buy horses for his regiment. She took one look at him and thought she had found love at last. He married her because his father got down on his knees and begged. The Turgenevs were aristocrats, their line so noble they could trace themselves all the way back to a Tatar prince. But they were impoverished. Varvara Petrovna's fortune saved them all from ruin.

Sergei Nikolayevich treated his wife with the deference his situation demanded, but made no effort to create even a false illusion of affection. He has been dead now for nearly a decade, but the grief of widowhood has done nothing to soften Varvara's imperious cruelty. She keeps her own police force, punishes her serfs ruthlessly and capriciously, and has made herself so powerful that even the local authorities are too terrified to cross her threshold.

When she travels from her country estate to her house in Moscow, the caravan of wagons and carriages stretches for two kilometers. She brings forty house serfs from Spasskoye, including her personal physician, whom she knows full well is the bastard son of her late husband, although no one has ever dared to speak of it.

At the moment, she is in her Moscow sitting room, berating Ivan Sergeyevich, who is pacing the floor.

"I don't know what you're talking about. Live your life! What is the matter with you? Have you gone mad? Your life is here in Russia. What was the use of all the tutors and instructors? This is my reward for sacrificing my own happiness, sending you away to university in Germany. You have become a foreigner. I no longer know my own son!"

She is a very small woman perched on the very edge of a huge armchair, her feet barely grazing the floor.

"What sort of man resigns a respectable position at the interior ministry to take up writing? Scratching paper, that's all it is! No better than a scribbler, a pen pusher, a tradesman! Vanishka, you are a squire, a Turgenev!"

Ivan's steps follow the border of the Tabriz carpet as carefully as a tightrope walker. "If I am a squire, why do you refuse to give me a respectable income?" He knows she will never answer this question, but his pride demands that he continue to ask it, just the same. "You force me to come to you for every small need. I had to beg a few kopeks from the footman to pay the cabdriver last night."

She falls back against the chair in despair. "Why must you walk incessantly? All this pacing makes me nervous. Sit down!"

"Try to understand, Mama. There is nothing for me in Russia. I am embarrassed by my own class, by the useless, idle serf-owners."

"Useless! Am I also useless? Who pays your tailor? Your barber? The useless serf owner, your mother! Does it occur to you, Vanishka, that you, yourself, are one of these useless people?"

"Perhaps I am useless. Very well then."

"So, you will abandon me. When you are gone, I live in darkness. I am blind. I don't even know where I am. You want to kill me! That's it, isn't it? You want to kill me with your selfish conduct! Then you will be a rich man and can do as you like! I am surrounded by enemies, people who envy me! No one has ever loved me! Not even my son! I have no son!"

"Mamika, all my life I have tried to love you."

"And am I so difficult to love that you leave me, leave your country?"

She shrieks, bent over double, clutching her chest. No matter how often he has seen her do it, it still frightens him. Maybe this time it's real. Maybe her heart really is beating too fast. Her face has turned livid.

"Oh, please, Mama. I'm going to call for the doctor."

"Call for the doctor then. Call Porfiry. He is your brother. Did you know that? You don't seem surprised. Why did you suppose your father paid for a serf boy's medical education? You are no better than your father was. Men care nothing for the suffering of women."

He kneels before her, covers her hands with kisses. She pulls away.

"What do all these kisses cost you, Vanishka? What do they prove?"

He sits back on his heels. He is suffocating. The immense rooms of his mother's Moscow mansion are too small to contain the enormity of his feelings.

"Please, Mama, be calm."

"How can I be calm when you are going abroad in pursuit of that Viardot? You are like a dog chasing a gypsy caravan."

"Yes, I am going abroad. If you refuse to help me, I will find a way to borrow the money or earn it. I am sorry, Mamika. This conversation has given me no pleasure."

"Pleasure! Do you suppose that I am enjoying myself? Look at you! Handsome like your father. You could have had a fine Russian wife. I have in mind the perfect girl, wealthy, beautiful, titled. But you want that damned gypsy singer, hardly good-looking. A married woman. You don't even try to hide it. Leave then. Leave me to die here alone."

PART TWO

THE SONG OF
TRIUMPHANT LOVE

As you grew greater in my eyes I felt that I could wait, because I knew I had to love you long, and I was not afraid of seeing my passion vanish before it was satisfied, as do the passions of feeble souls. We were two exceptional characters; our loves had to be heroic; the common path would have led both of us to ruin.

George Sand, *Mauprat*

Château Courtavenel, August 1845

THE NARROW TOWER WINDOWS ARE SO deeply recessed into thick stone walls that Pauline has seen no need for curtains. This afternoon she has opened them all, and the breeze crosses the room in a steady stream, rustling the papers on the table where she works. She has been composing a song, a villanelle, but it has become impossible to continue. A chorus of starlings, squatting on the roof, are obstinately repeating their own melodies in a raucous counterpoint that drowns out the tune in her head.

She drops her pen into its porcelain holder, loosens her chignon, and shakes her head, unfurling her thick, black hair, and rubs the spot at the nape of her neck where the pins have begun to annoy her. She leans back in the mahogany chair, stretching her legs out under the table, and the warm river of youth courses through her body.

Through the open windows, a flapping of wings rises up from the poultry yard. The breeze cools her cheeks. The sun dances across her eyelids. How fresh the air is! How delicious the odor of trees and grass, the scent of apples ripening! How happy she is alone in her tower, sitting at her writing desk or at the square Pleyel piano the workmen so laboriously winched in through the window with ropes.

She needs to prepare her mind for the evening. Soon she will descend the staircase that winds in stone slabs. She is sure that when she reaches the great hall, her uncle Paolo will still be reclining on the chaise where he has been smoking and coughing all day. His wife, Tía Mariquita, will still be reading quietly beside him. Maman, stationed in her armchair, will look up from her needlework to worry about something she thinks might be going on in the kitchen. Her brother, Manuel Patricio, will be somewhere in the house, lamenting the misery of his disastrous marriage, smashing furniture to cheer himself up when he can find no one to listen. Little Louisette will be running wild in the garden, chasing Mignon the goat, while the nanny, Jeanette, futilely calls for her to stop.

Soon Louis will appear at the door with Ivan Turgenev, both of them tracking in dirt. They have been gleefully shooting pigeons all afternoon at the behest of the mayor, Monsieur Guignot, who has been receiving complaints that the birds are taking over the village.

The entry hall will fill with the barking of dogs, still delirious from the hunt. Maman and Tía Mariquita will try to shoo them into the scullery with *ces oiseaux horribles*. Louisette will race in to greet Papa and "Tourguel," pursued by the nanny, whose mobcap will be askew. Manuel Patricio will dash in to clap the two men on their backs.

And when he sees her, Ivan will stare at her, his eyes burning with such ardor she will have to look away, to turn to her husband, to reassure herself that she is blameless.

She feels Ivan's eyes on her constantly—as she gathers roses in the early hours of the morning, as she crosses the corridor on the way to the pantry, as she sits with her family at the breakfast table. He is, somehow, always waiting for her when she turns a corner, greeting her with a surprise she knows must be feigned. He annoys her sometimes. And sometimes, he even frightens her a little.

She wonders if Louis has managed not to notice, or if he has noticed but does not mind, or if he minds very much but is so kind, so selfless, and so proud that he will never mention it. And she thinks that her husband may be blinded by his own fondness for Ivan Sergeyevich, his *cher ami*.

* * *

"Dear boy!" Louis Viardot looks up from the papers spread over his desk. He can see from a distance of one hundred yards that Ivan Turgenev is enamored of his wife, but a man in his position has to be a pragmatist. He would never stoop to the pathetic behavior of the jealous old husband, but he will not lose her. So he neutralizes his young rivals in the kindest way possible, by befriending them.

Befriending Ivan Turgenev has been a pleasure. He is an agreeable conversationalist and an excellent shot, a favorite hunting companion. Viardot appreciates Turgenev's brilliant mind, his passion for justice, his playfulness—the same qualities he adores in Pauline.

In Saint Petersburg, he'd asked Ivan Turgenev and Stepan Gedeonov to dictate a translation of some of Gogol's stories for a volume he would edit and publish himself, and he has invited Turgenev to complete the work during a three-week stay at Courtavenel. This morning, the proofs have arrived from the printer in Paris.

"Come in! Have a look! Plain, honest typeface. Keep it simple, I'd rather thought."

Ivan pats the breast pocket of his linen jacket in search of his spectacles as he leans over the wide desk.

Nicolas Gogol

NouvelleS RusseS

Publiée par Louis Viardot

Traduite du Russe par

Louis Viardot, Ivan Sergueï Tourguenieff et Stepan
Alexandrueï Gedeonoff

Louis watches a grin spread over Ivan's face, like a boy whose tutor has just patted him on the head "So, there you have it! Your name in print in a French publication for the first time. We shall make your Gogol famous in France. Eh? Shall we plan on spending a few hours this afternoon reviewing these pages?"

Ivan Sergeyevich straightens up. "Your wife has been kind enough to invite me to walk with her. Would it be terribly inconvenient to plan instead for tomorrow morning?"

Ah, his wife. He cannot compete with the attraction of his wife. "I see. Of course. Pauline. Well, no matter. Tomorrow morning then. Shall we say immediately after breakfast?"

* * *

Pauline has taken Ivan to her favorite spot, a quarter of an hour's walk from the château, beyond the kitchen gardens and the henhouses, beyond the willow-lined canals, on a little rise above the plain, where the fields roll uninterrupted all the way to a distant horizon.

"The steppes at Spasskoye are like this," he says.

She nods. "It's the way you described them to me, the way I imagine them. Wherever you turn, the sky surrounds you. I have never seen so much sky. It's as though you could walk off the edge of the earth."

An immense old elm stands alone there. It has survived the winter winds and summer storms, sheltered the larvae of moths, tolerated galleries of spiderwebs, witnessed the births and deaths of thousands of wood mice, legions of squirrels, finches, and jays. With the years, it has grown gnarled and humped with warty knobs, but what beauty it might have lost has been compensated for by an indisputable majesty.

The summer afternoon stretches out, becoming more golden with each hour, and the tree, thick with leaves, casts a long, dense shadow. Ivan's eyes wander through its branches, which cross one another like the jumbled streets of an ancient city. He says, "How beautiful this dark green elm is against the deep blue of the sky. How much indestructible life and strength there is in it." He reaches up to grasp a low-hanging bough and swings slowly, his feet in the air.

She worries that he might injure both himself and the tree. His body, stretched out long, is so young, so inviting, she has to tell herself that he reminds her of an ape to keep from throwing her arms around his waist. She says, "How mighty the elm that can bear the weight of a great Russian bear," and laughs, lifting her shoulders and turning her head to one side.

He grins, jumps to avoid falling over as his boots hit the ground.

She is sitting on a flat rock in the shade, the skirt of her gray-checked dress spread around her. He lowers his big body to sit beside her on the soft ground where it is cushioned with mossy patches, opens the knapsack in which he has been carrying her things, and hands her a book. Then he lies on his back at a discreet distance, just far enough from her rocky perch that should their bodies touch, it will not be by accident.

They have been reading George Sand's *Mauprat* aloud to each other, and she opens the book to the page where she placed a ribbon the night before. Ivan, his hands folded behind his head, speaks as though he is addressing the tree above him.

"Have I told you that during the brief but tedious year when I was employed at the ministry of the interior, I spent most of my office hours reading Sand's novels? I read *Indiana, Valentine, Leila*. Her books are so full of tenderness. She uses words the way a painter uses colors, to capture the most subtle impressions. There is no writer in Russia, in England, in France, in America, in the world whom she has not influenced. It makes me quite ashamed of my own feeble scribblings."

Does he take his writing so seriously? Perhaps there's some justification, then, for her attraction to him, for the sweetness she feels in his company. But she can read only the little Russian he has taught her. She has no way of judging what value his work might have.

He rolls his head in her direction. She is becoming too accustomed to his smoky eyes. He says, "I'd like to ask you something, but I am very embarrassed. I have nearly given up on myself as a poet, nearly given up on my literary endeavors altogether, but I am writing some stories—I should say *a* story—at the moment. At least one. If I were to make a rough translation from Russian to French, would you have a look at it?"

She covers her smile with one hand. In company, he is an easy conversationalist, almost too voluble, but when they are alone together, he often seems to stumble, and his voice takes on a high, comical pitch.

"Now you are flirting with me, Ivan Sergeyevich. You have your Russian literary friends. Why not let them advise you?"

"Perhaps I will have the courage to show the story to them if you decide it's worth pursuing. I have no idea if it's any good or not. I find that reading my own work is like being forced to drink tepid, dirty water."

"And so, you ask me to drink it?"

"Every artist needs a first critic. Do you see?"

"I do see, yes. I have had a first critic in Maman. And I have had a mentor in George Sand, who has taught me what it means to be an artist. A great deal of work, a little talent, the development of certain skills will make you a musician. But to be an artist requires a kind of sacrifice, a willingness to share your innermost self."

He is smiling, but trying not to. Although his lips are barely curved, his cheeks have risen to meet his eyes.

"I have been enormously curious about that 'sacrifice,' as you call it," he says. "You seem to me so innately calm and cheerful. I have found nothing in your being that is strained or affected. Yet when I saw you on stage in Petersburg you were another woman, a creature of overwhelming passions—horror, desperation, sorrow, joy. While the other singers merely stand and gesture, you transform yourself."

She laughs. "The tenor Rubini has warned me not to act with such passion. He's afraid I will actually die onstage. But, really, I have no idea how I do it, or how to do it less."

"You don't surprise me. To do a thing with such brilliance must be completely natural. You cannot possibly be aware of it."

"I have never really examined it—how I become another person onstage. I don't try to experience strong emotions while I sing. I am too busy thinking of producing perfect sounds, keeping an eye on the conductor, an eye on where the light falls, an eye on the other singers, who are rarely where they are supposed to be. I work in advance to understand the character, to plan my movements, my gestures. What I feel while I am actually performing is simply what I hear in the music, which is in my body, moving through me and out of me. If I could discover how the music enables me to find those passions buried within myself, to call them up when I need them, I might be able to trust it, like any other skill.

"It may be that onstage, when I'm portraying another person, I'm free to express emotions without taking responsibility for them. Great passion has great consequences. In my own life, I might not wish to know such joys and sorrows. There might be no escape from those feelings. But onstage, I can experience them in perfect safety. On my character's behalf, I can suffer torments, and then walk into the wings, returning to the calm and ordinary life of Pauline Viardot-Garcia."

Finely veined lids cover his eyes for a moment. When he opens them again and looks at her, something has changed between them. They are closer together now, although neither of them has moved.

He turns to her, raising himself on one elbow. "I have no such outlet, no alternative but to feel the great passions that overwhelm me. I can become nearly senseless with joy, but I am also subject to long bouts of melancholy. I don't think you have seen that in me.

Not yet. I'm one of those people who enjoys brooding over his own feelings—although I cannot bear such people myself."

The moment has passed. He has made a joke, showered confetti over their heads. She laughs. "Isn't it the same for a writer, who needn't suffer from thoughts he can pass on to his characters? Goethe might have thought of actually shooting himself in his despair over the married Charlotte Buff, but instead he created Werther, desperate for the married Lotte, to do it for him."

Ivan tries to hold her eyes. She is afraid that if she returns his gaze, she will acknowledge something unspoken, and quickly looks away. "So! Let's see what passions George has sublimated in her novel." She begins to read aloud in her rich, dark voice.

"The evil is that I love him. The symptoms are that I think of none but him; I see none but him; and I could eat no dinner this evening because he had not come back. I find him handsomer than any man in the world. When he says that he loves me, I can see, I can feel that it is true. I feel displeased and at the same time delighted. Monsieur de la Marche seems insipid and prim since I have known Bernard. Bernard alone seems as proud, as passionate, as bold as myself and as weak as myself, for he cries like a child when I vex him, and here I am crying, too, as I think of him."

Ivan on his back on the ground, listens, gazing up at the sky and the leaves, the intarsia of light and shade.

She closes the book. "There are only a few pages more. We should save them."

For an instant she thinks she might lose control, might stretch out along his body, her legs on his legs, her belly on his belly.

But he sits up in time to save her, leans forward, and takes the book from her hand. Their shoulders touch. *Move away from him, Pauline.*

She gets up quickly, shakes out her skirts, stoops under the tree's low-hanging branch, stands with her back to him, staring straight ahead at the fields. *Do not look at him, Pauline. Do not turn around.*

She wills him to disappear, leaving her alone with the old elm. If she is too weak to extinguish the sparks, at least she ought to be strong enough to avoid inflaming them. The air is clean and tinged with green. She pulls it down into her body, cooling, cleansing.

A cloud, tugged by the breeze, changes shape as it moves like an inchworm measuring the sky, and she flies to it, riding astride it, crossing the fields. The heat has silenced the birds, but the wheat sighs and murmurs in a gust of wind, the tips of the stalks moving from side to side as though shaking their heads. *No, Pauline, no.*

She does not hear him get up. How can a man so large move so silently? But she feels him behind her, his breath on her neck.

"This is happiness," he says.

She has been gently dropped from the sky.

"Yes," she admits, "happiness."

She cannot help turning to look at him.

A smile hesitates on his lips, then disappears in fright.

She holds his eyes, and his smile hurries back. Shyly, he squeezes her hand, then lets it go. She weaves her fingers through his. *Pauline, what are you doing? This cannot be happening.* A dog barks on a distant farm. A mournful bell tolls a long way off. "What, five o'clock already? They will be ringing for dinner at Courtavenel." The breeze flutters her skirts.

He says, "I'll just gather your things."

* * *

Louis wants her. Always, he waits for an invitation, a smile, a hand caressing his cheek. There are nights when he sleeps on the bed in his dressing room, nights when she goes upstairs ahead of him, closing the door behind her, nights when she stays away until she is sure he must be asleep, then quietly slips into bed beside him. There are nights when, overcome with gratitude for his kindness, she kneels over him on the bed, her loose hair a dark curtain around their heads. But tonight, he almost demands his conjugal rights.

He takes her by the shoulders, pulls her toward him, "My wife," he says. "My wife . . ." And she lets him do as he likes, up on his elbows, satisfying himself between her legs. She sends her mind over the fields and into the sky, listens to the song she has been writing, considers adjusting the chord sequences. And then it's over, and she is free to pull down her nightdress, to turn away and say softly, "Good night, Loulou."

* * *

Ivan began a game of chess with Pauline's brother, Manuel Patricio, and five hours later, when Pauline followed Louis up the stairs to bed, they were still playing, refusing to stop even for supper. Neither of them appeared this morning, so when she returned from her walk, she inquired of the cook and was told that Manuel Patricio had come down for breakfast and gone back to bed, and that Ivan Sergeyevich had just asked for his bed tea.

By the time he finds her in the summer room, the air is swollen with the heat of an August afternoon and the household is napping. Pauline never naps. There is always too much to do, too much that intrigues her. Since she was a child her family has called her *hormiguita*, little ant, because she is always busy.

When Ivan appears, she puts her drawing tablet aside and opens her fan. "Sit with me."

"We were at the chessboard nearly all night," he says.

"And who was the victor?"

"To be perfectly honest, I don't remember. Your brother plays very well."

"What did you two find to talk about?"

"Oh, we are foolish fellows, your brother and I. For a long time, we said nothing of consequence. We . . . you heard us . . . we made each other laugh. But as the hours wore on, we became less invested in our game and more at ease with one another. Toward dawn, Manolito began to talk to me about your sister Maria."

The house is so silent she can hear Ivan breathing softly in the armchair beside hers. Even the flies are too weighed down by the heat to buzz.

"I remember so little of my sister—the smell of violet water on a handkerchief, a softly powdered cheek that bent down to be kissed, hair that fell like a velvet cloak when the pins were removed, the porcelain-headed dolls she kept hidden in the costume chest. I was the child of my parents' later years. Manuel Patricio and Maria were nearly grown when I was born.

"When I was very small, our father organized an opera season in New York. Maria sang the leading roles. Manolito must have told you that she married while we were in America. I hardly saw her after that."

Pauline is fanning herself slowly, looking out at the rose garden.

"It was her great misfortune to have met Charles de Bériot when she was already a married woman. I cannot fault her for falling in love with him. De Bériot was considered the greatest violinist in the world until Paganini came along. He was a man Maria's own age, handsome.

"Maria paid a terrible price. When she began openly living with de Bériot, the aristocratic snobs who had showered her with invitations closed their doors to her, and when she became visibly with child, even our father refused to receive her. He was teaching by then, you see, and good families would not permit their daughters to frequent the studio of a *maestro* whose own daughter behaved so recklessly. She was unable to get an annullment from Malibran for years. And then . . . did Manolito tell you how she died?"

She turns her head just enough to catch a glimpse of him. He is sitting very still, hands resting on his thighs, and although his eyes are closed, she can tell that he is listening and that she can tell him everything, talk all afternoon.

"I was fifteen years old, still entirely devoted to the piano. Maman and I were in Brussels, looking after little Charles-Wilfrid, and Maria had just returned to to the villa from London. I found her lying on the bed in complete disarray. She had tried to dress herself, but she was too weak. Her camisole was undone, her stockings rolled down around her ankles. 'Listen to me, Paolita,' she said. 'I am dying.' Maria was very dramatic. She always said she would die young. I could not believe that she would really die this time. 'You are the only one who will know,' she said. She made me swear not to tell anyone. '¡Júralo!' Her voice was still strong. '¡Júralo!'"

"If Maman or de Bériot had known how unwell she was, they would have called the doctor, who would have confined her to bed, but she desperately wanted to go back to England. She was sure that if she canceled the festival, the impresarios would say she was unreliable, and she already had a reputation for capriciousness.

"She was with child again and Charles had forbidden her to ride. He was afraid she would lose the baby, but she wanted to lose it. She knew that no one would hire a prima donna with a swollen belly. So, she defied him. She was in the habit of defying everybody. And she went riding in Regent's Park, driving the horse as fast as it would go. The horse threw her, but the stirrup was twisted about her ankle, and the terrified animal dragged her for thirty yards. She was bruised, but able to stand up and walk, so she went back to the hotel and told Charles she'd fallen down the staircase on her way to their room. By the time they arrived back at the villa in Belgium, she was suffering terribly.

"She didn't dare let her *femme de chambre* see how badly she was injured, so she asked me to bring her a cup of strong coffee with rum and plenty of sugar. She said it would revive her, and it did a little, but I had to help her dress. When I hooked her corset, she groaned, and I saw that her waist and chest were covered in black bruises.

"After a few days, the bruises had faded, and she managed to climb into the carriage that took her back to England. The rest of the story I heard from Maman. Her final performance in Manchester was a duet with Madame Caradori-Allan, who added spectacular flourishes they hadn't rehearsed. The audience went into raptures, screaming for an encore. Maria whispered to the conductor, 'If I sing it again, it will kill me.' But she was so furious with Caradori-Allan, she wanted to annihilate her, so she sang it again, adding even more spectacular flourishes of her own, then she crumpled, unconscious in the wings, while de Bériot, who had no idea his wife was mortally injured, played his violin solo onstage.

"When her personal physician, Belluomini, arrived from London, he found her lying on blood-soaked sheets in a drab room at the Moseley Arms Hotel. De Bériot lost all courage. The moment she died, he rushed back to Belgium, abandoning her corpse. Maman had to cross the channel alone to retrieve her daughter's body, and I was left at the villa in Ixelles. When Maman returned from England, she ordered the long dining table moved into the drawing room. Maria's casket was placed on top, covered with flowers and surrounded by candles. De Bériot, who had abandoned Maria's body in Manchester, now refused to leave it, and I wandered from room to room alone, trying to convince myself I hadn't killed my sister.

If I had broken my promise, if I had told Maman how injured she was, she might have lived. She might still be singing, and Pauline Viardot, the acclaimed mezzo-soprano, would not exist."

Ivan Sergeyevich no longer sits silently beside her. He hovers over her, but she cannot bear to look at him. She has trusted him with her most terrible secret, and it has frightened her. He takes her hand in his and raises it to his lips.

"You had better find Louis in his study," she says. "He will be wondering where you have been all day."

She picks up her drawing pad, but Ivan does not move. Reluctantly, she raises her eyes to his for a moment. "Now I have confessed," she says.

* * *

When his three-week invitation ended, Ivan Sergeyevich joined Russian friends who were touring the South of France, and a few days later, Louis went to Paris, taking with him the proofs of the Gogol translation. As he stepped into the tilbury, he turned to Pauline for one last, sorrowful look, and she feigned a little sorrow of her own, hoping she was not lying when she protested that she would miss him.

As she watched the carriage roll down the long allée toward the Fontenay-Vaudoy road, all the muscles in her body loosened. She smiled. She laughed. She skipped over the drawbridge and ran into the château and up the winding stairs to her tower. At the tall narrow window, she stood with the palms of her hands on the deep sill, leaning into the sun. Free of Louis's attentions, she could find herself again.

The day before, he had appeared in the porte cochere, leading a white stallion. "I would give you anything in the world, Pauline," he said, "but I bought this stallion for you, because I know that you love to ride, and because, although it pains me beyond words to be away from you, I know that there are times when you need to be away from me."

What was she to say? His selfless love weighed on her. There was no honest way to refute him.

Maman was terrified of losing another daughter to a stallion, but this afternoon she has left the groom at the stable and ridden out alone. Mounted astride, her skirts bunched between her strong thighs, she flattens herself against the horse's neck and they fly across the endlessly flat green fields edged red with poppies, woman and stallion, hearts racing, joyfully singing together.

When she reaches the village of Vaudoy-en-Brie, she stops for a moment to cool the sweating animal at the well by the old church. It is early evening now, and in the fading light, hunting is good for the little birds that swoop low to catch insects, while crows complain to one another from the treetops.

She mops the dust from her face with her handkerchief, remounts, and heads back through the fields to the edge of the forest, to the old elm, where she leaves the white stallion to browse for tidbits on the ground. She stretches out on the soft moss, half expecting the earth to be warmer where Ivan Sergeyevich once lay.

For all she knows, he is no more than a dilettante, at most a writer of real talent but little discipline, but he has invaded her thoughts. She wants to banish him, to drive him out of her mind the way a housewife drives a mouse out the kitchen door with her broom.

He has written to thank them. She wonders if he has written separately to her. Surely, he must have. Has Louis always been the first to receive the mail? If a letter arrived from Turgenev addressed to her, would he have opened it, read it, discarded it? Was the stallion the gift of a jealous man who is courting his own wife?

It's her nature to maintain a calm clarity. She has always been able to count on singing, drawing, reading, writing music, a solid mental challenge to allay any undesirable emotion. But now, in the shadow of the old elm, she is unsettled, thinking of Ivan's body, and she wonders if Russian men are particularly hairy. The soft, pale chestnut hairs she saw on his lower arms when he rolled back his sleeves must also cover his chest, creep downward from his navel to . . . ¡Ay! *Pauline!*

George Sand would be appalled. George told her that a passionate love would be the worst fate that could befall her. Passionate love! What a disastrous idea! The complications it would cause in her life are too frightening to contemplate. Nearly every operatic heroine she portrays suffers agonies of love. Surely, whatever feelings she might have for Ivan Turgenev are not love, but something better, a passionate *friendship*. It's as though he is still with her, as though he never left, never could leave, as though they have become inextricably linked, one to the other. There is something pure in it, something comforting.

Does she love Louis Viardot? She often asks herself that question, but she has no real answer. She admires his honesty, his kindness, his generosity, but he lacks spontaneity, imagination, the remnants of childishness that lift the burden of adult life and that are always present in the heart of an artist. She suspects that it is this lack in his own character that drew him to her, to George Sand and Ary Scheffer.

She agreed to marry him because George convinced her he would make an ideal husband, and because she herself could see that he loved her quietly, with an interest in her every word, an eagerness to grant her every desire. Even at the age of eighteen, she had already observed that a woman in love is a slave to her own heart. But as it was Louis, not she, who had fallen in love, she reckoned she would have the security of marriage without the inherent chains.

The wedding was a small civil ceremony at the Mairie of the 2nd arrondissement, the bridegroom, a resolute nonbeliever, having refused to marry in a church. Louis resigned his post as *directeur général* of the Théâtre-Italien and took his bride to Italy. She was delighted to be a wife on the arm of an adoring, jubilant husband. Affectionate as a puppy, she kissed his cheeks at every moment. She was his giggling, happy girl. He was her *bon papa*. From Rome, they wrote a joint letter to George Sand, thanking her with all their hearts for having brokered their marriage. *Not a day passes when we don't send you a prayer of gratitude.*

And then they were back in Paris, in the Viardot apartment on the Rue Favart, living with Louis's aging sisters who were missing teeth and smelled of camphor, spinsters who covered their thinning hair with old-fashioned wigs, his sisters who allowed their turtledoves to fly uncaged through the rooms, leaving a trail of bird droppings in their wake. His sisters, who had never dreamed that another woman would become mistress of their home, pouring coffee from the fluted spout of their late mother's silver pot into their brother's porcelain cup every morning.

Mademoiselle Garcia, the great prima donna, the talk of Paris, became Madame Viardot, counting sheets in the linen closet and fussing over a newborn baby.

She wrote to George, less sure she should be thankful this time. George wrote to Louis. *Pauline's genius is a sacred flame, and you must protect it, encourage it, so that it blazes in all its glory. I beg you not to smother it in a blanket of domesticity.*

He was persuaded to devote himself to managing his wife's career, to make himself indispensable to the practice of her art.

After her spectacular Paris début, Pauline's rivals, Giulia Grisi at the Théâtre-Italien and Rosine Stoltz at the Opéra de Paris, made sure that the stage doors of Paris were firmly closed to her, so Louis arranged contracts in Vienna, in Prague, in Berlin, in Saint Petersburg, where her successes were stupendous. It made her deeply fond of him, but it did not make her fall in love.

Now she watches the leaves of the great elm turn from green to gray, while a red glow lingers on the horizon. She finds her horse nibbling the grass a little way off, remounts, and rides back to the château, leaving the sun to set behind her like a reluctant farewell.

* * *

Ivan Turgenev carried those twenty-one days at Courtavenel with him, his head tightly packed with precious memories. To try to think of anything else would be like trying to add one more garment to an already overstuffed trunk.

He took the new southwest train line from Paris to Orléans with two of his "Russian literary friends," as Pauline called them—Vasily Petrovich Botkin, art and music critic; Nikolai Mikhailovich Satin, poet and translator—wealthy young men on holiday. From Orléans they went on to Tours, Bordeaux, and as far as the end of the rail line at Bayonne.

His friends lost patience with him. He constantly aired his memories, spoke of nothing but Pauline and Courtavenel. She was goodness itself, simplicity, honesty, genius. Courtavenel was like nothing they had known in Russia, not in families like theirs. The Garcias had embraced him—the brother, the old uncle and his wife. The mother was a charming woman, so warm and so capable, so intelligent. He even enjoyed the precocious little daughter.

But Ivan Sergeyevich, it's easy enough to enjoy other people's children.

Ah, he says, but he really knows Pauline, now that he knows her family.

And the husband? Viardot?

Such a decent fellow. At times, he must confess, he wished Viardot would behave badly, that he would be less attentive, less devoted to Pauline, less selfless in his love for her.

You are deceiving yourself, Ivan Sergeyevich, if you think she will love you enough to forsake all of that. She is a great prima donna, and you are just a Petersburg dandy. What can you mean to her? You will marry a woman to your mother's liking soon enough. Don't become enslaved by this infatuation, we beg you, and for heaven's sake, stop repeating yourself so tediously. You are driving us both mad.

Finally, they forbade him from mentioning Pauline again, and he silently disappeared into his memories.

Ivan Sergeyevich, where have you gone? Excuse me, does anyone know what has become of Turgenev? He was last seen wandering aimlessly in his own mind. We may be forced to give up on the poor fellow.

They did give up. They traveled on to Spain, leaving Ivan to roam the French Pyrenees alone.

He is happy to be alone. Happy to wander mountain trails, to discover wild horses grazing beside an abandoned stone cottage, happy not uttering a word from morning to night except to greet an old goatherd. His happiness is so great it erupts into senseless grinning or provokes foolish tears. He is loved. He has seen it. At Courtavenel, beside the old elm, he caught her looking at him with an expression that was a more honest declaration than any words she might have written or said.

All day, as he wanders mountain trails, he conjures her. In the mornings, as his feet follow the banks of a stream, his mind hovers over the desk in her tower. In the afternoons, as he scrambles down a steep, rocky path, he watches her reading under the great elm. At night, as he falls asleep breathing the resinous fragrance of pinewoods, he wanders the château. And should he chance to pass the room Pauline shares with Louis Viardot, the door is always closed. He has no wish to peek inside. She sleeps—perhaps she sleeps beside her husband. But when that thought intrudes, spilling ink on the perfect image he has drawn, he turns the page to find her smiling at him.

T HE FOLLOWING YEAR SHE WROTE TO him from Berlin, while Louis was away in Paris for a few days and she could be sure of receiving his reply. She wrote because, although she had received no letter from him, she had been unable to banish him from her thoughts, and because she hoped that by writing as she would to any friend, she would prove to herself that that was all he was. She wrote because she was preparing a new role for the German audience, Iphigénie, a character whose passion she could not find in Gluck's music, nor in Racine's text, and she has come to believe in Ivan's artistic sensibilities, to trust his advice.

She calculated the days until the letter reached him, until he wrote back, until his letter arrived. She told herself to be patient, to put it out of her mind. But he wrote back at once.

How happy he was to receive her letter, to know that her attitude toward him had not changed! He does not wish to, can not, change his own feelings. How strange that none of his letters had arrived! Yet, he has had his suspicions.

Now that the dam has been broken, he will flood her with letters. He writes in German, in the language of Goethe, of Werther. *Ich bin immer der selbe, und werde es ewig bleiben.* I am always the same, and shall forever remain so.

He writes that she ought to study Goethe's *Iphigenie auf Tauris*, which all Germans know from memory, that the qualities of Goethe's character are inherent in her own nature. She will need to make no effort to find the passion of Iphigénie, who was, after all, a Mediterranean woman, simple, calm, great and true, like Pauline herself. He begs a thousand pardons for offering such pedantic advice, but she knows (doesn't she?) what a strong interest he takes in her every move. Oh God! How he would love to hear her sing!

She had almost succeeded in convincing herself that it would be better not to hear from him again. She is bound to her music and married to Louis Viardot. She ought to let Ivan Sergeyevich find a wife of his own. He may be no more than a spoiled Russian aristocrat, like all the other lions, the beautifully dressed dandies whose knowledge of art and music is just enough to carry them through a brief conversation.

But now his letter has arrived, and she very nearly regrets receiving it. His voice is there, in those pages. Not the voice of the Ivan she has imagined for so long, but the voice of the Ivan she has tried to forget.

He writes that he is contributing to a new journal, *The Contemporary*, and is working hard to settle his affairs, to fulfill all his obligations so that he can leave Russia again. She should not be surprised to find an extra spectator in her audience after the New Year. "How beautiful it is to be able to write *au revoir*, until we meet again, knowing that we will meet again, and soon."

How beautiful, and how frightening.

DRESDEN, MARCH 1847

PAULINE HAS TO READ ABOUT HER triumphs in the newspaper to discover how well she has been received. The Germans are so restrained in their emotions, they are almost embarrassed to applaud. And she needs to hear a lot of very loud applause. The transcendent joy of holding the attention of thousands of people lasts three hours, perhaps four. If the ovation is truly enthusiastic, she floats on billows of adulation until the early hours of the morning, when exhaustion wins its battle with excitement and she sleeps at last.

The next day she faces her own, brutal review. No matter the flattery of admirers, the praise of critics. She knows. She knows that she lost her concentration in the middle of the duet, that she budgeted her breath poorly in the cadenza, that she substituted a mezzo forte for a pianissimo because her throat felt a little tight. Her elation turns to the sort of emptiness some women experience after the birth of a baby. So much energy, so much preparation, only to find herself alone in a hotel room, resting the voice, not speaking too much, passing the day sketching, reading, studying.

There are conductors who drag the tempi, forcing her to take unwanted breaths mid-phrase, fat, sweaty tenors who deafen her, singing straight into her ear, clasping her too closely with their damp hands and sprinkling her with their spittle. There are so many receptions—smiling, chatting, saying the same things in different languages to an endless parade of fatuous men and women.

And there is fear, the relentless, heartless enemy that makes her mouth dry and her throat tight when she needs more than

71

anything to be expansive and free. She has never forgotten her part, but she knows it could happen to her, as she's seen it happen to her colleagues, who search wild-eyed, for a cue from the prompter.

She has to compete with the memory of her sister, Maria, to surpass the memory of every singer who has performed the role before her. She is alone, with no instrument but her own body, her own meticulously groomed voice. And her voice might fail her at any moment—if she does not sleep well, if she speaks too much, if she speaks too loudly, if she eats something that disagrees with her, if bad air or infection clog her nose or irritate her throat.

When she steps onstage and begins to sing, when she hears her voice ringing across the heads of the audience, filling the hall, the power of it, the visceral thrill of creating so much glorious sound with her own body always overcomes her. Still, she suffers, dreads the waiting to go on, trembles as she sits in her dressing room gazing at the ugly little woman in the mirror. The more famous she becomes, the more audiences expect greatness at every performance, the more reason she has to fear.

But when she looks across a room and catches Ivan smiling at her, when she arrives back at the hotel, exhausted, and finds him waiting for her in the lobby, when after a long and discouraging rehearsal, he appears shyly in her rooms to talk to her, reassure her, advise her, the sight of the thick chestnut hair that grazes his collar, the softness in his eyes, the way he moves his hands when he speaks, make everything else less important.

If Louis Viardot resents Ivan Turgenev's presence, he will never admit it. He has usurped him, taking him off to the Grunewald forest to hunt or to the Dresden galleries to buy art. He has made Ivan Sergeyevich his own companion, welcomed him like the coming of the Savior.

* * *

May. The banks of the Elba are green again, and the dome of the Frauenkirche seems carved into a cobalt sky. Pauline's season at the Semperoper has ended, and her season at the Frankfurter Nationaltheater will soon begin. She is sitting on a tufted chair in her suite at the Hotel Taschenbergpalais watching Geneviève sprinkle her gowns with sprigs of lavender and fold them into tissue paper. Her trunks have been brought up from the hotel storage rooms and stand open, gaping like hungry animals. Packing is the most tedious part of the tour. It demands a summing up. On that last day in a city, she always feels that something has ended, that whatever will come next has yet to begin, and she is in danger of falling into a melancholy void.

Geneviève holds up a velvet cloak trimmed in silver fox. Pauline clucks her tongue. "That will go in the trunk we are sending back to Paris."

For three months, Ivan Sergeyevich has been discreet, always available when she wants him, invisible when she does not. Now she will have to do without him. He is leaving her to escort his mentor, the critic Vissarion Belinsky, to the spa at Salzbrunn in the hope that the waters will relieve the poor man's consumption.

In the light of early morning, when the last trunk has been loaded onto the carriage, she will take her place beside Louis and tell herself that she is perfectly happy with her *bon Papa*, as happy as she has always been. Then she will catch sight of Ivan, racing across the gravel of the porte cochere to repeat the fervent farewell he bid them both the night before. He will bend his big Russian head into the carriage window and she will offer him her cheek to kiss. And as the carriage begins to move, she will turn to watch him standing there until he disappears in the distance. Then she will remove her gloves, unpin her hat, take her husband's hand, and bend her head toward his. Without Ivan, her life might sometimes be lonely and tedious, but without Louis, her life might be impossible.

When they arrive at the hotel in Frankfurt, she will almost expect to find Ivan waiting for her, and the lobby will seem curiously empty. Upstairs, she will leave Geneviève to count the trunks as they are carried into their rooms, change out of her traveling clothes and crawl onto the curtained bed for a bit of a lie down, and when she closes her eyes, she will see Ivan Turgenev smiling at her.

Three weeks later, when he receives her letter, he will leave his trunks with his friends at Salzbrunn and take the next train to Frankfurt.

Paris, October 1847

I van traveled with the Viardots from Frankfurt to London to Paris to Courtavenel. Now fall has arrived, and he no longer has the funds to follow in the tracks of their carriage. Pauline and Louis have set off for engagements in Brussels and Berlin, and he has taken cheap rooms in Paris for the season, where he awaits her return, assiduously following reports of her triumphs in the newspapers.

His mother keeps forgetting to send his allowance. He imagines her playing at Patience in her Moscow mansion, remarking as she turns over a card, "Oh, I must send money to Vanishka," but never troubling herself to give her manager the instructions that would alleviate his difficulties.

He is living on modest advances from *The Contemporary*, sending stories off to Saint Petersburg. Ideas assault him faster than he can record them with his pen. At Courtavenel, he'd gazed across the flat green fields of wheat and written of emerald rye, softly waving across the steppes of Orel province. He'd seen clouds drifting toward Provins and written of their shadows gliding in long streaks toward Mtsensk. Now, in this city of Manon, Pierre, and Pascal, he writes of Natalka, Pyotr, and Khor, of the Russian serfs, the mass of souls owned by his mother, whom he knows as persons like any other, often clever, sometimes noble, people who suffer and rejoice while they live and die with dignity.

In the mornings, he takes breakfast at the Café de la Rotonde in the Palais-Royal, observing the other patrons, making friends with their dogs, scribbling in his notebook. Then he returns to his rooms to write.

Nearly every afternoon, he calls on Pauline's mother, who is living with her brother Paolo and sister-in-law Mariquita in the Rue Laffitte. She treats Ivan, if not like a son, at least like a favorite nephew. He suspects that although she says nothing, she knows everything. One afternoon, she looks up from her embroidery hoop and says, "Pauline is no less passionate than her sister Maria was, but she is more disciplined. She treads a narrow path, like a horse with blinders." And then she presses her lips together and smiles, and he understands.

Pauline encloses letters to Ivan among the pages of those she sends to her mother, who asks him to read them aloud, allowing him to find the folded messages as he might. And Maman asks him to post her replies for her, tacitly allowing him to add a letter of his own before sealing the envelope.

He writes to Pauline in his head all day. All that he sees, all that he thinks or feels, he carefully stores in his memory until he can write it down and send it to her.

Guten Morgen und tausend danke, teuerste Madame,

How good are long letters! Like the one you just wrote to your mother, for example! How glad we were to begin reading! It is as if we had entered into a long allée in summer, very fresh and very green. Ah, one says to oneself, it is good here, and walks with small steps, listening to the warbling birds. You warble much better than they do, Madame. Please, keep on writing, knowing that you will never find readers who are hungrier or more attentive. Imagine, dear Madame, your mother in her corner by the fire, asking me to read your letter aloud—a letter she already knows nearly by heart!

Lately, I almost do not leave my rooms. I have been working with incredible fervor . . . Ideas come to me in such abundance,

I feel like a poor devil of a provincial innkeeper who is suddenly overwhelmed by visitors and ends up losing his mind.

Ah! You are laughing at my choice of simile. Laugh, show all your teeth, raise your right shoulder and turn your head as you do. It is your habitual gesture and I advise you to keep it, as it is very lovely, especially when you accompany it with a certain face that you make.

I must finish this letter as I've promised to take it to your mother so she can add it to her own.

Seien Sie auf ewig gesegnet, Sie edles, liebes, herrliches Wesen. Be forever blessed, you noble, dear, glorious being.

Your devoted,
J. Turgenev

Bonjour, cher Monsieur, liebster Freund, caro, дорогой, querido amigo,

Maman will already have read you my letter (or will you have read it aloud to her?), so you know all my news.

I make my début as Romeo in Bellini's I Capuleti e i Montecchi on Tuesday next and I am already trembling in fear that I will not get it right, which is to say that I will not perform the role to my own satisfaction. Never mind the Berliners, they will applaud even if I sing badly. They have already been convinced that they ought to like me. The men will sit politely beside their wives thinking of the bond market, politics, the railways, anything but music. And the wives will be comparing their dresses and jewels to those of every other woman in sight. But that is of no importance. What matters to me, above all, is to be true to the music, to Bellini, to Shakespeare, to Romeo. I will send you the details after the second performance, because the first one never goes well for me.

I am working ENORMOUSLY! Thursday, rehearsal till 3 o'clock, outing in a carriage till 6. Grrrrand dinner at 7 with the Archduke. Friday, concert at 2 o'clock. Evening at 7 o'clock, *dress rehearsal of Les Huguenots till midnight (Meyerbeer himself is conducting!). Yesterday (Saturday) I did not rise until 1 o'clock. That evening, Les Huguenots was a great success. But I have been obliged to learn the role of Valentine in German!!!! First I had to arrange the text, pruning wherever possible the cruelest words that tore at my mouth like brambles through which my poor voice could hardly emerge. Then I had to get the words onto my tongue and into my voice. It was work! You say that I pronounce German well, and I believe it! I go to enough trouble to accomplish it! Never mind. Afterward, I sang a little in Italian. It has the effect of salve on a burn.*

You have taken a liking to work. It is the best thing in the world, especially in your position, as you find yourself a wealthy son in Paris, that abyss, etc. etc. Take advantage of the favorable breeze that Apollo is blowing over you. Work like an artist. You will never regret it. You will always be young and all the pleasures of life will be new to you. It will make you strong in the face of misfortune. I also work. It is my only distraction, my only pleasure. If it is not the purpose of my life, it is the means by which I am able to live.

Will you do a small favor for me? Ah, you are smiling and nodding, but you don't know what it is yet! Will you write to my good Louis? He is wondering why he has heard nothing from you, whom he calls his "cher ami." You have said that you would write him "one of these days," but please send a letter to him now, so that he is happy and does not constantly ask why you haven't written.

Auf Wiedersehen, Monsieur. I fervently press your dear, big hand in both of mine.

Pauline

Paris, February 24, 1848

A RY SCHEFFER DROPS ONTO A PILE of straw on the ground under the royal apartments in the Tuileries palace. When was it that the drummers beat the rappel, calling up the National Guard? When was it that he put down his brushes, took up his rifle and left his studio? It was at dusk, he remembers. He'd never seen Paris like that. Doors closed. Shops shuttered. People crowded at second and third floor windows, watching, shouting as the National Guardsmen filled the deserted streets with singing.

Scheffer is the royal portraitist, art teacher to the king's family, confidant of the queen, but like all men with a certain income he is obliged to serve in the National Guard. Eighteen years before, he and his circle had supported the liberal Louis-Philippe d'Orléans, the "Citizen King." How he has disappointed them! The economy has collapsed. The working poor are rioting in the streets. Scheffer is risking his life now, to prevent the king's army from massacring its own people.

Close to where he sits, an enraged mob is storming the Tuileries gates. He closes his eyes. It's Thursday. Thursday morning. He has been fighting since it all began.

On Sunday, when he entered the royal apartments to teach the king's grandson, the little Comte de Paris, the queen summoned him to her private cabinet. She knew, even then, what was about to befall her family. Now Scheffer is sitting on the ground under her windows.

On Tuesday night, the barricades began to go up—overturned carriages, piles of cobblestones, trash, broken bottles. The old trees that lined the boulevards were felled, sacrificed. Casualties of war, they block the narrow, ancient streets.

On Wednesday morning, on the Boulevard des Capucines, a nervous protester shot his pistol in the air. His bullet, by chance, grazed the leg of a colonel's horse. An order was given in haste. The fourteenth regiment fired their muskets. Crowds of Parisians rushed in terror in every direction, colliding as they ran. Husbands dragged their fainting wives away. Fathers snatched children into their arms. A squadron of cuirassiers charged the retreating crowds, trampling the dead and wounded. Sixty-two men, women, and boys lay in bloody pools. Not all the bodies were claimed. Seventeen nameless corpses were stacked on a cart, the body of a half-naked woman on top. There were no horses. Men strapped themselves into the harnesses and paraded their ghastly load through the city, shouting and sobbing, "Give us arms!" Give us arms!" The cart rolled through the streets, trailing blood, while behind it, new barricades rose in every quarter.

Now it's Thursday. The third day. Ary Scheffer has seen it all. He has seen too much. He lies back in the hay, conjuring the smiling face of a benevolent Christ.

The crowd has dragged all the royal carriages into the Place de la Concorde, piled mattresses over them, and set them alight. Even in the chill of February, the heat from the fire is terrible. His eyes are closed, but his nostrils are filled with the stench of gunpowder, his ears deafened by shots from both sides of the fighting.

"Scheffer! Scheffer!" There is so much noise. Muskets, shouting, shrieking. "Scheffer!" He looks up. The queen is a pallid face in the window. "Scheffer! I want you to escort us out of the château! The king has abdicated!"

He meets them on the wide marble staircase, fifteen of them, three generations robed in the black of deep mourning. The queen descends. King Louis-Philippe, betraying all of his seventy-five years, is leaning on her arm.

"Scheffer!" she says. "Stay close to the king. Your uniform will inspire respect."

He walks at the side of the king he helped to throne and dethrone, through the gardens to the grill that opens out onto the Place de la Concorde. Cuirassiers flank their little cortège, but the enraged crowd surrounds them, threatens them with pistols, rifles, kitchen knives, fists. Scheffer manages to stop two public hackneys, and calls out "*Le roi parte! Vive le roi!*" The hackneys began to roll, the crowds fall back, and Louis-Philippe is on his way into exile again.

Two hours later, Ary Scheffer is in the Hall of Deputies as the Second Republic is declared.

George Sand, hearing the news at Nohant, writes to her son, Maurice, in Paris, fearing for his safety, demanding that he return at once. When he fails to appear, she leaves for Paris and finds him drinking wine, drunk with joy, celebrating at Eugène Delacroix's studio on the Rue Notre-Dame-de-Lorette. The streets are wild with crowds of people singing the forbidden "Marseillaise."

Louis and Pauline Viardot were in Berlin when the news reached them. By the time they manage to return to Paris, their republican friends have already become officials in the interim government. Louis has thoughts of being elected to the new National Assembly, but George Sand discourages him. She persuades Pauline, her beloved *fifille*, to compose a cantata, a "Marseillaise" for a new era, to be sung at the opening of the renamed Théâtre de la République.

Pauline is convinced of the republican ideals shared by Louis, George, Ivan, and Ary, but she is too pragmatic to be overjoyed. "The cowards will retreat into their shells," she tells George. "They will whisper their fears to one another."

Ivan Sergeyevich is filled with optimism. He tells Pauline that this is the beginning of a new European order. There are rumblings in Poland, Hungary, Austria. In Sicily, there has been an uprising against the Bourbons. Perhaps there is hope, even for Russia.

A few months later, the ideals of the Second Republic disappear in the smoke of dozens of bonfires that plague the streets of Paris. Workshops are set up for the masses of unemployed citizens who are paid to plant trees, build roads and railway stations. But there are not nearly enough jobs for the 90,000 who apply. When the money runs out and the workshops close, the protests begin.

In the riots of June 28, more Frenchmen are killed than in any single battle of the Napoleonic wars. Thousands of bodies are recognized and buried. An unknown number of nameless corpses are tossed into the Seine.

48 DOVER STREET, MAYFAIR, LONDON, JULY 1848

L ONDON IS OVERRUN WITH FRENCH REFUGEES. The abdicated
king, Louis-Phillipe, has escaped to England and the bourgeoi-
sie who helped topple him have followed in his wake, fleeing the
chaos of the streets.

Pauline's brother, now a professor at the Royal Academy,
has managed to rebuild Jenny Lind's shredded voice, placing her
back on the throne at Her Majesty's Theatre. And Louis Viardot,
shrewdly taking advantage of the situation, has persuaded the com-
peting Royal Opera to engage Pauline in order to draw audiences
away. They have brought their entire household along—Louisette,
Maman, the nanny, Geneviève, even the cook—and none of them
dare to return to France until they are sure it's safe again.

This morning Pauline is administering comfort to her beloved
Chopin, who is miserable because George Sand has grown tired
of him and because he detests England. She thinks he ought to
be comfortable enough in the Mayfair flat he has managed to let,
with a salon large enough to accommodate all three grand pianos
sent to him by their various manufacturers—Pleyel, Broadwood,
and Érard.

At the moment, Chopin is bent over the Pleyel, coughing. He
is always coughing. Pauline stands facing him in the crook of the
grand piano, patiently waiting for him to finish complaining so
that they can rehearse. He has been hired to perform at a private
matinee, but he is too frail to play the entire program himself,
so he has asked her to sing some of his mazurkas, which she has
arranged as songs.

He presses a handkerchief to his lips. "Sometimes I think I will cough up my very soul," he says. "I am like an old cobweb and the walls are beginning to crumble beneath me."

Pauline moves around the piano and stands behind him. Her arms around his neck, she kisses the top of his head. To make music with her dear Chip-Chip is the greatest pleasure she can imagine. When he plays the opening bars of a song, the poetry of the music opens before her like a wide door, and she enters a new and beautiful world.

She says, "This dreary city can do your lungs no good. The air is so black one hardly dares to breathe it."

He leans his head back to look at her. "We are exiles! In Paris, I lay in bed, too weak to get up and dress, listening to the fighting. Even on days when I was strong enough to go out, it was difficult to get around. The cobblestones were torn up and there were barricades all over the city. My students were afraid to come for their lessons. At least here in the abyss that is London, one can navigate the streets."

"The English idolize you!" she says.

"If they do, it's because my shoes are clean and I don't hand out cards advertising my availability for lessons at home, for weddings and banquets, and so on."

"You know that's not so. You charge them a guinea a lesson, and they line up to pay it."

"Oh yes, the Duchess of this and the Marquess of that and a dozen others whose names go in and out of my ears. The great ladies whose fees pay for these rooms all look at their hands and play the wrong notes with great feeling."

"And you are in demand as a concert artist."

"Demand, yes. You know how I loathe playing for strangers, but there is money in it. I made nearly a hundred guineas for my first concert. If the London air were not so black, the people not so heavy, if there were no smell of coal and no fog, I might start learning English. Next week, we will *entertain* at the mansion of Lord Falmouth, who fancies himself a violinist. If you heard him play in the street, you might give him threepence. He has dozens of servants, all dressed better than he is himself."

Chopin examines his hands, flexes his long fingers. "I shouldn't be unfair. They are good people, the English, but so bizarre. To them, the arts are just a costly indulgence. If you tell them you are an artist, they think you must be a painter at best. They will never call a musician an artist, because to them, music is just another line of work. They require music at every occasion, from a flower show to a banquet, but no one listens to it. It's background noise."

He begins to cough again, and she begins, quietly, to cry.

"I'm failing, Pauline. Consumption will kill me soon. You have been kind to me, but I am alone. I became accustomed to George and her family. There were always people around me. I always knew how the day would go."

She doesn't want him to see her face, bends over him, speaks softly, "You and George have listened too intently to the gossip of meddlers. George asks after you whenever she writes, Chip. She is concerned for your health."

He takes her hands in his. "Perhaps she feels guilty. Perhaps she genuinely cares. It gives me little comfort in either case. She said she was weary of nursing me, of living like a nun. She said that to me! You see how frail I have become. She was afraid that if I made love to her it would kill me. Well, perhaps I tired of her, too. What does it matter now?"

He releases her hands, and she steps back, wipes her eyes, rearranges her face so that when he turns to her, he finds her smiling.

"George has become absurd," he says. "Do you know that since she was named the official pamphleteer of the interim government, she addresses all her correspondence to 'Dear Citizen'? Shall I hope for a letter addressed to 'Dear Citizen Chopin'?"

He is examining his handkerchief, folding it to conceal the spot of blood he has just coughed up, but Pauline has seen it.

"George is a fervent republican, Chip, you know that. She asks for you because she will always love you."

"There is so little left of me to love," he says. "What use do I have for a mistress now? My manservant has to carry me up the stairs, to dress me and undress me, to lift me into the carriage if I venture out of an evening. I have infuriated the English by refusing an offer from the Royal Philharmonic. But where would I find the strength to play with an orchestra?"

Pauline reaches over his shoulder, opens the folder, and places the first song there. He knows it from memory, of course, but perhaps if he sees it, he will be inspired to begin playing it.

"You will hear for yourself," he says. "I play the soft passages delicately, barely grazing the keys, so that when a passage requires a strong forte sound, I have the strength to play loudly enough to make a contrast. I can only play Mozart now, or my own compositions. Beethoven is beyond me."

She moves back to the crook of the piano and begins to sing, hoping to distract him. "*Voici que j'ai seize ans, On dit que je suis belle . . .*"

And he begins to play, finding the strength to sit straight now. They are both too meticulous to put off rehearsing any longer.

In August when the London season ends, Paris is quiet again. It's safe to return to France, but the republicans—Louis Viardot, George Sand, and Ary Scheffer—are in despair. Pauline is disillusioned but she is consumed, as always, by music. And Ivan Turgenev is waiting for her at Courtavenel.

Courtavenel, August 1848

A RY SCHEFFER IS A MAN WITH secrets, a man who keeps the depths of his soul well hidden. He suffers all the concerns and weaknesses common to humanity, but he prefers to confide them only to his Lutheran god, through Christ, whom he worships with a deep and sincere devotion.

In his youth, he fathered a daughter with a woman who died soon after childbirth. No one, not even Louis Viardot, knows the woman's identity. Scheffer kept the very existence of the child secret until his own mother discovered that he was sending money to a family in the country and insisted on retrieving her grandchild.

At the age of fifty-three, he can no longer remember all the secrets he harbors. The secret he is carrying to Courtavenel this summer morning has been closely guarded since the day he fell in love with Louis Viardot's bride while painting her portrait.

He has prayed for God's guidance, struggled to transform his love for her into the affection of a friend. He is certain that God granted him this opportunity to practice self-sacrifice, and takes comfort in the knowledge that he has never given Pauline a moment's discomfort. He hides his love the way a monk wears a hair shirt hidden under his robes. She trusts him, confides in him.

Even after her portrait was finished, she came to his studio nearly every day to play his piano while he worked, escaping her sisters-in-law. There was talk. The idle Parisians will seize on any opportunity to gossip. It was, perhaps, unseemly for a young woman to go alone to an artist's studio. But Viardot has never shown the slightest concern. Why should he? He knows Scheffer to be a man of rigorous moral character who believes that self-sacrifice is the key to happiness.

Ary willingly sacrificed his life to nurse his mother through a long and difficult illness. He rejoiced for his daughter when she married a fine and gentle man, although her absence has left him lonely. But despite all his sacrifices, he is not happy. After all the riots and bloodshed, the February revolution failed. When the fighting ended, he shut himself in his studio on the Rue Chaptal, his only weapon a paintbrush. He has no wish to walk the boulevards of a Paris he no longer recognizes. And then, the Paris spring was particularly damp and dismal.

If Viardot had not been so relentless, so insistent in his invitations, Scheffer would be in his studio now, instead of bouncing along toward the Brie in this diligence. Perhaps Viardot is right. Perhaps he has been putrefying in Paris, festering with self-pity.

He has just enough light at his window seat to read the from his Bible, thereby discouraging the conversational attempts of his fellow passengers. Looking out from time to time, he watches gray skies sweating drizzle, fields flattening. As the carriage rolls into the little town square at Rozay-en-Brie, he spots Viardot waiting for him in the tilbury, and the heaviness he has felt for so long lifts a little.

* * *

From a wicker armchair in the summer room, Ary stares out at the Courtavenel rose garden. Something is wrong with Louis. They have both been trying hard to be jolly, but it's become increasingly obvious that their laughter is hollow. They are like a pair of prisoners trying to dance with shackled feet. He would never invade his friend's privacy with indelicate questions, but perhaps a well-placed comment might open closed doors.

"This Turgenev seems an interesting fellow. Exceedingly intelligent, I'd say. Have you read his work? What is your opinion?"

Louis Viardot uncrosses his legs and leans forward. "Of course, I cannot fully appreciate him in Russian, but he has made some rough translations for Pauline, and I believe he is gloriously gifted. I'd like to publish a volume of his stories here, properly done. The French should know him."

Ary strokes his tidy beard, nodding. "This is the young fellow you met in Petersburg in '43, the fellow who worked with you on your volume of Gogol. I remember him now. He is with you a great deal?"

"He has become one of us. Everyone is attached to him. Pauline's mother has all but adopted him. He spends hours at chess with Manuel Patricio, takes the old uncle fishing, gives German lessons to Louisette. I, myself, find him an optimal hunting companion. He has been staying at Courtavenel all summer, but he makes himself useful. I gave him some small responsibilities while we were in London so he would have a sense of earning his keep. He organized my library, kept an eye on the gardener, worked at clearing the moat, that sort of thing. And, well, you see, Pauline . . ."

"Pauline is fond of him?"

"She is."

When Ary entered the hall that afternoon, Pauline rushed toward him, arms open, laughing. He is always lost at the sight of her, at the warmth that flows from her smile. And when he came down later, she was waiting for him, chattering like a sparrow. So much to tell him, she said as she took his arm, leading the way to the dining room. They all embraced him—Pauline's mother, her aunt and uncle, her brother Manuel, Louis's sister Berthe. He felt a new man, en famille, no longer knocking about his big empty studio in Paris. Viardot introduced him to a young man he called "a good friend of the family," a Russian who spoke flawless French.

Ary reaches into his jacket pocket for his cigar case. "And this Turgenev, is he a good sort?"

"A good sort, yes. Nature has denied him nothing. He is amiable, aristocratic, handsome, intelligent. He can be rather childish at times. He plays pranks with Pauline's brother, clowns and makes faces and behaves foolishly, but his spirit is very gentle, which is what has endeared him to everyone here. I believe he has a genuine love of the family, of each of us.

Ary is unconvinced. "And his constant presence here has not been in any way . . . inconvenient?"

Viardot coughs out a forced little laugh. "Yes, I see what you're asking. You have already noticed that he monopolizes Pauline, but it would be ungenerous of me to resent it. She's so happy in his company, and I enjoy him, as well."

At the table that afternoon, Ary told himself that he was a jealous fool, but there were too many moments when Pauline and Turgenev exchanged glances as though they were reading each other's minds. And as they all folded their napkins and pushed their chairs back, Pauline hurried off to her tower, the young Russian in pursuit.

And now he sits beside Viardot, two men growing old, both in love with a young woman who thinks of them as her closest friends. Ary has always believed that Pauline is incapable of passion for anything but her music. Seeing her with Turgenev, he wonders if he has been wrong. Viardot, who loves her so deeply, so unselfishly, must be suffering terribly from the loss, not of her love, but of the hope of achieving it.

In late summer, the roses are tired, dripping petals, pink and red and white, like garments carelessly tossed on the ground. Through the open window, their sweet aroma drifts in with the buzzing of bees. Ary clears his throat, afraid that his long silence may be construed as an admission of unspoken emotion. It won't do. "Perhaps a stroll is in order," he says, lighting his cigar. "I haven't seen what you've done with the orangery."

* * *

Pauline is thinking of neither Louis Viardot nor Ary Scheffer. She is a happy woman. In London, she received huge ovations for her Amina in Bellini's La sonnambula and five encores for her Valentine in Meyerbeer's Les Huguenots. The accumulated applause of half a dozen cities still resonates in her body. She doubts herself less, pleases herself more. She feels as though she can do anything, sing anything. The terrified adolescent who made her début in Paris has become the prima donna of Saint Petersburg, Vienna, Berlin, Dresden, Prague, and London. Now, when she looks in the mirror, she thinks it's as well the good Lord made her ugly, or she would never tire of admiring herself.

These last weeks in the country, she has decided to allow herself to rest. She will be back at work soon enough. All her life she has been consumed by work. This summer she is consumed by Ivan Turgenev.

In the mornings, she performs her daily hour of study. She can do without exercising the voice for a week, two or three if she has no engagements, but more than that and she would have to begin again with a few simple exercises, adding more difficult vocalises day by day, slowly rebuilding the muscles. The voice is a delicate instrument, twin membranes in the throat, requiring constant maintenance, so that even now, on vacation in the country, she is at the piano every day. She wants to sing everything, and she can. She has the glittering upper range of a soprano, the luscious lower range of a contralto, the flamboyant virtuosity of a coloratura, the weight and volume of a true tragedienne. No music has been written that her formidable voice cannot accommodate.

In the afternoons, she allows herself to do as she likes, to walk the fields with Ivan, following the trails the farmer's plow has carved between rows of sturdy green wheat, already waist high. Sometimes a fat hen waddles beside them, strutting as though it knows how splendidly it's dressed, in coppery feathers and a red comb. There is nothing they don't wish to discuss with one another, no fear, shame, joy, or sorrow too intimate to be revealed, no thought too trivial to share.

Far from the house, away from curious eyes, they sit together along the willow-shaded banks of the canal or under the great elm, reading aloud from George Sand or Goethe or Homer, or whatever Ivan wrote the day before. She encourages him, demands that he write, and he writes a great deal.

She allows him to lie with his head in her lap. She covers his eyes with her hand. Blindly, he whispers, "You have made me dizzy with happiness." She laughingly nudges his forehead with hers, rubs noses and then quickly pulls away before he can kiss her.

And that's all. That's all there can be.

"I can't imagine anyone kinder than you," she says. "We have known each other a long time."

"Yes, almost four years. We are already old friends."

"Friends . . . no, we are more than friends."

He turns his head away. "Be careful what you say to me. My happiness might slip through your fingers and be gone."

In her body, if not in her heart, she is faithful to Louis Viardot, willingly performing her wifely duty. It had been painful at first, then simply untidy. She is not at all sure that it can be anything more, although she has heard stories. When she bathes in the stream with George at Nohant, she feels an intense pleasure as the cool water rushes over her belly, under her arms, between her legs. When she gallops with her horse Cormoran, the saddle bumping beneath her makes her breath come fast and heavy. She is alive to the wind on her neck, the sensation of her petticoats rustling around her thighs.

Singing is a sensual art. The muscles tense in her groin, supporting the breath, the sound resonates in her head. It's physical effort, physical pleasure.

Since the moment she was born, her Spanish mother and father, sister and brother, aunt and uncle have held her tightly and covered her with kisses. Her own expressions of affection are naturally physical and effusive. She embraces George Sand, planting a dozen little kisses on her neck. She's forever kissing the hands and cheeks of her family, her friends, her colleagues.

Her feelings for Ivan Turgenev ought to be no different, no less innocent, but her eyes explore his body, linger in places where her hands long to go. She needs somehow to be closer to him, to become a part of him.

Even when they are in the same room, he seems to be too far away from her. And if he is very close, if by chance or by design they should touch, her breath becomes shallow and she feels as though she might begin to cry. At times these feelings frighten her so much she avoids him, finding safety at the side of her husband.

And when Ivan asks her if she is avoiding him because his company no longer pleases her, she replies, "No, I avoid you for the opposite reason."

It occurs to her that Louis might feel neglected, but he is unfailingly cordial toward Ivan, even warm. Now Ary is here to distract him, to talk with him. And Ivan is lying with his head in her lap, in the shade of the old elm.

The sun doesn't even consider setting until nine, and only bothers to dim at ten. The blue of the sky, the green of the forest grow deeper while the light still wavers over the fields. In the evenings, Pauline loves to be out of doors. She dances across the lawns, winding through the rose garden, Ivan following her, little Louisette bouncing on his shoulders. The summer breezes draw her on and on, and she smiles, encircled by such love that her heart begins to beat faster, stronger and stronger until she's breathless and has to stop, to press both hands to her chest, rub her eyes, close her ears tightly, and wait for the inner storm to calm down.

If the evening is especially warm, they take the rowboats out onto the murky waters of the moat, Ivan, Pauline, and her brother Manuel Patricio, all singing, little Louisette chiming in. Hidden in the shadows of the overhanging trees, she feels Ivan's eyes on her face and pretends not to notice.

Later, she watches her husband sleeping, his nightshirt buttoned to the throat, his hands clasped across his chest, and she thinks of Ivan, the big Russian bear. She imagines him sleeping naked beside her, chestnut hair splayed across the pillow. She longs for him. She knows he longs for her. But she tells herself that the consequences would be too great. She would lose her reputation, her engagements, her invitations to the great houses and royal courts.

She asks herself what would be the harm if they were exquisitely discreet, if no one ever discovered what had happened between them. Still, she would lose her peace of mind. Already, he disturbs her thoughts. Let this friendship remain as it is, innocent, blameless.

She is too grateful to Louis, too fond of this admirable, whole-souled man to hurt or humiliate him. It's enough to sit beside Ivan, her head resting, now and then, on his shoulder, enough to lay her hand on his, to touch him lightly, as though she is merely making a point. And if, at times, her eyes should happen to graze the mound rising between his legs, she quickly looks away, and reminds herself to breathe deeply.

* * *

Ivan watches her constantly, stealthily. Sometimes, the knowledge of her unspoken love for him seems like a potion he has too willingly swallowed, enslaving him forever. He is intoxicated by her gentleness, her lingering gazes, by the hope that again, this morning, she will smile and offer him both her hands, that she will lightly touch his shoulder as she passes behind his chair, that she will lean toward him and whisper some small, shared opinion, her breath teasing his ear.

He has always known that the women into whom a man pours his lust are serf girls, or the high-priced young beauties found at fashionable bordellos. The women a man loves, the women a man might hope to marry, are precious creatures to be respected, revered, treated with the utmost delicacy. But Pauline is not like any other woman in the world. She appears on the greatest stages of Europe, sings for kings and queens, yet she ran barefoot through the wet grass after the evening storm, lifting her skirts and showing her ankles. She weeps at the pain of the smallest living thing, yet she rides her stallion through the fields alone, galloping like a cavalry officer.

That first night in Saint Petersburg, peering through his opera glasses, he saw the *prima donna assoluta* who brought thousands of Russians to their feet. But now that she has taken his head in her hands, when he looks at her, he sees slender thighs dancing under thin muslin skirts, small, firm breasts lightly bound. He sees her exquisite pale fingers, imagines where she might place them. And he feels ashamed and delighted and afraid.

* * *

Louis Viardot sees that Ivan Turgenev is in love with his wife. He hopes that his wife is not in love with Ivan, but he knows that neither is she in love with him, her husband of seven years. He sometimes wishes he had a less agreeable rival, a man less intelligent, less kind. If Ivan has stolen Pauline's love, he cannot fault him for taking what has never been his to lose. He defends his position by embracing his wife's affection for the man, by nurturing a relationship of his own with him. Louis shares her every enthusiasm—for music, fine art, literature. He is determined to share her enthusiasm for Turgenev, as well. Pauline bears the name Viardot and has made it famous. She is the mother of his daughter. So long as she observes the conventions, so long as she behaves as though she is his wife, he will endure the pain.

Rue de Douai 48, Paris, October 1848

PAULINE IS SITTING ON THE ONLY chair in the room, twisting her handkerchief as though she is trying to strangle it. This will be her music room, large enough to seat thirty or forty people. But at the moment, only the piano has arrived. And a single chair.

She wonders if she should have agreed to buy this house on the slopes of Montmartre at the edge of the city where farmers still grew artichokes. Louis convinced her that the air is clearer here. But one has to pass streets lined with saloons and dance halls to reach the place. George Sand asked her where the devil it was.

Louis wants to build a gallery to display his art collection. He wants to add an additional floor under the roof to accommodate guests and servants. The very thought of workmen pounding over her head demolishes her. It will be difficult enough to furnish this big empty house. How will she manage it?

She is preparing the most exciting season of her career. Giacomo Meyerbeer has unlocked the door to the Opéra de Paris for her. He heard her sing in Berlin in '43, before Saint Petersburg, before her biggest triumphs, and even then he believed in her. He told her that he would not permit his new opera, *Le prophète*, to be produced in Paris without her, and he has kept his promise.

She was full of joy when she signed the contract. Now just thinking of it makes her anxious. The first new Meyerbeer opera in fourteen years will be the most important event of the season. The Parisians, exhausted by fighting and bloodshed, talk of nothing else.

She cannot afford to be distracted by furniture and draperies. She needs peace of mind. She needs music to push all other thoughts away. But Meyerbeer has shown her only bits and pieces of the score, and while she waits to hear more, Ivan's letters play in her head like a persistent melody.

I tried to write some poetry for you, but it all fell to pieces. All I can do is stare, dream, remember.

¡Ay! Pauline! Are you really so foolish? Perhaps you are.

Maman is standing by the window, her hands on her hips, supervising two workmen who are loading lengths of deep green brocade onto a brass rod. "Who measured these windows? This fashion of fabric dragging on the floor is not to my liking. In a month they will be full of dust, grease, and dog hair . . . *Entonces* . . . I suppose they will do for the moment. The rest of the decorating can come later, Paolita. When, who knows? When you are not so occupied with engagements, and that will not be for a very long time . . . Why are you sitting there? What is happening in that busy mind? Tell me, how is our Russian friend? Does he write from wherever he is?"

"Lyon! Ivan is traveling through to Avignon and Marseilles. He will be in Paris on the fifth and will dine with us. He writes, always before he goes to sleep at night."

"And when he awakens, he finds a letter from you, no doubt. Perhaps Viardot has good reason to keep you occupied with decorating."

"*¡Ay, Mamita!* Do I have no secrets! All I meant to say was that Turgenev is a faithful correspondent."

"No, *m'hija*, you have no secrets. Not from your mother who always knows what's in your heart. We all love our Ivan, our *Jean*. I think even Louis loves him more than a little. But take care. You are not so unbridled as Maria was, but neither are you immune to passion, and Louis Viardot is a good, kind creature, whose blood runs too slowly and carefully through his veins."

"*¡Mamacita!* What are you saying?" Laughter rushes through Pauline's body. Laughter spills from her eyes, and nose until she coughs and chokes, and has to untwist her handkerchief in order to mop her face. Then, seeing her mother still bent over with laughter, she begins to laugh again. *You can do this, Pauline. You can conquer the Parisian audiences. You can survive Ivan Turgenev. You can even live in this house with Louis Viardot.*

Rue de Douai 48, Paris, November 16, 1848

THE MUSIC ROOM IS STILL NEARLY empty, but Louis has placed some of his sculptures here and there and Ary Scheffer's portrait of Pauline has been conspicuously hung on one wall. The brocade curtains have been pulled aside, revealing windows that look out onto the garden—a little desolate now that winter threatens. Pauline is seated facing the piano, the score in her lap.

Meyerbeer, who has finally agreed to play through her role in its entirety, is organizing his copies of the pages, preparing to begin. He always looks slightly unkempt, although anyone can see that he frequents the best tailors and that his barber appears every morning to curl his thinning hair. He is the most successful opera composer in Europe. George Sand says his music is akin to great dramatic poetry. Liszt admires him so greatly he has written piano transcriptions of some of his melodies.

Meyerbeer's power and success are unparalleled, and his enormous wealth allows him to do as he likes, without bowing to the compromises other composers are forced to make in order to survive. He uses his sheer brilliance and penchant for flattery to neutralize his jealous adversaries, but Pauline sees that he is not so sure of himself as he appears to be, and she finds it endearing.

He is a Jew, a fact he neither conceals nor repudiates, but the operas he has created with the librettist Eugène Scribe have Christian themes. Scribe quarried this new libretto from the pages of Voltaire's *Philosophical History* and carved it to suit Meyerbeer's purposes. To the story of the sixteenth-century false prophet John of Leiden, pawn of the Anabaptists, he added a saintly and devoted mother, the abduction of the prophet's virginal fiancée, an extravagant coronation scene, the conflagration of the palace, and the fiery death of the three principal characters.

The Opèra de Paris is the only theater in Europe with the technology to produce the spectacular stage effects Meyerbeer wants for *Le prophète*. But the *directeur général*, Léon Pillet, insisted, as he always did, that his mistress, Rosine Stoltz, take the leading female role. Meyerbeer insisted that no one but Pauline Viardot could sing it. Despite all his influence and power, he has had to wait seven years, until declining ticket sales brought the house to financial ruin and Pillet and Stoltz were finally banished.

In exchange for his opera, he obliged the new *directeur générale*, Nestor Roqueplan, to offer Pauline a contract for the entire season, accomplishing what Louis Viardot had not had the power to do. But he has refused to allow her to see the score until he has adjusted the role to perfectly suit her voice.

Ready now, Meyerbeer has seated himself at the piano. "Madame Viardot, you will see that I have written three momentous arias for you, each contrived to inspire furious ovations. The music encompasses your entire range, descending to G below the staff, repeatedly rising to B and C above it. I have written coloratura passages so difficult, no other singer is capable of executing them, and tragic passages so powerful only a voice as monumental as yours could sing them credibly."

She laughs. Meyerbeer is nearly as well-known for his hyperbole as he is for his music. "Maestro, I'm not sure whether I should be flattered or terrified."

As he plays, she sings softly to herself, following the score. For the first time, the dominant female character in an opera will not be a romantic young woman, but an elderly mother who sacrifices herself to save her son. No other composer would have dared to attempt it.

The premiere is still months away, but articles are already appearing about the enormous cost of the sets, the extraordinary stage effects. The rising sun will be represented by a new sort of light—not a gas lamp, but a beam that never flickers, lit from behind by a platinum filament encased in glass and charged with electricity. In the ballet scene, the dancers, who will appear to skate on a frozen pond, will, in fact, be gliding on the newly fashionable roller skates.

Meyerbeer himself courts journalists, plants stories, starts rumors. He annoys Pauline by guarding his singers, attempting to control the manner in which they appear in public. An absurd rumor is circulating—started, she suspects, by Meyerbeer himself—that he insisted she have a protruding front tooth extracted and arranged for the dentist to send it to him, so that he might later present it to her as a brooch, enameled and encrusted with diamonds.

She is ready to forgive him even that, now that she is hearing the music at last, growing more excited with every measure. He has written beautiful melodies, moments when she will need to express the most poignant human emotions, arias that fit her voice like a flawlessly tailored coat. It will be the greatest challenge of her life. She will need to envelop herself completely in Le prophète, to forget everything else.

Opéra National de Paris, Rue Le Peletier, April 16, 1849

<hr>

A FTER THE FINAL CURTAIN, PAULINE STANDS in the wings, listening to the crowd chanting, "Viardot! Viardot!" She is nearly twenty-eight years old, the age Maria was when she died. Every moment of her life has led to this. Every childhood hour spent accompanying her father's students. Every tear she shed when her mother told her to close the piano. Every note of every boring scale she has ever sung, every minute of every rehearsal, of every performance on every stage. She has not appeared in Paris in seven years.

Listening to the ovation crescendo, she thinks of herself at eighteen on the night of her début, when her sister's voice still rang in the ears of Paris, and she walked onstage with the dread of a prisoner approaching the guillotine. She thinks of Grisi and Stoltz, her rivals, so threatened by her success they made sure her contract would never be renewed. The critic for the *Revue des Deux Mondes,* who adored her at her début, was paid to wonder "if there can be any point at all in the engagement of Madame Viardot at the Théâtre-Italien." That critic is in the audience now, listening to the frenzied applause.

She steps out into the spotlight. The audience is on its feet. She crosses her hands over her chest, bows her head, closing her body as she curtsies in the customary, humble acknowledgment of applause. Then she straightens up and raises her arms wide, opening herself to a torrent of adoration. She has reconquered Paris.

Dozens of bouquets fly through the air—white roses wrapped in satin streamers, violets encased in lace, laurel wreaths entwined with orange blossoms. She takes a few steps and realizes she is walking on a carpet of flowers.

The audience calls her back again and again, until the gas lamps have to be raised in the house. In the wings, her eyes adjusting to the dark, she finds Geneviève waiting with a lavender-scented towel. She is hot, but she is not tired. She floats down the hall toward her dressing room, trailed by compliments.

And there is Ivan. She has had so little time even to think of him. She looks up at his face, grinning.

He kisses her brow, the top of her head. She walks into him as though entering a familiar room and his arms close behind her like a door.

In the lobby, Louis, Maman, Manuel Patricio, Tío Paolo, and Tía Mariquita are mired in congratulations. Ary Scheffer and his daughter Cornélie stand to one side, trying to avoid the crush of the crowd. Chopin, weak and struggling for breath, is already on his way home in the carriage with Princess Obreskoff. "What a horrid rhapsody that was," he says. Richard Wagner left in disgust after the first act. The Prince-President Louis Napoléon Bonaparte and his entourage are still drinking champagne in the royal box. Hector Berlioz, walking home with his friend Joseph Méry, is thinking of the review he will write for the *Journal des Débats*. "What a fine opera!" Méry laughs. "If only it were set to music!"

At two in the morning, in the house on the Rue de Douai, Pauline sits up in bed, bent over her lap desk, scratching out a note to George Sand at Nohant.

Victory, my dear Ninoune. VICTORY! And good night.

Boulevard des Italiens, Paris, June 1, 1849

THE BLUE DEVIL CHOLERA SWIMS IN the gutters of the narrow muddy alleys, feasting on excrement, garbage, and misery. It floats in foul pools, in the filth that passing carriages spatter on pedestrians. For seventeen years, it slept with legions of fleas, with drowning rats, until this spring, when rains flooded the gutters, and Cholera awoke in a blast of thunder. Now it roars through Paris, clawing at the legs of its victims, erupting from their bowels. Fever, chills, vomiting, diarrhea, eyes like stones, tongues like ice, violet feet, red hands, blue faces, black lips. A woman who stumbles in the street is dead before the stretcher can reach her. A child complaining of leg cramps is put to bed and never gets up. Too many corpses. Too few coffins.

Paris is hot and sunless. Heavy skies, gray air thick with the stench of death. Anyone who could manage it has fled, leaving only the poor and the doctors behind.

But in the green gardens of the Rue de Douai, there are no vile pools, no muddy gutters. Cholera, having no place to hide there, sweeps through the shady avenue, leaving only a shadow. Louis Viardot called it the "cholera effect" and refused to be frightened away until his mother-in-law insisted that he was endangering his family.

On the wide Boulevard des Italiens, Ivan Turgenev is busy packing the last of his cases. Clean running water is delivered through iron pipes to his rooms, but fear of the blue devil drifts in through the windows. He's been terrified of cholera since he was a child, when an epidemic raced across Russia's vast expanses, leaving nearly half a million dead.

The lease on his rooms is up. The next morning, he will take the diligence to Rozay-en-Brie. The next evening he'll be at Courtavenel. This last sultry night in Paris, he will stay with his friend Alexander Herzen.

While the carriage carrying Ivan and his cases rolls toward the Herzens' apartments on the Champs Elysées, fourteen Parisians fall dead. One is a little girl the age of ten, one an old man of sixty, one a scrubwoman who collapses over her wash pail, one an egg dealer who never comes home from his shop; one is a peddler whose wares are stolen the moment she dies; four are infants at the Orphan House in Faubourg Saint-Antoine; one is a courtesan who dies on silk sheets in the Rue de Rivoli; and the other four, all women, die under a single blanket in the same bed at a makeshift hospital in the Hôtel de Dieu.

While Ivan lunches with his friend, two dozen more fall. In the hour he spends napping after his meal, the death toll is thirty. And when he awakes, he is damp, dizzy, and frightened.

"It's the heat," Herzen says. "It's this damned heat. We will all do well to get out of Paris. Why don't you go to the baths, have a good soak and a scrub?

And later: "Still feeling poorly, old fellow? Take a glass of soda water with a little wine and sugar. Hold on! You will be on your way out of this swamp soon enough."

In the darkest hour of the night, Ivan Turgenev stands over Herzen's bed, pale and shivering, whispering, "I'm done for."

COURTAVENEL, JUNE 2, 1849

PAULINE IS BUZZING AROUND THE DINING room, counting the place settings. She has sent the tilbury to Rozay-en-Brie to collect Ivan. Perhaps she just has time to clip a few more roses. She stops in the cloakroom to collect her bonnet. Ah, but there's the crunch of hooves and wheels on the drive.

She sends the maid to fetch Louis.

The great wooden door creaks open onto the bright light of the summer sky. Louis comes up behind her. The driver is standing on the threshold. Where's the luggage? He is holding only an envelope.

Pauline slides her finger under the seal, steps away from Louis as she unfolds the paper.

"Cholera. Jean has contracted cholera."

She hands the letter to Louis, moves past him into the grand salon, finds the nearest chair, and sits very straight, seeing Jean, cholera's blue mask covering his face.

"No one who enters a Paris hospital leaves alive," she says. "Thank the Lord he's with Herzen. He is too unwell for visitors. I . . . we cannot go to him. He will write when he's better . . . or he will never write again.

"Tell cook to serve dinner, Papa. Ring the bell. I'm going up to the tower." He is hovering, her husband.

"Pauline, we know Jean. He's always complaining of something, checking his pulse, taking his temperature. Last year it was his bladder problem. Mention cholera and he will imagine the symptoms. He will become feverish and start retching. Soon enough, he will find that being ill in stifling Paris is too much of a bore and he will be on the Thursday coach. Please, *chérie*, join us at the table."

She is already on her way up the curving stone staircase.

In her tower room she stands looking out over the fields. He must be suffering. Chills, fever, tearing pain in the feet, the calves, the thighs, violent cramps in the stomach, torturous thirst, diarrhea, vomiting.

This is what will come of your willpower, Pauline, your pride, your restraint. He will die and you will never know what it is to lie with this man, young and in love with you. If only once, just once, you had gone to him, touched him. Once would have been enough. You could have returned to your life with Louis, borne it gladly, having known passion. You were too frightened, too afraid you might learn what it is that compels a woman to forsake everything, to abandon herself completely to love.

How often she has imagined his body, his breath on her neck, his lips on her nipples, his tongue tracing a line down her belly, his big hands between her legs, stroking her.

She has always believed that there might be a god, some power one could call supreme. Now she wonders if there is any point in praying. The sun is beginning to fade. Doves coo smugly in the eaves below her window. How is it possible that the world goes on, oblivious, while Turgenev suffers, dying?

Maman's hands on her shoulders startle her.

"I didn't hear you come up!"

"You were far away, *m'hija*. Louis showed me the letter. Jean is ill, but it's you who are trembling."

Pauline takes her mother's hands without turning around. "Cholera is an impatient killer, Maman. It ravages the body without pausing to listen to pleading or arguments. I know how it is. Everyone in Paris knows. The body becomes cold, icy, but the mind remains alert."

"Hush, it's not so awful as that. Jean has always been terrified of illness. He is always imagining something."

"He should have left Paris with us last week. Now, it's too late. He will die soon. He may already be dead at this moment."

"Paolita, listen to me. Jean is alive! Herzen will have found an excellent doctor for him. There are medicines—laudanum with mint water, injections of opium, chamomile tea, paregoric, starch enemas, rubdowns with camphorated spirits, rubdowns with ice."

"Yes, Mamita. We have all heard of cases in which the victim improves with these treatments. The cramps and discharge cease. The body warms. And then he dies, a death so subtle it's almost impossible to be sure of the moment when it occurs."

Champs Elysées, Paris, June 26, 1849

TWENTY-FOUR DAYS LATER, PAULINE IS IN Paris, wearing a thick black veil over her bonnet, a style taken up, in spite of the heat, by women who are convinced that cholera is airborne. She was afraid that the old porter might recognize her in spite of it. But he barely glances up from his newspaper.

"The family has all gone to the country, even Monsieur," he says, slowly turning a page. "Their friend is still there, that's all."

"Yes, it is the friend I wish to see."

"They say there's cholera there, Madame. The friend's been ill."

She had counted on the fact that the city would be empty, that the Herzens would be gone, that she could slip into the apartment unnoticed. But when she stepped out of the carriage, not knowing whom she might meet on the street, she nearly turned in panic to search for another cab. Ivan won't be expecting her. He hasn't asked her to come. But to turn back having risked so much was impossible.

The porter walks ahead, lighting her way up the staircase. He knocks at the Herzens' door, then steps behind her, waiting at a discreet distance. Silence. She stares at the door, willing it to open. Footsteps. The latch unlocking.

Ivan fills the doorway. He's a little disheveled, hair awry, dressed in Russian tunic and nankeen trousers. She lifts her veil.

"Dearest Madame!"

He looks thinner, drawn, but there's no more gray in his eyes than she remembers, no less color in his cheeks. She steps inside, unties her bonnet.

He moves toward her to close the door.

She leans her head into his chest.

"You mustn't die, Jean. You mustn't die and leave us."

And she wonders at herself for having said those things, for having admitted them. She has been frantic, waiting for letters, only to be told not to visit, waiting for the letter that never arrived, telling her he hoped she would come to him.

He takes her head in his hands. She lifts her chin, kisses his lips. After years of watching and waiting and denying, she wants to swallow him up, to wrap herself around him, to hold him inside her body.

He pulls away, looks at her, questioning. She touches his face.

The Herzens' apartment has been closed. Windows are shuttered, carpets rolled, furniture draped. Cloth bags encase the chandeliers.

"They have all gone to the country? Even the servants?"

"I suppose I will have to leave myself soon enough," he says. "I'm quite alone here."

"And where do you sleep then?"

"Ah, the scene of my suffering. It's through there."

"This way?"

"I wouldn't like you to see it. It's in disarray. The servants have all gone, and I . . ."

But she is already walking across the parquet floor, down the dim passage. She decided, days ago, that if he lived, when he was well . . .

Along the corridor, the doors are shut, all but one. She steps inside. A shadowy light filters in through closed shutters. A leather-topped desk, an upholstered chair, a mirrored armoire, an Aubusson carpet, a curtained alcove, a rumpled bed. His bed. She unties her crinolines and lets them fall in a heap of horsehair and lace, sits in a jumble of sheets and coverlets. She cannot control her trembling. She grasps the edge of the mattress. crosses her feet at the ankles, clenches her jaw. She doesn't want to call his name, to have to ask.

He calls hers. "Pauline?"

He is standing in front of her, looking at her, incredulous. She points a toe in his direction.

"Help me take off my boots."

Wordlessly, he kneels, unlacing them, pulling them off, one, then the other. He reaches under her skirts to unroll her stockings. He kisses her feet, each toe. He kisses her ankles.

She covers his hands with hers. He kisses her fingers one by one. Then he stops. Rocks back on his heels. "Are you sure?"

Impatient, she grasps his hair, and she feels the weight of his body, this big Russian body, and he is reaching for the buttons on his trousers, and then his smooth, cool skin, hard between her legs.

Her mind, her breath, leave her. There is no more bed, no more sheets, no pillows, no light, no air, only Jean. There is no more music, no husband, no mother, no daughter, nothing, nothing, nothing but a desperate need to feel him inside her. He rubs his cheek against hers, his soft beard. "Give me your mouth," she whispers. "I want to kiss your mouth."

Afterward, he stands up, trousers around his ankles, and she laughs a little at how silly he looks. He sits on the bed edgewise, watching her as he kicks off his drawers, sweeps his tunic and undershirt over his head.

Later, much later, she will feel guilt, remorse, even horror at what she has done. But in that moment, in that room in the Herzens' empty apartment, she feels only wonder. His face is so familiar, his voice. But now that he is naked, he is almost a stranger. His body, the fine hairs that cover his chest and run down from his navel, is it as she imagined? She looks but does not want him to notice that she is looking. For the first time, she feels a little shy with him, with this big, naked man.

How must she appear to him? The buttons of her bodice are undone. Her skirts are crumpled over her thighs. Her hair spills out, pins and combs loose on the pillow. She is damp under her arms and wet between her thighs. She takes a long, slow breath.

They always had words for each other, so many words. But now, they are quiet. The things they might have said—the promises, the declarations of love, the expressions of gratitude, tenderness, endearment—seem pitifully inadequate, trite. He lies on his side. She turns to face him, and they stay like that for a very long time, without saying anything.

* * *

Paris, Monday, July 9, 1849

Hello Madam, Guten Morgen, Dearest of Beings,

I am writing this in the parlor of your aunt and uncle Sitchès on the Rue Laffitte, while they are out shopping for last minute things. I don't know when we will leave for Courtavenel, probably tomorrow. I have been busy all morning moving my cases, but I have had time to read the papers. They are referring to you now as "la Viardot"! Does this mean that you are really a celebrity?

It is 4 o'clock in London and you have been there for six hours, after a good and happy journey. You are in London and I am writing to you there. I cannot believe it, but it's true!

Liebes, teuerstes Wesen, beloved, dearest creature, I think of you every moment—of the joy, of the future. Write to me, even on bits of paper. You know what I mean. You are the best thing on earth. Two months is a long time to be apart . . .

I woke up several times last night thinking of you. I saw you leaning over the edge of the boat near the paddle wheel, looking down at the white foam on the green sea. May God watch over you and bless you. How happy you have made me!

your J.T.

* * *

Pauline leans over the edge of the boat near the paddle wheel, looking down at the white foam on the green sea, remembering. How many times has she imagined Jean in the dark, while her lithe little husband pumped himself into her?

Louis is standing beside her, smoking. He removes his cigar from his mouth. "My dear, you have been very quiet these last few days, and I have not wished to interfere in your thoughts, but I have been wanting to say that sometimes, between a husband and a wife, it can happen that one or the other must go her own way . . . or his own way, for a time . . . that is, just in a manner of speaking, but we would never let anything interfere with our marriage, would we?"

She continues to look at the water. He is waiting.

"No, Papa *chéri*. You mustn't worry about that."

"Of course, I mustn't. Whatever made me mention it? Forgive me."

COURTAVENEL, JULY 24, 1849

O UTSIDE THE WINDOWS OF THE GRAND salon, the poplars rustle in the wind. The soft noise they make, and the spitting of the oil lamp on the table, are the only sounds Ivan hears. Alone at the château, he has been writing to Pauline off and on since morning. He picks up the pen again and then puts it down, too excited to write any more.

He calls her name, stretches out his arms, trying to feel her somehow, physically feel her presence in the room, feel her sitting beside him there at the table. All day, he has been imagining her movements.

She is awake now. She has had her breakfast. She is calm. Is she calm? Yes, yes, she must be calm.

This morning, as he entered the poultry yard in search of the copper hen who followed them on their walks, she was in London, trying out her voice with a few scales. It was eleven o'clock. In nine hours, the curtain would go up in London. In the afternoon, as he sat reading in the summer room, she was resting. At five o'clock, when cook brought him his tea, she was preparing to go to the theater. As he stood up from the table, she was stepping into her carriage. Now, while he is writing to her in the grand salon, she is onstage at Covent Garden. "I thought of you at eight o'clock, London time, as I promised," he writes. "I thought of you all day. I am always thinking of you."

A circle of light shimmers around the oil lamp. He reaches into the left pocket of his trousers and produces a watch, engraved with his father's initials "S.N.T." Fifty minutes past the hour. From the

119

right pocket of his trousers, he withdraws the watch his mother gave him when he went off to university in Berlin, a Lepkovsky engraved with his own monogram encircled by cupids. Fifty-one past the hour. From the proper watch pocket of his waistcoat, he withdraws an enameled watch on a gold chain and flips open the cover. Forty-nine past the hour.

In ten minutes, it will be midnight in London. The first curtain call. The audience will be shouting for her. Of course, they must be. He has seen *Le prophète* in Paris ten times, knows the precise length of each act. Subtracting the cuts Meyerbeer made for the London production, and accounting for the promptness of English audiences, at this moment she will be standing behind heavy velvet curtains, listening to the ovation, preparing to step back into the spotlight.

He pulls a handful of red roses from the vase on the table, shakes the water from the stems, and hurries out of the room, out of the château, Louis Viardot's dog Sultan rushing at his heels.

He pauses on the drawbridge over the moat. Cicadas carouse in the darkness. Water laps against stones. The breeze bothers the rushes. An unbelievable number of stars blink around the tops of the poplars with a blue light, while the crescent moon peers through the black branches.

He is shouting, "Brava! Brava, my queen! Most beloved of women! May God bless you!" And he throws the roses high into the starry sky.

Onstage at Covent Garden, Pauline plunges into a swell of applause. Dozens of bouquets fly through the air. Bending in a deep curtsy, she catches sight of a bunch of red roses on the stage floor and lifts them to her lips.

* * *

At the house they habitually rent in Maida Vale, Pauline is sitting at her dressing table. She is no longer Maria Malibran's unattractive little sister, the great tenor Garcia's talented little daughter. She is a prima donna. She has changed, and she hates it.

She is amazed to hear that this person fears her, that that person is too awestruck to approach her. She tells herself that it has nothing to do with her. It's all perception. She is still the simple, generous girl she has always been. Perhaps she has been forced to adopt a realistic attitude toward her accomplishments and their consequences. Perhaps she has been too busy surviving her fame to notice that she has closed off parts of herself that had always been open. But she has had to defend herself. She is ceaselessly pursued by people of all ages and classes who want to take a small bite of her before going off satisfied—with an autograph, a handshake, an anecdote.

She picks up her hand mirror to more closely examine her dark, hooded eyes, her thick black brows, the squat little nose she has always despised. She rolls her dark hair into a bun on top of her head, trying it out, looking at herself from one side, then the other. She is asked to sit for portraits, all of them idealized to the point of caricature so that she hardly recognizes herself. The shops are full of flattering likenesses, Pauline Viardot plates, teacups, silk fans. Figurines depict her costumed for her most famous roles. She is so much more beautiful in porcelain than she is in the flesh that when she meets someone for the first time, there is often an uncomfortable moment as a look of incredulity is quickly hidden.

She rehearses, performs, appears at receptions. She agrees to sing, just a song or two, at the Earl's matinée. She knows that Louis protects her, that he must have declined dozens of requests without telling her.

She would like more time to rest, to read, to write music, more time alone, more time to think of Ivan. He sparkles through her body whenever her mind slows down—in the half hour when she closes her eyes before going to the theater, in the minutes when she lingers over breakfast or sits idly in a carriage stalled on a crowded street.

Ivan writes to her every day, sometimes twice. She knows everything he does, everything he thinks or feels, and in the unexpected quiet of an afternoon, she writes to him.

He writes to Louis, too, friendly letters about the lazy gardener, the yearly clearing of the moat, the prospects for shooting quail in the fall. Sometimes, she casually adds her own little "*bonjour*" in an empty space at the bottom of Louis's replies.

The days and nights roll on like a caravan of overloaded carts, and it seems to her that it will be a very long time before she sees Ivan again.

The London papers announce everything she does, everything she wears, from the moment she arrives on British soil. They applaud the beauty of her singing, the passion of her acting, the elegance of her person. And they applaud the correctness of her behavior—a gentlewoman, her husband at her side, a woman of fine moral character, not at all the unfortunate sort of person one so often associates with the theater.

* * *

Louis Viardot is finding it difficult to suppress his irritation. Ivan Turgenev, who might well be his wife's lover, is living in their château with great expectations but almost no ready funds. Ivan has taken a proprietary attitude, complaining about the gardener, suggesting repairs to the drainage of the canals. And twice, he has rather apologetically suggested in his letters that should Louis have the time to find one for him, he would fancy an English hunting dog.

Crossing Trafalgar Square, Louis tilts his silk top hat over his eyes. It has begun to drizzle just enough to annoy him without actually justifying the opening of his umbrella. As he ascends the marble steps of the National Gallery, his mood begins to lift. The paintings he is about to visit are old friends, works he has studied and written about.

Another thick envelope arrived that morning from Courtavenel. He watched with the jealous eyes of a bourgeois husband as Pauline opened it, and he detests himself for it. It horrifies him to think that he might be ungenerous. Selfishness is, after all, at the root of jealousy, is it not?

Sometimes, as she reads one of Turgenev's letters, Pauline mentions that he has written this or that—a rat in the kitchen caught by the cook, or a poor crop of berries—or that he sends his friendliest regards. But she only sometimes hands him the letter so that he can read it for himself, and then only to point out a particularly glorious bit of writing.

I should tell you that I noticed something, which is that the motionless poplars are like schoolboys, wild at heart but standing proudly still in the sun. Yet in the evening breeze, against the deep rose of the sky, when the leaves seem almost black, it's as though these wild boys have been given permission to move about.

What irritates Louis the most is that he looks forward to spending time with Ivan. There is nothing better than tramping through the woods at Courtavenel with a gun in his hand and Turgenev at his side, chattering on with his agreeable stories, his literary opinions, his politics. He understands why Pauline loves him. He understands why Ivan loves Pauline. What he cannot understand is the manner in which Ivan manifests his love, the agonizing care with which he strives to avoid causing pain. What must it cost him to be so discreet, so respectful, so affectionate even, to the husband who stands in the way of his happiness?

As he reaches the second floor of the museum, Louis begins to feel almost jovial. The galleries are nearly empty this morning. He can savor the space unimpeded—the wide halls, the light, the echoing sound of his boots and walking stick. There are too many minor works in the Italian galleries, but a pair of Canaletto paintings of the Grand Canal, hanging side by side, take him to Venice. He can almost walk straight out of the London gloom into the Italian sunlight. He imagines himself on the bridge where the artist must have stood sketching. Canaletto, he thinks, was a painter of portraits, depicting not the Venetians, but the city itself. *Ah, that's good!* He retrieves a notebook from the inner pocket of his jacket and writes it down. "He left views of his city, painted from every aspect with such truth, talent and love, that if ever the Queen of the Adriatic should sink into the marshes, she might still be known from Canaletto's portraits of her." *Yes, that's very, very good. No, not quite.* "The <u>discrowned</u> Queen of the Adriatic." She would have lost her crown. He is feeling much better now. He will use those phrases in the book he is writing on the museums of England.

There has been gossip in Paris about Pauline and Ivan, but he cannot possibly be bothered with that. There is always gossip in Paris. The city is plagued with an idle class of people who derive a perverse pleasure from a wholly unwarranted sense of superiority. There have even been rumors that Pauline and George Sand are lovers, which is nonsense. Whatever proclivities George may have, they have never included Pauline in that way.

Canaletto's Italian sun, reflected off the Grand Canal, has warmed his day. After all, there can be no point in tormenting himself. Pauline is as friendly and affectionate to him as she has ever been. Perhaps he should begin to make inquiries about an English hunting dog for his dear friend, Ivan Turgenev.

COURTAVENEL, AUGUST 10, 1849

IVAN HAS PLANNED THE WAY IN which he will greet them. He will approach Louis with a firm handshake, a few words, a broad smile, genuinely glad to see him. He had thought of kissing Pauline's hand, but then he decided that it might seem odd, too formal. Instead, he will take both her hands, squeezing them firmly. He will be seeing her again for the first time since their afternoon alone at the Herzens' deserted apartment, and her husband will be with her. How should one behave? He will be careful not to look at her too much. He is afraid he won't be able to prevent himself from staring at the face he has been imagining for more than two months, but he will have to do it for her sake, for their sake.

She will be distracted by other ecstatic greetings. Maman, Tío Paolo, and Tía Mariquita have just returned from a family wedding in Brussels. Louis's sister Berthe has returned from Paris, bringing along little Louisette and the nanny. There will be a crowd at the door when the carriage drives up.

The family are waiting eagerly in the grand hall, but he is in his room, on the excuse that he needs to work. No one can see him here. No one will know how anxious he is. No one will catch him looking at one of his watches and then another, pulling them out of his pockets and putting them back again. No one will notice that he is leaning so far out the window, trying to glimpse the approach of the carriage, he is in danger of falling.

He hears the sound of hooves in the distance, hears Maman clapping her hands, hears her tell the maid to fetch Monsieur Turgenev. He pulls his body in from the window, stands behind the door of his room, grasping the handle. He counts to twenty, then takes slow, excruciating steps down the stairs. They are all outside, already standing near the threshold. He breaks into a run.

His plan falls to pieces. The driver jumps down to open the carriage door and Louis emerges, smiling and waving, reaching in to offer a hand to Pauline, who appears laughing. Her eyes greet each one of them, linger on his as though she is passing him a message. And in her arms, she cradles—black and tan and very small—a puppy. When she puts it down, Louis's dog Sultan, who has been jumping all over, pauses and comes up to sniff it. They are all crowding around now. Little Louisette reaches up to her mother, and Pauline, holding the child by the hand, turns to Ivan.

"Your dog is very sweet and very good, but she peed all over the boat during the crossing, so you must watch her carefully until she is better educated. In England she was called Diana."

There are rare moments in life when a man knows real contentment. There are even rarer moments when he is truly jubilant. But very few men have ever been so overwhelmed with joy as Ivan Turgenev is at this moment, when Pauline Viardot looks at him with such love. He feels light-headed and can neither speak nor breathe, until her husband greets him with a thump on the back.

* * *

The harvested wheat has been piled into golden stacks, arranged in rows like a village of straw huts, but Pauline still walks the fields with Ivan, the puppy Diana at their heels.

At dusk in her tower room, she leans against the cool stone walls while he covers her with his body, his lips on her neck, on her shoulders.

At night she lies in bed, at times alone, at times beside her husband, and if Louis rolls toward her, she thinks of Ivan a few steps away, down the hall and across the landing.

In September, when the shooting season begins, Ivan and Louis set off together to Blandureau or to the woods at Maison-Fleur—boots and knapsacks and rifles and dogs, tramping and talking and hunting quail. And always, buried under a leafy blanket of camaraderie and mutual affection, they hide their struggle for Pauline's love.

In October, the Viardot household packs up and leaves for Rue de Douai. Ivan, who really has no money at all, stays behind at Courtavenel with only the houseman, the cook, and his dog Diana.

When he can manage it, he comes to Paris for a few days, staying at the passably genteel Hotel Byron on the Rue Laffitte. And when she feels the need, at great risk and with the utmost discretion, Pauline comes to him there.

Rue de Douai, Paris, October 1849

Ivan is sitting next to Pauline on the settee in her Chinese blue drawing room, listening carefully, while his fingers play idly with the folds of her gown.

"I had no idea Chopin was back in Paris. I assumed he was still in Chaillot. Of course, we knew he was dying. He has been dying for years. When they came to see me—really, I knew none of them at all—and to be asked to sing at the funeral of such a dear friend, to be told of his death by strangers . . ."

Ivan puts an arm around her, draws her close to him, but she pulls away. "Please, Jean, no. I'll begin to cry again, and I have only just managed to get control of myself.

"These men said that some wealthy friends had arranged an apartment for him on the Place Vendôme, a sunny ground floor, and they moved the Pleyel there, but he was too weak to get out of bed and play it. His students played for him. He could at least hear his music.

"All the grandes dames of Paris felt obliged to come and faint in his room. There were so many of them, they had to be kept waiting in an anteroom. Ludwika, his sister, came from Warsaw. George's daughter Solange never left his side, but her mother . . .

"George has not been to see him?"

"There is a rumor that Solange asked if her mother might come and that the doctor advised against it. I wrote to George, but I could only tell her what I'd heard from others.

"It has happened to me, Jean. I have been swallowed up. I have become La Viardot, the great prima donna. Pauline Garcia is lost.

You must help me to find her again. Pauline would have been there to say goodbye to him. To Chip-Chip."

She reaches under a lace cuff to pull out a linen handkerchief and dabs at her eyes and nose.

"He planned his own funeral. Some of his preludes, then the Mozart Requiem. I will sing and Lablache will sing, God bless him. They had to beg special permission from the Madeleine to allow women to sing there, and we will be obliged to sing behind a black velvet curtain at that.

"To keep the crowds away, they are issuing invitations. *¡Dios mios!* That church holds three thousand people! Berlioz will be there and Meyerbeer, Theóphile Gautier. Delacroix will be a pallbearer. Louis will see that you receive an invitation." She glances at his face to determine if Louis's kindness pleases or embarrasses him.

"Chopin wanted to be buried at Père Lachaise with Héloïse and Abélard, but his sister Ludwika is to take his heart back to Poland. He was always terrified of being buried alive, you see, so with the heart . . . *¡Ay!*, it's too awful! To think, if cholera had taken you, as well!"

COURTAVENEL, APRIL 1850

IVAN TURGENEV IS IN AN EXTREMELY pleasant limbo. He is at Courtavenel, waiting for Pauline to return from Berlin, where she is singing in yet another production of Le prophète. She has asked him to look after her new protégé who is staying at the château while he is composing an opera for her. Charles Gounod is a man of Ivan's own age, thirty-two years old, and he finds him quite agreeable if a bit overwrought. Ivan has a chess partner in Pauline's Tío Paolo. He is giving German lessons to little Louisette. Maman is giving Spanish lessons to him. The château is beginning to warm up after its winter slumber. The boats have been slid back into the moat and as soon as the wood swells a bit, they can all go rowing.

He has to copy out a story and send it to Saint Petersburg, but the weather is too fine to waste sitting indoors at his writing desk, and the dogs are restless. He is wearing his old gray jacket, his straw hat, his loose cotton trousers. Hands in his pockets, he wanders the grounds, idly kicking the odd stone. Louis's dog, Sultan, who is getting old now and a little lame, dawdles behind him. His Diana, who has grown into a worthy huntress, runs ahead of him, nose to the ground, tail wagging ecstatically. When he looks at his dog, he still sees the puppy Pauline gently stroked, speaking softly in a language too silly even for babies.

He should have left for Russia, and that worries him. His mother has written that she is ill. If she is to be believed, she is dying. She sent him the money for the journey back, and he hasn't quite managed to spend it all yet, but he is short of the fare for the boat from Stettin to Saint Petersburg. He has had to ask for another advance

131

from Krayevsky, the editor of *Notes of the Fatherland,* to whom he already owes five hundred paper rubles, and in exchange has sent two plays—at least one of which will easily be passed by the censor—and a story, "The Conversation," which by rights belongs to the editor of *The Contemporary,* Ivan Ivanovich Panayev, husband of the insufferable Avdotya.

This means he still owes Panayev a story, but he has one finished. He just needs to make a clean copy. Perhaps after supper, not now. The important thing is that he is here, at Courtavenel. His health is fine. The sun is shining gently. And Pauline will arrive before long.

He has decided to visit all the places he will have to say goodbye to soon enough. He knows it's a silly, sentimental thing to do, but he is determined to make it more sweet than bitter. He wanders along the canal in the shade of the willows, wondering how he will be able to endure leaving. He has become a writer here, spent the happiest days of his life with the most extraordinary woman on earth. He has become part of a family—Maman, Manuel Patricio, little Louisette, are all dearer to him than any blood relation.

It's not unlikely that once he leaves France, the czar will make it impossible to return. He will never see this path, never watch the lacy shadows of the willows on the waters of the canal. Even now, in this beloved place, he can feel Russia bearing down on him, an immense, dark figure, as still as Oedipus's Sphinx. He can feel her great eyes fixed on him, dull and inert as stones. *Be patient, Sphinx, I will return to you soon enough and you will devour me as you please if I cannot guess your riddle. Leave me in peace a little longer.*

The dogs have run toward the henhouse. They must have scented something.

His "Russian literary friends," as Pauline calls them, have been hammering at him for months. Pavel Annenkov, that fat little hippopotamus, is leaving France himself. He will be in Saint Petersburg by Easter. Annenkov came to visit him at the Hotel Byron in Paris. He settled his substantial haunches into an armchair and twirled the ends of the black mustache that hangs over his full lower lip like a marquee. "We have been amphibians, living between two worlds," he said. "The time has come to choose between land and sea, the West and Russia."

Alexander Herzen thinks it's madness to go back to Russia now, when the czar is so terrified by this latest French revolution he is arresting anyone who breathes a dissenting word. Herzen warned Ivan that he might be arrested at the border, that the czar's secret police will know he has been close to the republican Louis Viardot, who is close to the radical George Sand, who is close to the socialist Louis Blanc.

Herzen thinks that Pauline is sending him away, that she has tired of him and dismissed him, which is far from true. Of all his Russian friends, only Annenkov is fond of her. All the others accuse her of separating him from his homeland. They think she has enslaved him. Perhaps she has, but he is a willing slave.

Pauline has begged him not to leave, for both her own sake and for his. As for her husband—perhaps Louis would be relieved if Ivan were no closer to his wife than the other side of the continent, but he would never say as much.

A hare must have outrun the dogs. They both have their noses to a mound of earth, trying to sniff it out. He calls them off. The hare won the race fairly enough.

Ivan finds a handkerchief in the pocket of his pants and mops the back of his neck. Pauline's elm is just up ahead, waiting for her.

What a comedy! He loves Pauline. He loves her more than anything on earth, and he is leaving her. If he stays away much longer, he could become an orphan, on the list of permanent exiles, like Herzen, unable to return to Russia for the rest of his life. The czar's government could revoke his passport and confiscate everything he owns or ever will own. If the banker Rothschild had not intervened, Herzen himself would be penniless.

Ivan is not at all sure that he can find the strength to go, even if he can find the money. It would be easier to tear off one of his own arms. He takes a long look at the elm tree, stares at it without blinking, trying to burn the image into his being. Then he whistles for the dogs. He had better get back to the château and try to jolly up Charles Gounod. He left him lying on the bearskin rug in the grand salon moaning like a woman in labor because inspiration failed him. That is a dangerous slope, and he has slid down it often enough himself, clutching at weeds to keep from tumbling into the abyss.

COURTAVENEL, MAY 1850

THE LAST OF THE AFTERNOON RAIN drips from the gutters in a sweet whisper, as the sun struggles to make its way through the clouds. Pauline can feel Ivan's breath on the back of her neck, feel the space between his body and hers. She has given up asking him not to go. Every day he changes his mind. He determines to leave for Russia, begins packing his things, then breaks down and unpacks them. Every day they spend hours in the tower together, talking, examining the possibilities, inventing a future.

She leans back into his chest. His fingertips brush her forehead.

He says, "I will be able to bear leaving because you will remember me. Won't you?"

"Remember you? I cannot think of this absence as different from the other separations we've had since we've known each other. You will be gone for a time, and then you will return."

He insists, and she disputes it, that he ought to leave her to her husband, return her to her peace of mind. He insists, and she does not argue, that he has no reason to hope, that to hope would be despicable.

He begins kissing her hands. He could kiss her hands for hours, as though hands were the most erotic parts of the female body. It's a chaste expression of passion, guiltless. He is merely kissing her hands, after all. But he is kissing every finger. She finds it oddly comforting. It demands nothing of her in the way of response.

* * *

Turgenev came to him for advice. At least, he called it advice. Louis thinks that perhaps it was absolution he was seeking, the right to leave France with a clear conscience. Or perhaps it was money. They are walking the narrow road from Jarriel to Vauchoy. Walking is the thing one does in the country, in the Brie, through flat fields, through patches of forest, from one village to the next. One walks, one talks, one wonders at the vastness of the sky. If it is raining thirty-five kilometers away at Provins, one can see the black clouds from Courtavenel where the sky is clear.

Louis knows. He has always known, but he has chosen not to know. He thinks that they all must know, that they conspire to protect him. Surely his mother-in-law assumes that Pauline and Ivan are lovers, but she will never say so. Pauline's aunt and uncle, her maid Geneviève, even the old cook must suspect it. They are all so fond of Turgenev. Kind, gentle, funny Jean.

He will not lose her. He is a respected art historian, a translator and a scholar. But to be the husband of Pauline Viardot, that is his real accomplishment, his pride.

Turgenev, walking beside him, has been talking since they left the château—on and on about why he has to leave, why he doesn't want to leave, why it would be suicide to go back to Russia now, why he has to go, in any case. It has become intolerable.

Louis grips Ivan's arm. "My dear Turgenev, I cannot endure listening to another word. Your indecision torments me more than it does you. Let us be perfectly open with one another, like two friends. We have been discussing your dilemma without saying what we have both been thinking. You love my wife, don't you?"

They stop walking.

"Of course, I love her. I love you all with all my heart. You are my only family."

"And we all love you dearly, but you understand me. What I want to ask is, do you love my wife in a way that would be difficult to admit to her husband?"

"Yes . . . I love your wife . . . in that way."

"Ah." Turgenev's words cause him more pain than he imagined they would. He stands stroking his beard, staring across the flat fields, composing himself.

"Then what are we to do? You are a younger man than I. You are intelligent, charming. My wife is very fond of me, but she is young. I'm sure she finds you attractive. And I must say something else. I have suspected your feelings before now, years before. But I have always had such faith in you both, and so long as I saw nothing that need concern me . . . but something has changed. I do know this much. It is a sin to ruin other people's lives. I won't be so selfish as to stand in the way of her happiness. I love her too much to punish her. We must decide, you and I, what is to be done."

"I must go."

"Do you really think so? You must leave us completely?"

"I must go, for many reasons, for all the reasons you and I have already discussed. I must go back to Russia."

Viardot begins to walk again. Turgenev does not move. Louis wonders if the man lacks the courage to continue the conversation, or if his determination to leave has had the reverse effect of rooting him to the ground. After a few moments, he hears boots crunching leaves and sticks. Turgenev is walking quickly, overtaking him.

Viardot hopes he hasn't spoken harshly. He stops, reaches up to put his hand on the taller man's shoulder. "Are you firmly decided, then? It will be sad here without you. Pauline will be very sad . . . and I will be sad, too, truly. All of us will be sad. But perhaps you are right. You should go. And . . . what I said before, about not standing in the way of Pauline's happiness. . . . The truth is that I'm not sure I could survive it. You are a danger to me now. I suppose you have always been a danger . . .

Viardot traces circles in the ground with the brass tip of his walking stick.

"We are an odd pair, you and I. A man marries a woman because she adores him. He becomes the center of gravity for her.

She defines herself by her husband. She is the general's wife, the miller's wife, the wife of the greengrocer. She is ambitious for him. She helps in his work in whatever way she can.

"Pauline is not that woman. She is no one's wife. She is La Viardot. I have no reason to complain of it. I chose it. Pauline is the center of gravity for *me*. She is my life, my world. But you are still a young man, Turgenev. I was a bachelor until I was nearly forty. You, you . . . well, we shall see."

They begin to walk again, slowly. The early wildflowers are in bloom, blue and yellow at the edges of the fields. The sun is beginning to drift toward the horizon, and the birds are singing frantically the way they do in the spring, when the males are all looking for a mate to get them through the summer.

"You are not going away for very long, are you?"

"I should think it will be a very long time. In any case, I won't come back unless she summons me."

Louis, who has looking at the ground, lifts his bearded chin to meet Turgenev's blue-gray eyes. "I see, well, dear boy. You've taken a great weight off my chest.

* * *

From her tower window, Pauline waits out the evening rain that bashes the gutters, pounding the stones below. The sky, her beloved, endless Brie sky is a volatile creature, subject to fits of fury. But these rages always pass, so she waits, watching as the black wall of clouds rolls slowly eastward toward Provins. She waits for the calming light.

She has been traveling since she was born, from opera house to opera house, city to city, with her parents, then with her mother, with her husband. She needs to find some sort of permanence in her life.

Ivan has been wherever she needs him to be. If she goes with Louis to Berlin or London, he waits for her in Paris or at

Courtavenel. Now, he is going back to Russia, cold, distant Russia, and for how long? They have talked endlessly about his going, if he should go, when he should go. But so long as he is here, at Courtavenel, she cannot really believe he is leaving. It's too painful even to think of it. What will her life be once he's gone? What was it before? She hopes she will find a way to content herself with dear, noble Louis. She will resign herself to performing her wifely duty, and he will be grateful for whatever affection she shows him. And that will have to be enough.

She turns away from the evening light and hurries down the curving stone staircase in search of her husband who will never leave.

Monday, June 24, 1850, Paris

9 pm. It is here, then, the last evening that I will spend in Paris, dear and good Madame Viardot. Tomorrow at this time, I will already be rolling along the road to Berlin, on my way to Russia. I won't speak of our anguish, of my sorrow. You can imagine it well enough, without my making you sad again by telling you. All my being is consumed by only one word—adieu, adieu.

Tuesday, 8 am: Bonjour for the last time from France, bonjour dearest Madame V. I hardly slept at all. I woke every moment, weighed down with sorrow. I felt my sorrow even in sleep. I am waiting for the post to arrive with a letter from you. I will have a letter, won't I? When you write to me in Russia, include as many details as you can. Tell me at what time you woke up, what you ate for breakfast. It will shorten the distance between us, and many leagues will separate you and me.

Two hours later: My head is on fire. I make myself ill with weeping. I no longer know what I'm writing. I'll send you my address. I'll write to you from Berlin. Thank you for your dear, good letter. I leave then, with courage and with hope. Come for the last time into my arms so that I can press you to my heart. I love you. I love you all. I will love you until the end of my life.

Adieu, adieu, your Turgenev

Monday, June 24, Paris

My dear Viardot,

I will never find the words to tell you how moved I have been by your expressions of friendship these past several days. I really don't know that I have deserved it, but I do know that I shall carry the memory in my heart so long as I live. I have come to appreciate the excellence and nobility of your character.

Iv. Turgenev

Wednesday, June 26, 1850 London

Dear, good Turgenev,

I had wanted to write you a long letter today, but your letter arrived from Paris and I feel as though my arms and legs have been broken. You are leaving! This sad news is not unexpected. Your decision, which is so painful for all of us, must have seemed inevitable. Go then, but go with the firm belief that you will return once you have arranged matters over there. May God care for you and watch over you constantly! And bring you back soon, well and happy. You will find us just as you have left us. No, better, because we will love you more from having suffered your absence. I give you all the blessings of my soul.

Your devoted Pauline

Wednesday, June 26, London

My dear friend,
I believe you have done well to return to Russia. Your affairs demanded your presence and your efforts. Your decision is commendable. I recommend you to the one I call the Just Being. May it protect you. I hope that in time, you will return, an independent man with a strong vocation. And may Diana bring you some moments of pleasure.

L. Viardot

July 1, 1850, London

My beloved friend,
Thank you for the letter you sent from Berlin. I hadn't expected a letter today, and it shocked me to get it, as though you yourself had entered the room. It was brought to me at ten this morning while I was still in bed, just as I woke up. You can well imagine how it was received! I have not stopped thinking of you. God bless you and guide you at every hour of your life. This is my prayer in the morning and in the evening. You are my first and last thought every day. If you knew how much I talk about you, you would know that your presence in my heart has not diminished at all in your absence.

July 2: Now we are separated by the sea. Your letter from Stettin was brought to me in my bed when I awoke. I think I am sleeping later than usual these days in order to awake with the delivery of the post, instead of waiting for it, tormented by the slightest delay. If you think that your departure has done me good, you are greatly deceiving yourself.

Your Pauline

PART THREE

ON THE EDGE OF
ANOTHER MAN'S NEST

I have had enough of perching on the edge of another man's nest. If I cannot have a nest of my own, then I do not need one at all.

Ivan Turgenev in a letter to the poet N. A. Nekrasov

Courtavenel, September 1850

EVERY NIGHT PAULINE TELLS HERSELF THE pain of losing Ivan will be less tomorrow. Every morning she awakens thinking of him. All day she wonders why she allowed him to leave, if she could have prevented him from leaving. She avoids Louis, hides her sorrow. She needs work. Work has always saved her, and Charles Gounod is about to provide her with it.

While she was away in London, Gounod sent incessant letters from Courtavenel. She was his good, very dear, very excellent, very much-loved friend. She was the girl of his soul. Together, united in the cause of art, they would create a masterpiece. He whined if he hadn't heard from her in four days. He waited for her, hoped for her, blessed her. He was working on "our" opera, playing "our" piano. He confessed to her that in her absence, he worked in her bedroom and slept in her bed.

She was surprised, a little annoyed, a little pleased. She knows that if he fancies himself in love, it's not with Pauline Viardot-Garcia, but with the prima donna who has the power to stage his work at the Opéra de Paris.

He is a handsome man who charms women and flirts shamelessly. Even Maman and Tía Mariquita open their fans to hide their smiles when he comes into the room. The whole family has embraced him. Even Ivan befriended him. Only George Sand is wary, protective of Pauline's generous heart.

145

My fifille,

*You will have a new role and a new triumph. You have a new
master up your sleeve, a genius whose music you will interpret.
But is he good? Is he humane? There are few great artists who are
also great men.*

The weary sun sets earlier now. The air is cooler, kinder than it
was during those hot last days with Ivan, when sweat mingled with
tears and she felt as though her body and soul were melting. After
supper, the women go upstairs to fetch their shawls. When they
come down the trees outside the grand salon are no more than
dark shadows on the window panes. The lamps are lit. They're all
there, the family and the dogs.

Pauline settles into an armchair. Gounod has promised to play
the entire opera. She lets her head fall back against the cushions,
preparing herself for pleasure. She reconquered Paris by creating
a role in Meyerbeer's new opera. Now she will create a new composer in Charles Gounod.

Since the success of *Le prophète*, young composers have besieged
her. They write, claiming that she has inspired them. Awed them.
The story is always the same. They want to make their fortunes
writing music. The only road to those heights ascends through the
realm of opera, and Pauline is enthroned at the very summit.

Nine months ago, she agreed to give thirty minutes of her time
to the organist of the chapel of the Missions Étrangères. It threatened to be a tedious half an hour. The young man, who had been
living with the Dominicans at Saint-Sulpice, signed his letter
"Abbé Gounod."

He arrived at the Rue de Douai laden with extravagant compliments, exhausted every superlative in the dictionary in his flattery
of her. She wished he would just get on with it. Finally, he sat at
the piano and began to play, singing in a sweet, thin tenor voice,
sacred music, hymns, cantatas.

Astounded, she asked to hear another composition, and another. Pauline is more than a singer. She is a virtuoso pianist, a brilliant composer. She is convinced that she is listening to the next Mozart. He must write an opera for her.

She had been thinking that she would like to play Ovid's *Sappho*, the great poet in love with the warrior Phaon, who sent him into the arms of another woman in order to save his life. Viardot's name sells more tickets now than Grisi's. She can insist that the Opéra de Paris stage the opera for her, and she can recommend the young composer to the most fashionable librettist in Paris, Émile Augier.

Louis negotiates all her contracts, but this time she went with him to meet the *directeur générale* of the Opèra de Paris. Nestor Roqueplan is a bit dandyish for her taste, an habitué of fashionable salons, but he's clever and she likes him. She is not afraid to ask him to stage a new opera by an unknown composer. If he wants her for the next season, he will have to take Gounod, as well.

Roqueplan knows when to be obsequious. He insisted that he was ready to do anything to please the greatest singer in Europe. Pauline wanted Gounod's opera to be a full-length vehicle. Roqueplan, afraid of investing too much in an unknown composer, said that it should be short, a curtain-raiser for a more substantial work. They settled on three acts. No ballet. She congratulated herself on her shrewdness and left for Berlin with Louis. Charles Gounod had six months to complete the opera.

Now he is at the piano in the grand salon at Courtavenel, preparing to present his work for Pauline's approval. She responds to his terrified expression with an encouraging smile, then closes her eyes and sinks into the music.

Ninety minutes later, having played the final, momentous chords, he looks up at her, a dozen questions in his eyes. She beams, raising her hands in enthusiastic applause. The family, who have been nervously waiting for her reaction, begin to cheer, and the dogs bark and chase each other around the chairs. She tells him it will be wonderful. She thinks it might become wonderful with a great deal of work.

The next morning, she sends a triumphant Gounod back to Paris, takes the score up to her tower and does not come down until she has devoured it. She plays it over and over again from start to finish, making notes, finding ways to improve the music, the drama. Three days later, she can play the entire opera from memory.

She thinks of nothing else, sees nothing but *Sapho*. The music plays in her head all day. In the morning, as she pulls on her stockings, she feels Sapho's love for the warrior Phaon. As she pins her hair, she feels Sapho's suffering. When she rides Cormoran out onto the fields in the evenings, the music follows her so relentlessly, she urges the horse faster trying to escape it.

She suggests changes, consults Louis, who suggests more changes. She describes the opera to Ivan in detailed letters. *I have asked the librettist and the composer to write a section of four verses with a sharp, animated rhythm. Yes, it will be a lament, that has already been decided, but it will serve as a purely lyrical aria, Sapho's last song. Her adieu to her lyre, to Phaon, to the sun, to her life, I will reward the audience with her agony, my head bent, drenched in tears.*

In her tower, one hand on the piano keys, she plays the opening arpeggios of the lament. She is Sapho, atop the Leucadian rock, ready to throw herself into the raging sea, to die for love. She lifts her immortal lyre to the sun, singing softly in quiet desperation, confused, lost, her strength, her will gone. As she begins to fully realize the horror of her fate, her voice rises in a crescendo of anguish, in a cry that descends to her dark lower register, then leaps once more, as she throws herself into the sea. She wills herself to experience the enormity of *Sapho*'s despair, falls against the tower walls with the weight of it, taking note of the way her voice rises and falls, the way the emotion compels her to hurry over some words and linger over others. She marks her score. She has suffered enough to understand the scene. When she stands onstage at the Opéra de Paris, she will calmly concentrate on her breathing, her movements, while the audience drowns in *Sapho*'s sorrow.

37 Ulitsa Ostozhenka, Moscow, September 1850

Ivan has gone down to the kitchens because he wants to greet the serfs, whom he hasn't seen since he left Russia. His mother disapproves of his going there. She enforces a strict line of command. If he requires something from the kitchen, he must speak to his manservant, who rings for one of the maids, who goes into the kitchen to speak to the cook.

He is long past obeying his mother's rules. He has known the kitchen serfs since they were all children together. He stands silently at the door, waiting to announce himself. It gives him pleasure to recognize familiar faces grown older. There are two large stoves in the room, a wood-burning oven in the wall, and a stone sink next to the back door, which is where he discovers her, a child dressed in a torn shift and dirty apron, her hair stuck to her head and neck, struggling with a full water bucket almost as big as she is.

"Who is that girl? Why is she made to carry such a heavy bucket?" Heads lift, floury hands mop sweaty brows. Aprons are hurriedly adjusted. Chairs scrape the stone floor in a commotion of standing, bowing and curtsying.

"Master Ivan!"

The little girl turns around. It's as though he is seeing himself—the same wide forehead, the same smoky eyes. He moves along the line of kitchen serfs, pressing hands, offering sympathy or congratulations in answer to his questions, but his looks again and again at the little girl, who looks at the floor. "And who is this little person, then?"

"She is no one, Master Ivan, the daughter of a seamstress whom your mother sent away last month."

"The father . . . ? No one tells us these things."

Swallowed laughter, pursed lips. Eyes quickly lowered. It's not impossible.

* * *

He finds his mother seated in a wheelchair at the card table in her sitting room. Varvara Petrovna is not the woman he remembered. She is shriveled, fragile, almost unable to move. She sits in sullen silence, gasping for breath until she decides to give an order. Then her voice grows strong, her face hardens, and the dropsy that is slowly killing her seems to shrink away in fear. When he first arrived, she wept and clung to him, her Vanishka, her Jean. How afraid she had been that she would die without seeing him again! How long he had left her alone! All the light had gone out of her life. She never succeeded in suffocating him with guilt, but she never ceased trying.

Now she is playing whist with her paid companions, women of good breeding who failed to find good husbands and women whose good husbands died leaving them in debt. They earn their keep by flattering Varvara Petrovna, by saying only what she wants to hear. The women look up when Ivan enters the room, but his mother's eyes are fixed on the cards in her hand.

"Mama, who is the little serf girl I just saw in the kitchen?"

A smile slithers over his mother's face. "Why on earth were you in the kitchen? How should I know what a little serf girl does? What sort of a girl?"

"A girl of about eight or nine, brown hair. She looks to be completely neglected and is being made to carry a bucket as heavy as she is!"

His mother's eyes never leave her playing cards. "Natasha, have the child brought to me—in the way that we usually do it. Sit down, Vanishka. You make me nervous standing there."

He sits, but he cannot sit still. He fiddles with his hands, his hair. He removes each of his pocket watches, checking the time.

This will be another one of his mother's cruelties. She enjoys tormenting her serfs. Sending a baby away from its mother, having a dog killed in front of its owner. What possible pleasure can she find in mistreating a small girl?

Half an hour later, the child is brought into the sitting room dressed in the manner of a fine little lady. Her hair, still wet from washing, has been neatly plaited and beribboned. Her stockings are white, her shoes polished, her calloused little hands clenched.

He watches, horrified, as the maid Natasha gives the girl a push, and she curtsies. Varvara Petrovna doesn't look up. She is still studying her cards, rearranging them. "Who does this child resemble?"

The paid companions sing out "Ivan Sergeyevich!"

Ivan stares at the little face.

"She is your daughter, Vanishka! Your daughter! I sent her mother away before you arrived and put the child to work in the kitchen. Remove her, Natasha. I'm tired. I am a dying woman."

The girl is removed like a brimming chamber pot and as Vavara Petrovna is wheeled out of the room, Ivan imagines shooting her in the back. He is a good shot. He could do it from a considerable distance. It amuses her to torment her own granddaughter.

He runs out in search of the child, his daughter. "Natasha, bring her into the street where my mother cannot see us. I must talk with her."

"But Master Ivan, what will you do? She is your mother's property like the rest of us."

He has no idea what he will do, None at all. But he cannot leave her there to be ridiculed by the serfs and abused by his mother. She is his daughter. His flesh and blood.

Rue de Douai, Paris, October 1850

"I was young. It was about nine years ago. I was bored in the country. I noticed a pretty seamstress whom my mother had just taken into her service. I said two words to her and she came to see me. I paid. She left. And that was all. It's the same old story.

If I had had—I won't say the slightest interest in the girl's mother—if I had even known her, I might have felt something more for the poor child who was so distressed there, standing in front of me."

AT THE BREAKFAST TABLE, LOUIS VIARDOT is hiding behind the pages of the *Revue de deux Mondes*, as he listens to his wife read Ivan's letter. Imagine Turgenev, fooling with the serf women! They all did that, he supposes. Turgenev is so outspoken about the rights of the serfs, but when it comes to this . . .

"*Bon Papa*, the child is only eight years old. There is no place for her in Russia. What will happen to her? He cannot leave her there to be tormented by the serfs and abused by his mother."

Louis hears the quiver in Pauline's voice. She becomes completely undone by the suffering of others. But this is more to her. She wants Ivan's child.

"I know what you are about to say, Pauline," he protests from behind his newspaper. "Please, don't say it. We have so little time for Louisette. You have the Paris season, the *Sapho* premiere, then we go to London."

Pauline pours herself another cup of coffee, brushes a few crumbs from the tablecloth. She is shaken, but her voice is steady. "The girl might be a companion for our little Louisette while we're gone."

Louis is pretending to read. "Louisette?" He turns a page. "Our daughter is intelligent, educated, she knows music, language. But she is impossible, spoiled by my sister and by your mother. How do you suppose she will receive this child? What will she say to a girl who has spent her life scrubbing pots and speaks only the most primitive Russian?"

He is sorry for having said something so unkind about his own child, and even sorrier for having made such a snobby comment about the lower classes. But it's true. Pauline knows it as well as he does.

She takes a deep breath and sighs loudly, rattles her spoon against her cup as she stirs her café *au lait*. "Papa *chéri*, the child is friendless, miserable, terrified, alone. The mother has given her up willingly and gone off with who knows how many lovers."

He lowers his newspaper a little so that he can peer over the top. Pauline is clearly distraught. It's too early in the morning to think about all this. He has barely finished his coffee. He cannot be expected to have such a momentous discussion at the breakfast table.

He folds the newspaper, folds his napkin. He says, "Perhaps Louisette ought to learn that all children are not so fortunate as she. I will think on it."

In his study, he tries to get on with his work. He is writing a history of the Arabs and Moors of Spain, but visions of a tearful, ragged little girl with Ivan Turgenev's eyes keep intruding on the scenes of Andalusia he is attempting to conjure. If Pauline is determined to rescue Turgenev's child, how will she feel toward the selfish husband who refuses her? For that matter, how will he feel about himself if he fails to help the child?

He puts his pen back in its holder and stands up to stretch his legs, runs a hand over his head. His dogs, who have been asleep at his feet, stir and yawn, and lazily beat their tails on the carpet.

With Turgenev back in Russia, he has managed to regain at least a little of Pauline's attention. She is distracted by Gounod, but that should fade once the opera has its premiere. It is the composer who fascinates her, not the man.

What in the world ought he to do? One cannot rescue every poor child in Paris, never mind all the poor children in Russia. But this is Turgenev's child. She might have an interesting mind, like her father. He might grow fond of her. She might be a grateful, affectionate little creature. How inconvenient this is! *Viardot, you're an old fool who has never been able to deny Pauline anything.*

Late in the afternoon, he finds her at the piano in the music room.

"Write to him then. Write to Turgenev and I will add a few words of my own at the end of your letter. If we don't rescue the girl, he will be forced to shut her up in a convent full of sour old nuns. Ask him if he needs money for the child's voyage."

Peterburskoye Schosse Road, November 1850

IVAN IS SEATED OPPOSITE HIS DAUGHTER in the carriage, rolling toward Saint Petersburg. He is leaning forward, hands clasped, earnestly interrogating her. Smoky little eyes look brazenly into his, challenging him. He sees in her face that the child is his, but he feels no connection to her. He has three days of travel to discover who she is before he puts her on a boat and sends her off to the Viardots in Paris with a French lady as chaperone.

The dog, Diana, whom he loves infinitely more than this strange girl, sleeps curled at his feet on the carriage floor. He needs to talk to the child, to find something of himself in her.

"Do you like music?"

"Yes."

She turns her little face away. She can have no idea whether she likes music or not. What music can she have heard? A serf singing in the fields? A balalaika?

"You won't mind going far away, will you? Of course, you won't mind. Your new mother is a great lady, and you will have her name, Pauline. We will call you Paulinette."

"My name is Pelageya Ivanova. My mother went away. I don't know where she is, but she is not in Paris and she is not a great lady."

"Yes, your mother went away, and so I have found you a new mother. A wonderful mother. You will love her very much."

The little face wrinkles, eyebrows nearly meeting over the nose. Ivan thinks this may be a sign of intelligence. Perhaps she is pondering the concept of loving, having had no experience of

157

it. He expected to find a savage child, shy, and badly behaved. But his daughter is a calm little creature, rather bold. She has been sharing a straw bed with two old women who have spoiled her, not in the way one would spoil a child, but as one spoils a pet, a plaything. He can hardly bear to imagine what her life has been, all the wiles she must have needed to acquire in order to survive.

Now he knows how criminal it is to bed a strange woman. Here is the result—all of his own faults and blessings combined with those of a woman he never knew at all.

He will have to confess his concerns to Pauline. At least, his daughter will be removed from the cruel atmosphere in which she has lived so far, and perhaps, when she has seen and felt goodness and affection, her withered heart will expand and her spirit will begin to flourish.

The little girl is staring out the window. What can she be thinking? She'd seen nothing of the world beyond Spasskoye until she was driven to his mother's Moscow mansion in the back of a wagon with a dozen other serfs. She is far too serious, far too intense for such a young child. She must be very frightened, but too proud to show it. Perhaps she is afraid to cry. She must have been beaten for crying.

My dear, good Turgenev,

The little girl has arrived, and I love her already. She looks very much like you, and this makes me very happy. She is doing well. She slept peacefully and she has been playing all day with Louise. Although they quarrel constantly, shouting in Russian and French, it leaves no more than a shadow between them. Good night, my dear Turgenev. Sleep the best of slumbers. A thousand blessings of my heart and soul.

Your Pauline

Dearest, most beloved, most adored woman,

I just received the letter in which you give me the details of Paulinette's arrival. My God! How good you are! Your letter has moved my heart. How much better it is if <u>our</u> little girl is good and loving. She will love you. She must adore you. She is, after all, my daughter. I beg you to permit her to kiss your hands often. Though they are not my lips, they are lips that are very near to me.

I will not speak to you of my gratitude. That word makes no sense between us. But you know that you can count on my complete devotion, absolute, eternal. You know that you could ask for my life and I would happily give it to you. I tell you this—and I know that you believe it.

Be happy and well.

Your J.T.

P.S. Thank you for sending the dear fingernail. I will send you a lock of my hair. I beg you for a petal that has been crushed by your foot. I kiss those dear, lovely feet a thousand times.

Moscow, December 4, 1850

Dear, good Madame Viardot,

I arrived here last night and found that my mother was no longer among the living. She died having made no provision for the thousands of souls who depended on her. God save us from such a death. On the night she died, in an attempt to delude herself, she ordered her serf orchestra to play polkas in the next room. One owes the dead respect and compassion, but I find it impossible not to tell you everything I know and feel. May heaven bless and keep you.

J. T.

Opéra de Paris, April 16, 1851

—————

TWO YEARS AFTER HER TRIUMPH IN *Le prophète*, Pauline stood on the stage of the Opéra de Paris as Sapho. Charles Gounod was so distraught before the curtain rose that she had to take him into her dressing room and hold him like a terrified child.

It was not a success. Few people knew the composer, and in the salons it had been whispered that the opera was a bore. The hall was only half full for the premiere, and audiences dwindled for the following performances. But so long as she continued to receive fervid ovations, Pauline publicly proclaimed the opera a triumph. She could not tolerate a failure. She sent an ebullient report to George Sand:

> *Ma Ninoune chérie,*
>
> *Rejoice, we have had a great and beautiful success. The response was enormous at the premiere and even greater last night. Every aria was applauded strongly, especially my final adieu to the lute. The work completely drowns all lesser music.* [end letter]

And to Ivan Turgenev:

> *Dear, good Tourgline,*
>
> *We played Sapho three times in succession, our success growing with each performance. You have undoubtedly managed to read all the notices in the French newspapers. Berlioz wrote a*

161

magnificent review. His exalted praise is laced with insults, but he places Gounod in the first rank of composers.

Privately, she worried that the reviews would devastate poor Gounod, who wrote the opera at her insistence. Perhaps she had done him a disservice.

Journal du Débats, April 22, 1851
  "The entire third act of Sapho seemed very beautiful to me, extremely beautiful, the height of poetic drama, but the quartet of the first act, the duo and trio of the second act, where the passions of the principal characters erupt with such force, positively revolted me. I found them hideous, unbearable, horrible. I hope that M. Gounod will not hate me for the ferocity with which I express myself."

                                                          Hector Berlioz

Rue Chaptal, Paris, May 1851

—————

Her eyes hurt. Ivan wrote that if he could take her pain on himself, it would cause him less distress than knowing she suffers. The doctors say it's neuralgia. She wonders if it's the pressure of unshed tears. At every moment, she feels she is about to cry. But she cannot possibly cry. What reason could she give for crying?

A great heaviness weighs on her limbs. She finds it difficult to get out of bed. Sitting up, even moving, seems too great an effort. She ignores the coffee tray Geneviève has brought in. Madame is unwell this morning. Madame no longer finds it possible to participate in her own life.

Everything is wrong. Gounod, whose persistent attentions had been a comfort, no longer has time to see her. Ivan is a continent away. She has tried to love his little daughter but failed. Louisette despises the girl. All day the house shakes with childish screaming, insults hurled in Russian and French. It's to Louis that Paulinette runs for comfort, Louis who adores her.

A square of light lands on her face as Geneviève draws the curtains. Pauline throws an arm over her eyes to block it out. She longs to disappear into the darkness, to leave this house, to leave Louis, the nasty little girls, the strain of smiling, of speaking in a calm tone.

George is at Nohant. Maman has gone off to Belgium. But Ary Scheffer is in Paris. She used to escape to his studio when she was newly married and living with Louis's sisters. He still keeps a piano there. He has always said that her playing makes him paint better.

The thought is enough to make her throw off the blankets and ring for Geneviève to help her dress.

It's spring in Paris. The sun is smiling down on the streets. The trees are all in bud. The birds sound a cheerful chorus. It's all of it far too bright to suit Pauline's mood. She walks with her eyes lowered, watching her boots traverse the gray cobblestones. For the first time in her life, she wonders how she will find the strength to carry on. Nothing interests her. Even work, which has always saved her, seems tedious, infuriating. But she reminds herself that she is out of the house, away from Louis and the little girls. She begins to walk faster. She is walking toward Ary, toward comfort.

She finds him at his easel, a small figure in the vastness of his studio. It's an enormous space, two stories high, half-empty, lit by high windows. The walls are hung with his works and works of painters he admires. Unfinished canvases are stacked against a staircase. The sound of Pauline's steps as she crosses the wooden floor echoes up to the ceiling.

He smiles at her, surprised, happy.

"Bonjour, Ary. How are you?"

"Me? You know me, Pauline. I'm the same. And you?"

"Better for seeing you."

Just to be there, to play the piano in his benevolent presence, will calm her. She thinks that in an hour or two she will feel well enough to go back to her house, to her marriage, her life.

She leans over Ary's shoulder to have a look at the painting on the easel. The poet Dante is seated beside his beloved Beatrice, who stands on a pedestal beside him. Her white gown is only sketched in, but her head and face are finished, her eyes gazing not at Dante, but at heaven.

Ary wipes his hands on a rag.

The piano is waiting for her. She begins to move toward it.

"Stay a moment, Pauline. What is it I see in your face? A cloud has hidden the light of those dear, dark eyes."

"It's . . . no, Ary, nothing. I have nothing to complain of."

"The Russian child? Turgenev's daughter? Does she give you pleasure?"

"Paulinette! The poor girl. Louis has fallen quite in love with her, which makes our Louisette terribly jealous and spiteful. You will see for yourself when you meet her. No, Ary, really, we are all well."

What can she say to him? Can she tell him that she wants to die? She has thought of it. It would be selfish, irresponsible to die, but living has become unendurable. Every moment she struggles to keep from screaming, from falling on the ground and never getting up.

Ary takes her hands in his and strokes them gently with his thumbs.

She doesn't dare look at him. No matter how she tries to compose her features, her face always betrays her. She knows she is being ridiculous. She cannot possibly start to cry now, like a two-year old.

"I know you have not been yourself," Ary says. "Is it so hard to tell me why?"

"What do you know? Has Louis spoken to you? No, forgive me, I have no right to ask that."

She closes her eyes, her head bent like a penitent in the darkness of the confessional.

"I have always come to you, you know that but . . . even the strongest will has its limits, and I have found what mine are. George says that passion has rights of its own, and I have denied it those rights. Perhaps I shouldn't admit this to you . . . I might have given my life to him, to Turgenev. At times, I wonder if I should have. But I chose loyalty over love. I know you will commend me for that decision. Oh, Ary, you cannot know. Love kills when it's not permitted to burst into flame. I try to extinguish it. I try very hard, but it's such cold, cruel torture."

His face is cloaked in the tender passivity of a priest.

She studies the wet brushstrokes on the face of Beatrice. She has had a little outburst. She must take it back now. "I'm speaking rubbish," she says. "Incomprehensible rubbish. Forgive me for burdening you. I'm only telling you what you must already know. Hard as I try, I can feel no more for my husband than friendship. Perhaps the heart can be silenced, Ary, but it cannot be compelled to speak. Louis is too good, too noble. He never asks questions or complains, but to see him suffer so undeservedly and to know that I am the cause of it breaks me to pieces.

"It has always been my nature to live in that calm, safe place where my every thought is for music, art, my vocation. If I could find my way back there, if I could find that place again, I would never leave it."

A profound melancholy settles over her, as though her confession has cut away the source of her agony, and nothing more than a painful incision remains.

Ary's hand grazes the top of her head like a benediction. "My poor Pauline, if you cannot feel passion for Louis, you must feel compassion. You have a duty to him, to your husband. There is no greater joy than the triumph of the will against the baser self. No greater strength, no greater power. I know that Louis does not believe in God. But you, Pauline, you must pray, if you can, for God's guidance. If you cannot find comfort in God through prayer, then find it in your devotion to art in its most divine aspect. Life, to be peaceful and worthwhile, must every moment be a sacrifice."

He is such a committed Lutheran, she thinks, so fortunate to be so unquestioning.

"I know you are right, Ary. My mind knows it and wills me to act accordingly. But knowing that I have made a noble sacrifice does nothing to ease my suffering. Nothing at all."

London, July 1851

M. Gounod's opera, Sapho, has suffered a fatal fall at Covent Garden. Mme. Viardot no longer sings. Each note that emerges from her intelligent throat is a shriek. The singer I admired is dead, or nearly dead, to art. Her broken voice no longer holds any charm, but is the mere shadow of a once beautiful picture.

La France Musicale

Pauline convinced the management of Covent Garden to produce *Sapho* that summer, hoping that the English would appreciate it more than the French. It was performed in Italian translation, according to the custom in London. She sang and acted brilliantly, and it was given a superb production, but it was a fiasco. The French critics, under the regime of Louis-Napoléon Bonaparte, attacked her because republicans were out of favor. The English critics, under the spell of Henriette Sontag, prima donna of the King's Theater, were not kindly disposed toward her rival, the prima donna of Covent Garden. Gounod found it convenient to blame Pauline for the failure of his opera. He spread rumors that she sang out of tune.

In the *Revue et gazette musicale* she read that her contract with the Opéra de Paris had been canceled. The *directeur générale*, Nestor Roqueplan, had not thought it necessary to notify her before he notified the press. She wordlessly handed the newspaper back to Louis. He looked at her with pity. She looked away.

"Papa, your outrage would be far more useful to me than your sympathy."

"It is not entirely Roqueplan's fault, *chérie*. His hand has been forced by Louis-Napoléon. You are paying once again for my political views and for George Sand's."

"Am I? And Pauline Viardot, composer of *Le Jeune République*, has undoubtedly been declared a dangerous republican, but that does nothing to diminish the talents of Pauline Viardot, prima donna of the Opéra de Paris."

She has risen and fallen and risen again, and now that she is falling once more, she wonders if it has been worth the fight.

In the house they habitually rent in West London at Maida Vale, she has chosen to sleep in the larger of the two salons with her piano, her writing table, her vases full of flowers, her books, and her memories of Ivan. In the blackness of a night when the furies fly in circles around her head and she cannot so much as close her eyes without seeing their ravenous faces, when the sheets on which she lies scorch her flesh and the coverlets strangle her so that she gasps for breath, she surrenders.

The cool floors soothe her bare feet. She brushes aside the loose black hairs that prickle her eyes, and pulls a shawl over her shoulders.

She enters the room where her husband sleeps and sits on the bed, watching him, finding nothing but gentleness in his features, in the narrow lips that have never spoken to her in anger. His closed lids hide dark eyes that have always looked at her with love. The pale hand on the coverlet has never touched her with anything but tenderness. She slips under the blankets, curls her body against his. Waking, he silently takes her in his arms.

The furies melt into a deep, still pool. She is safe.

Dun Castle, Lammermuir Hills, Berwickshire, Scotland, October 1851

———————

IN THE MORNINGS, THE LAWNS ARE already covered with frost, but if Pauline wraps herself in layers of shawls she can walk the park surrounding the castle, past the docile cattle that roam the fields, the flocks of sheep that forage among the grasses, down to the lake where ducks and swans dip their heads in search of a meal, then waddle up onto the dry, cold ground, fluffing their feathers to warm themselves.

She reminds herself that Louis is noble, generous, kind. If the face of Ivan Turgenev rises before her eyes as she looks out over the gray-green slopes of the Lammermuirs, she finds the strength to replace it with the face of Ary Scheffer, and reminds herself of the joy of self-sacrifice.

Louis has announced that Madame Viardot is retiring from the stage for a year of rest. The little girls, Paulinette and Louisette, have been sent to separate boarding schools in France. William Hay, Earl of Tweeddale, invited them to spend a few weeks here at Duns Castle. And as there is no reason, now, to return to Paris, they accepted. Louis has been keen to try the hunting, and he has his dogs with him.

George wrote wondering what the devil Pauline would find to do in Scotland. Pauline wonders what point there would be in doing anything at all.

In the afternoons, she makes her appearance at the tea table, and when the chatter begins to bore her, she excuses herself. She writes letters. She reads Shakespeare, Goethe, Balzac in English,

German, French. From time to time, she finds it necessary to consent to sing for the household.

She has begun to leave the door open between her room and the room where Louis sleeps. In the dark, she does things now she knows embarrass him, things he says he would never have asked of her. She touches him in a way that few wives touch their husbands.

They are still in Scotland in December when they read in the newspapers that Louis-Napoléon Bonaparte has dissolved the National Assembly and declared himself Emperor of France. It means the end to any lingering hope of a French republic. The death and destruction of the 1848 revolution has succeeded only in placing another despot on the throne.

Pauline watches sadness overcome poor Louis, who has worked all his life to promote republican ideals. He feels he is estranged from his own country, a relic of another decade. As it's too cold now to hunt in the Lammermuir hills, Pauline is his only consolation. He needs her affection more than he ever has, and she admonishes herself for resenting it.

There are riots in the streets of Paris again. Ivan Turgenev, frantic in Saint Petersburg, writes that he has heard that the barricades reach almost out to the Rue de Douai. Lord Hay has no choice but to insist that they remain at the castle. And they have no choice but to accept.

When Pauline's ankles begin to swell, she no longer walks the grounds but sits by the hearth with her feet on a stool. The doctor tells her she is with child again, and she hears the sound of a door slamming shut.

The news that you announce, dear Madame Viardot, is so important that I had to write to you immediately. I cannot share the dark presentiments you have about this child and I have a kind of certainty that I love him already, and that his entry into the world will be very fortunate. My only desire is to meet him before he is speaking fluently. In the name of heaven, take care of yourself. Let the Hay family pamper you there. And ask Viardot to write to me as soon as the child is born. I hope that he is a boy, and that he is a good and beautiful boy.

This news has so absorbed me that I am unable to write you about anything else.

IVAN SEALS THE LETTER, PUTS IT in his pocket, and goes out to walk the frozen streets of Saint Petersburg, thinking of nothing and of everything, his mind flickering from image to image, from Pauline's arms around his neck, to Pauline lying with Louis. He sees her looking at him with undeniable love, and he sees her turning to her husband with the same expression. He struggles to understand what she must be feeling, while his own emotions roil unexamined in his body. His feet, encased in heavy boots, become numb with the cold. He bumps into passersby, seeing neither where he is nor where he is going, until the lamplighters begin to lift the curtains of dusk.

At home, his servant takes his coat and, noticing the letter still in the pocket, asks if it should be posted in the morning. Ivan hesitates, trying to remember what he wrote, then nods, and sits to have his boots removed. Huddled in an armchair, he sinks into the profound loneliness of a man whose love is hopeless.

The Viardots were able to return to France for the birth. The baby, a girl, is called Claudie, after her father, Louis Claude Viardot. Louis requested it, and Pauline wisely obliged. In the salons, it is whispered that the name was chosen to affirm the child's paternity. The gossiping wags, who have difficulty counting backward from nine, claim that the child is Turgenev's. Those who are slightly more adept point out that the father must be Gounod.

Far away in Russia, Ivan is alone. The birth of the child has left him with even less reason to hope. But Pauline never leaves him. At a cousin's house, he sees a serf woman whose plain face and delicate hands make his heart stop for a moment. He buys her freedom in the way that a woman who has lost a child might buy a puppy, and moves her into his apartment in Saint Petersburg, into his house at Spasskoye, into whichever bed he happens to be occupying. But she is illiterate, ill-tempered, and has no patience for his attempts to educate her. He makes a comedy of his tragic situation, joking to his friends that even immorality has proven to be no cure for boredom. And when he can no longer bear the sight of her, he gives her a sum of money and finds a minor official with the Naval Ministry who is willing to marry her.

Rue de Douai, Paris June 1852

Sitting up in bed, Pauline strokes the perfect little face with her finger. The baby is staring at her, its dark eyes unblinking, its mouth moving about like a fish. How is it possible that she and Louis could have produced such a magnificent creature? The little chin, slightly pointed, the little nose so finely formed. Everything about Claudie Pauline Marie Viardot is delicate, feminine, flawless.

"Claudie, my little Didie. How your mother loves you! You have been spared her bulging eyes, your father's preposterous nose. You are as beautiful as your poor lost aunt Maria, and I am mad with love for you."

Ten days later, she hands the baby to the wet nurse and rings for Geneviève. It's no good lying about when she has a new season to prepare. She needs to go back to the music room, to the comfort of work. She is learning Mendelssohn's *Elijah* for a concert at the London Sacred Harmonic Society, and she is not used to singing in English.

"Woe, Woe," she sings, "unto zem who forrrsake heem."

From the corner of her eye, she notices that Louis has come into the room. Still singing, she signals him to wait, raising her right hand while playing the bass chords with her left. She turns her head. He is holding up a letter.

Ivan's long, slanted penmanship.

Her hand slides off the keyboard.

He says, "Sorry. I just thought you'd like to know that Turgenev has been arrested in Saint Petersburg."

"Has he written to you?"

"To us. He found someone to smuggle the letter out of Russia."

"But why? Why was he arrested? We should have prevented him from returning there, Papa. *I* should have. I should have insisted. He knew this would happen. He knew."

"I suppose . . . I suppose, but he brought it on himself. He published a few lines in a Moscow newspaper on the death of Nikolai Gogol, whom he knows perfectly well is non grata there. Ironic, isn't it, that this should happen when he has finally come into his inheritance and could have traveled wherever he liked? He could have returned to France. Ah, well then, sorry to have disturbed you."

> *I am being held at a police station by order of the emperor for having had a few lines about Gogol published in a Moscow news-paper. It is no more than a pretext. The article, in itself, was perfectly insignificant. I have been watched for some time, and they simply seized me at the first opportunity. I cannot fault the emperor. The case was put to him in such a treacherous manner, he could not have acted otherwise. They wanted to put a stop to all that was being said about the death of Gogol, and, at the same time, they were not sorry to put an end to my literary activity.*
>
> *In fifteen days' time I will be sent to the country, to Spasskoye, where I will be under house arrest indefinitely. To be honest, my misfortune is not so great. The year 1852 will simply not have had a spring for me, that's all. The saddest thing is that I have to say goodbye to my hopes of traveling abroad—but I never had any real illusions about that. When I left you, I knew that it would be for a long time, perhaps forever.*

She reads the letter. She reads it again. And then she really must get back to work. She inhales deeply, raising her soft palate, low-ering her larynx, relaxing her jaw, flattening her tongue. But what issues from her mouth is a wail. Why, why did he go back to Russia? What can she possibly do for him now? Nothing, nothing. When she realized that she was pregnant with Louis's child, she promised herself that she'd keep her eyes on her own nest, that she'd stop glancing eastward over her shoulder as though the future might be waiting for her there. *Now look at the music, Pauline. Try again. Get a really good breath this time.*

"Woe, woe unto dem who forrsake heem. Forrsake him. Forr dey have trrransgrres-sed."

* * *

Pauline still writes to Ivan, but not often. Knowing that her letters will be intercepted by the police before they reach him makes it impossible to write anything meaningful, and what use is there in keeping alive a love that may never be more than ink on paper? The less frequently she writes, the shorter her letters become, and fewer events in her daily life seem worth sharing.

That summer in London she hears that her rival Giulia Grisi has been signed for a winter season at Saint Petersburg. She is sure that Louis must have known, must have chosen not to mention it. She is enraged, but she says nothing. She was the greatest prima donna Russia had ever seen. The czar himself came backstage to kiss her hand. Stepan Gedeonov might still be infatuated with her. She sees no need to speak to Louis. She writes to Gedeonov herself.

Gedeonov replies to her letter, offering three of the roles she sang during her first Russian season—and he agrees to stage *Le prophète* for her, if the text can be altered enough to pass the czar's censors.

When she presents the letter to Louis, he is too proud and too clever to protest that she has taken his job from him, that he is, after all, in charge of her affairs. He simply, calmly points out that with only those performances, she won't earn enough money to justify the journey. She argues that she will surely be offered engagements in Moscow, as well. He reminds her that the opera house in Moscow has burned down, and she won't be free to leave Saint Petersburg until Lent has begun. She reminds him how much he enjoys hunting on the Russian-Finnish border, and that Princess Golitsyn will surely arrange concerts for her in Moscow during Lent.

Spasskoye, Mtsensk, Orel Province, January 1853

THE SNOW BEGAN FALLING IN OCTOBER, and now it's as deep as a man is tall. Whenever he sees a sleigh coming down the drive, he hopes it contains someone interesting with whom he can talk. He begged his friend Annenkov to drive out from Moscow to share in his rural ennui, but Pavel Vasilyevich is busy editing a new edition of Pushkin's works and cannot spare the time.

In order to survive the excruciating tedium, Ivan keeps to a schedule that moves the day along like an engine. He rises at the same time, breakfasts at the same time. If the snow is not too daunting, he walks for an hour after breakfast, reads and writes for precisely four hours before dinner, then works again until supper, which he takes precisely at nine. The nights begin early, the mornings late.

He sends and receives letters, but one can say more and learn more from an hour's conversation than from a year's correspondence. He waits, with little hope, for a letter from Pauline. He feels as though he has already become an old man for whom memories replace experiences.

The wind moans outside his windows like a sick child. He is trying to begin a story, to distill his characters into essences that can be bottled up and served to his readers.

He has found a mate for his Diana. He kneels over six black and tan puppies as they open their eyes for the first time, and Diana growls when he tries to touch their tiny heads.

He spends his thirty-fourth birthday alone in the great house, while outside, snow hurls against the windows in white darkness.

In spite of his inheritance, he is not nearly so rich as he had thought he would be. He has freed the house serfs, and offered the others maximum freedom under the law, which brings him minimal profits. He has given all the serfs at Spasskoye their houses and the land around them, built a school, a hospital, and a home for the aged. In order to send Viardot the money for his daughter's keep, he has recently sold a few verstes of wheat fields to a merchant who offered him half his asking price.

At the end of December when Pauline arrives in Saint Petersburg, he reads about it in the newspapers before he receives the letter she wrote him from Paris a month before.

She is in Russia. It's as though he has been abruptly wakened from a profound sleep. His eyes see hers wherever he looks. He feels her presence with every inch of his flesh. His body, which he had willed to numbness, is suddenly, excruciatingly alive. After months of lethargy, loneliness, and boredom, he is restless, inflamed. If he could reach his arms as far as Saint Petersburg, he would pull her close to him. If he could go to her, if he could see her, he would fall on his knees, weeping.

Every few days, the police come to his house to be sure he is still there. Sometimes he tells his servant to say that he is sleeping or ill. He is, after all, the son of Varvara Petrovna. Every soul in the province still trembles in fear at the thought of her.

He writes to everyone he knows in the capital. Have they heard Pauline sing? Have they seen her? Is she well? He writes to her.

> *You are already in Saint Petersburg and I cannot be there. It's hard for me, and I will have to get used to the idea before I can write you a more extensive letter. I beg you to take care of yourself. My God! The things I would say to you if I saw you again! Write me often, I beg you.*

He imagines her at Spasskoye in May when the gardens are splendid. He sees her walking down the allée lined with birch, the young leaves still slightly folded, showing the marks of the bud which encased them like the pleats of a dress. It's not impossible, is it, this dream?

The Imperial Theatre,
Saint Petersburg, January 1853

―――――――

PAULINE BEGINS AGAIN IN SAINT PETERSBURG, as she did nine years before, with Rosina in *Il Barbiere di Siviglia*. In Paris, they might have said that, at thirty-one, she was too old for the role of a saucy young woman. They might have said that her voice lacked a certain freshness now. She knows this, but she is in Russia, where she is still idolized. She makes her entrance on the great stage with the calm confidence of a goldsmith who has created the same flawless ring dozens of times before.

When she steps into the spotlight, there is thunder. There is lightning. There is a storm of applause, a torrent of flowers. For ten minutes she stands there, head bent, hands crossed over her heart. They are applauding a performance she has not yet begun. Their Pauline has returned to them.

She begins to cry before she begins to sing. Her voice, at first, is weak, shaking, her throat closed. Then the music lifts her like a wave and carries her along on its crest.

Five nights later, at the final curtain of *La sonnambula*, the czar himself appears onstage and offers his arm. Nicholas, who personally banished Ivan Sergeyevich to Spasskoye, leads her to the royal box to meet the czarina and all the assembled court.

She is thrilled, giddy. She is back at the center of the whirlwind, and she forgets everything else—until she returns to her dressing room and Turgenev is not there.

* * *

Louis has been trying to enjoy himself. He went off to the Finnish border with a hunting party in search of bear, but fever and stomach pains forced him to turn back. Before he had fired a single shot, he was wrapped in furs and bundled onto a sleigh, shivering and miserable, dragged over the endless ice and snow. In Petersburg, doctors were called. He was advised that the harsh Russian climate has afflicted him with an attack of nerves. Pauline has offered to cancel the rest of her engagements and return to Paris with him, but he cannot bear to deny her the pleasures of a brilliant season, and he has no reason to believe her when she swears that her only care is for him.

Not that she hasn't been caring. She appealed to the Grand Duchess Elena Pavlovna who sent her personal physician. Dr. Mikschik diagnosed catarrhal fever, located in the *plexus nervosus* below the *epigastrium* and prescribed powders of nux vomica and wolfsbane.

The illness does not frighten Viardot. He is merely bored, annoyed with himself for having allowed Pauline to persuade him that this Russian trip would be worthwhile. Confined to his bed with nothing to do, he writes long chatty letters filled with gossip. He even writes to Ivan Turgenev. Pauline has repeatedly pointed out that Ivan is alone, isolated, in need of friends. She urges him to take her to Spasskoye. Why in the world does she think he would consent to it? It's out of the question. Too far off and too dangerous. Yet she persists. This morning she suggested that as Spasskoye is such a great distance from Petersburg, perhaps they could meet Ivan in some village near Moscow. This time he really will have to deny her. It's hardly a question of jealousy. He has excellent reasons. Hoping to put the matter at rest, he has offered to explain the situation to Ivan himself, and has decided to take the precaution of writing in Spanish, assuming that Turgenev remembers the language and that the czar's secret police know not a word of it.

We had thought if we went to Moscow, we might continue on to some village where you could meet us from your side, and stop there for a day or two. But I was advised not to even think of it. I have been officially warned to be very prudent. We must consider that there is cholera in the area and that my health is not good, and that I am under constant surveillance, my every gesture monitored. If it is true what they say, then your friendship will cause me great harm, and mine will be even worse for you. Were we to organize a meeting and fix a date, it could have disastrous results, not for those of us who are leaving the country, but for those who are forced to remain here.

Ivan responds with a gentle irony that is not lost on Louis.

My dear friend, what distinguishes you most is your sound judgment. We will meet when it is God's will. Cuando Dios quiere.

SPASSKOYE, MARCH 1853

I**N TWO MONTHS, IVAN HAS RECEIVED** four long letters from
Pauline. Knowing that her hands have touched those pages,
that for an hour or two she thought of him, fills him with joy out
of all proportion. He scans the newspapers for her name, turning
the pages so anxiously they rip. His aristocratic friends in Saint
Petersburg supply him with news of her social appearances, her
escorts, her gowns. Pavel Annenkov, who is no connoisseur of
music, has nevertheless been pressed into reporting on her performances.

Now Princess Mestchersky writes that Louis Viardot has left
Russia and that Pauline is going to Moscow alone. Ivan tears at
his beard, at his hair. He paces through the house, unable even
to sit or stand still. Moscow is a three-hundred-mile drive from
Spasskoye, and the snow is beginning to melt, miring the roads in
mud. If the czar's police learn that he has left his estate, he will be
sent into exile in Siberia, perhaps for the rest of his life. But If he
does not go to her now, he might never see her again. If he could
see her smile in shocked delight, if she offered her magnificent
hands to him . . .

When he is calm enough to hold a pen, he writes to her. *Is
it true that you are going to Moscow, and that you are staying with
Princess Golitsyn? Without in any way criticizing you, I must tell you
that I would have preferred to have heard this news directly from you.*

Then he sends for his steward, a bald man of about seventy who
held the title of "Prime Minister" while Varvara Petrovna was alive
and who still wears the black coat, white cravat, and waistcoat of

his office. Ivan Sergeyevich has known him all his life. His loyalty is beyond question.

Ivan is rocking on his heels, his hands clasped behind his back, concealing his nervousness in his best imitation of a pompous nobleman. "Tell me, Mihail Savelitch, the merchant who bought those verstes from us, you must know where he is staying. He travels a good deal in his line of work, does he not?"

"I am sure he does, *khozyain*."

"I see. So, he has an interior passport? I ask you this in strictest confidence because I know you won't mention it to anyone."

"On my soul, *khozyain*."

"Look, I need to go to Moscow . . ."

"Forgive me for saying so, Ivan Sergeyevich, but in Russia, money can buy anything."

Golitsyn House, Moscow

———

PAULINE HOPED TO SEE HIM, OF course she hoped. Hope compelled her eastward across the continent. She'd hardly thought how she would manage it. Traveling to Spasskoye without her husband was out of the question. If the czar's secret police are not following her, as Louis insists, surely the journalists are.

In glittering, cosmopolitan Saint Petersburg, she had been distracted, whirling on a carousel of rehearsals, performances, receptions, endless music and noise. Now the whirling has stopped, throwing her to the ground. She is in Moscow, in the alien East. She has been ill, feverish, confined to her bed, thinking too much, remembering.

That morning, as the fever had broken, Geneviève drew back the curtains. Tremulous sunlight banished the images that tormented her in the dark. She sat up, asked for her tea. She was strong again, clear. Perhaps it was as well that she has not seen Ivan. She has fought too hard to regain her peace of mind.

There is a note on the tea tray.

"What is this now? Haven't we told the majordomo that I am too ill to see anyone? Why is he still sending up notes?"

"But Madame . . ."

"I see . . ." His handwriting. "Thank you, Geneviève."

He is in Moscow. She refolds the note and places it under her pillow to keep it safe and warm, rolls onto her side, pulls her legs up, and wraps her arms around herself, one minute whimpering with fear, laughing with joy the next. How has he managed to escape house arrest? How desperate he must be to see her. How he must love her.

Stop crying, Pauline. Think!

At nine in the evening, when the sky is black and the weak light of the streetlamps is easy to avoid, Geneviève approaches the gate of Golitsyn House with fifty kopeks to pay off the guard.

Now the agony of waiting. Pauline is sitting up in bed, leaning against a bulwark of pillows, willing herself to concentrate on her book, to convince herself she is not so anxious, after all. She has finally found the time to read George Sand's new novel, *Les Maîtres sonneurs*, but it is impossible to concentrate. At every small sound, she starts, convinced she hears his heavy footsteps coming up the back stairs.

¡Ay! This must be him now, the sound is too loud to be anything else. She can hear him getting closer, talking in a low voice to Geneviève. *Sit up straight, Pauline, smooth your hair! Pick up the book again. You mustn't appear too eager. You must breathe easily, speak with a firm voice. The knock on the door!*

But it's just Geneviève's face, peering into the room, her plump cheeks red from the cold.

"Where is he? Is he here?"

"He's waiting on the landing, trembling like a fawn. He had to grasp the railing to manage the steps."

"*¡Dios mio!* Bring him in before someone sees him!"

She forces herself to turn back to her book, then raises her eyes slowly. And he is standing in the doorway, looking helpless, a giant of a man with the sweet face of a boy, his hands large yet elegant, his shoulders a little hunched.

"Jean, you are mad to have come!"

Is she smiling too broadly? He has been so impossibly far away for so long, and now he is kneeling beside the bed. It's really him, his face, his hair, his beard, his body. The way he meticulously kisses each of her fingers.

"Pauline, you are ill!"

"Shh! We must whisper. They are all at supper, but someone could come into the passage at any moment. I am recovering from the grippe, from your cursed Russian weather. But I am better now that you are here. I have forbidden every visitor. You are the only person who can make me well. Come, sit down, bring that chair close to me."

She examines him, searching for the face she remembered, the lavender scent of his cologne. His hands, big and soft.

His voice is high, squeaking. "I'm dreaming a dream that I'm striving to remember even while I'm dreaming it. I cannot really be here, looking at you."

"And how do I look? Not very well, I'm afraid."

She is wearing her best peignoir, a peach silk extravagantly embellished with Brussels lace. Geneviève has loosened her braid, brushed her hair into a shining black mantle draped over her shoulders.

"You are magnificent," he says.

"Talk to me, Jean. Tell me about Spasskoye. Tell me about your work. Talk to me the way we used to when we sat together at Courtavenel under the old elm."

He leans over the bed and lays his head in her lap. She cannot help laughing. It's been so long, yet it feels so familiar. She strokes his hair. "It was like this, wasn't it?"

"I could stay like this forever. Will Geneviève come back soon?"

"Not until I ring for her to show you out. The night guard has been made to believe that you are her paramour. Imagine, fat little French Geneviève on the arm of a big Russian in baggy pants! Shhh. We mustn't laugh too loudly."

He raises his head. He is impossibly close to her, this bearish man who can make her happy, make her laugh. She touches his soft, hairy cheek.

He kisses her forehead, her eyes, the tip of her nose. He kisses her mouth.

"Jean, no."

His forehead is against hers. His staccato breath.

Pauline, you promised yourself that just to see him would be enough.

"I will have to tell Louis that I have seen you. If I choose not to tell him, I will have to ask Geneviève to keep a secret, and, you know, I cannot in good conscience ask her that."

He sits back. "I don't know what I thought. I shouldn't have assumed."

She takes his hand. "Talk to me, Jean. You have been gone for two years. Are you working? Are you writing?"

"No . . . yes. I started a novel inspired by my mother and her family. You know, I wrote you that I had discovered her diary after she died. What a woman she was! Annenkov has the first pages. He will give me good advice. But really, I don't have much hope for it. Pauline . . ." He kisses her fingers, her wrist.

"Forgive me. I thought . . . I cannot help thinking, that if I'm caught, sent to Siberia, if I'm never able to leave Russia again, if I never see you after tonight . . ."

She puts her hand in his hair.

"May I kiss you," he asks, "just once more? Just one last memory of a kiss?"

She has a sudden awareness of her body, as though she has never noticed before that she has breasts and buttocks.

She says, "Take off your boots."

Later, her head on his chest, her fingers play with the fine hairs on his pale, damp belly. She whispers without looking up, listening to his breath, his heartbeat. "Whatever I may feel for you, whatever you may feel for me, must remain hidden away, like the most precious possession. In a day, two days, I will return to my life, my work. I will sing Glinka's music at my farewell concert, and then I will return to France, to Louis and the children. And you will return to your life, to your destiny, whatever it is. I will learn that you have written many marvelous things, and I will be proud that you loved me. And someday, you will come back to us at Courtavenel. But it will never be as it was. You know it cannot be."

They are both crying, in the way that lovers cry together, the helpless, frustrated tears that come when both are in pain and there is no one to blame, so they cling to each other in mutual regret, memorizing the sensations of their mingled flesh, knowing, even then, that they will replay that moment over and over again, until the memory wears out and becomes dim from overuse.

* * *

For three days, Ivan wept as he drove the merchant's cart through the melting snow and mud back to Orel province, not caring that it might get stuck or overturn, lurching half-blind through the countryside. He had been clinging to a thin thread of hope that slipped from his grasp in Moscow, leaving him with empty fingers, twitching in agony.

Now that he is imprisoned once again at Spasskoye, sorrow has attacked his body with stomach pains so violent he thinks it must be cancer. He looks out at the gray curtain of freezing rain. In a matter of weeks, days perhaps, the white-beaked ravens, the larks and thrushes will announce the spring. Sparrows will begin to squabble and chatter again. One morning, a flock of wild geese will fly across the sky, and a gust of wind will seem warmer than usual. Tiny buds will begin to swell on the branches of the willows. But the muddy roads leading to his estate are still impassable, and there are few visitors whose company he can endure, in any case. He willingly succumbs to misery and loneliness.

* * *

On the boat from Saint Petersburg to Stettin, on the train from Stettin to Warsaw, in the diligence from Warsaw to Dusseldorf, and from Dusseldorf to Paris, Pauline gazes through windows streaked with dust, still feeling his skin beneath her hand, his soft beard brushing her cheek, knowing that every moment is taking her farther from him, from a part of her life that must be left in the dark now to shrivel and die.

As she crosses the border from Germany into France, she begins to think of Louisette, of Claudie and the dogs. All of them will be running and jumping when she comes through the door. She thinks of Louis, and vows to be kind to him. She thinks of Paulinette, too, but with more suffering than pleasure. She has failed to make the daughter love her, just as she has failed to make the father forget her.

In June, when she is back in London for the season, she visits Alexander Herzen, who has relocated his exile to a house in the Richmond district. She needs to speak of Ivan Sergeyevich with someone who shares her knowledge of him. She will tell Herzen that she saw him in Moscow without divulging all that transpired. She will be able to laugh at Ivan's hypochondria, his passivity, his foolishness, and praise his generosity, his kindness, his humor, his brilliant mind. She will speak of Ivan in a way that will help her clarify what her relationship to him must be.

Herzen publishes an expatriate journal in London, *The Bell*, which extols Russian culture while it savages Russia's repressive monarchy. "We constitute the whole of Russian publicity," he says. "I write, your husband translates, and you sing in Russian."

She raises her thick, dark eyebrows. "So, you are not among the many Russians who call me a crafty 'Jewess,' who accuse me of keeping Turgenev chained with love to get at his money? Am I not the heartless witch who tore Ivan Sergeyevich from his homeland and prevented him from writing?"

"If I ever thought so, Madame Viardot, I beg your forgiveness now."

Knowing that she has had the willpower to overcome her passion brings her a kind of happiness. She tells herself that although choosing the right path has nearly broken her, it has raised her up a step toward goodness. Her sacred art, her music, will be her antidote.

In September, the allied forces of France, England, and the Ottoman Empire land at Eupatoria in the Crimea. And in the extremity of his hubris, Louis-Napoléon has declared sovereignty over the Holy Lands. Russia is at war. Even if Ivan Sergeyevich were permitted to leave Spasskoye, foreign travel would be impossible.

In November, his house arrest is lifted, although he is to be kept under constant surveillance.

Pavel Annenkov has found him furnished rooms in Saint Petersburg on Povarskoy Lane near the Anchikov Bridge.

He is determined to make a new life for himself, devoted to literary work, friends, music, and the occasional game of chess. If there is nothing left for him but to write, he had better take another road with his work. He wants to produce something on a larger scale, and he worries that he is incapable of it. He sets out to destroy the "literary man," the stylist, to draw, instead, with clear and simple lines, with the skill and craftsmanship that results from certainty. He begins work on a *povest*, a short novel, burrowing through it like a mole. For the first time, he writes a careful outline before he sets to work, makes a list of characters, and writes a detailed biography of each one. He finishes the *povest* in seven weeks. Convinced that the thing is worthless and that his career as a writer is over, he sends the manuscript to Annenkov and other literary friends for their judgments. Then he spends six months revising it.

* * *

When *Rudin*, the *povest* over which he has so earnestly labored, appears in *The Contemporary*, it becomes the talk of every drawing room in the capital. He has portrayed a man with a brilliant mind but a weak character, a man meant to typify his class and generation—educated, idealistic, but superfluous, a man who serves no useful function in society.

The volume of his collected stories, which the editor has titled *Sketches from a Sportsman's Notebook*, sold out immediately, and now that the book is out of print, copies continue to be passed from hand to hand. Ivan Turgenev is a celebrity among the intelligentsia. Everyone wants to meet him.

He corresponds with Louis Viardot about the care of his daughter, Paulinette, but although he continues to write to Pauline, he hears very little from her in return. Occasionally, she dashes off a few lines, letters, which seem to him so hurried that each word strives to be the last. It's time for him to build a nest of his own.

For a few weeks, he spends long nights with a Polish woman who finally exhausts him. For a month, he courts Olga Alexandrovna Turgeneva, a bright, blonde, nineteen-year-old distant cousin whom he briefly considers marrying. He pursues an intense, flirtatious friendship with the Countess Mariya Tolstoya, whose estate is near his. None of his affairs ever amount to anything. He knows that a woman has a right to a man's whole heart, and that he is unable to offer that to anyone.

When he learns that Countess Tolstoya's brother, Lev Nikoleyevich, a writer of twenty-six, has dedicated a story to him, he invites the younger man, newly returned from the Crimean War, to stay with him in his Petersburg flat. He calls Tolstoy the troglodyte for his debaucheries, his wild suspiciousness, and his buffalo-like stubbornness. They have furious arguments over democratic reforms and the merits of George Sand's novels, and after a time, they can barely tolerate each other's company.

On nights when melancholy overcomes him, when he feels himself the saddest man in the world, he unlocks the drawer in which he keeps Pauline's letters and takes out the sheaf of pages. Sometimes, just the sight of her handwriting is too much for him, and he puts them away, swearing he will never unlock the drawer again. But on other nights, he stretches his long body out on the divan and carefully, lovingly reads them one by one, reliving what had been between them, floating in the warm waters of melancholy. In those hours, he is with her, cherishing her.

Pauline returned from Moscow determined to make the best of her marriage, no matter what it cost her. When a daughter, Marianne, is born, even the most vociferous Parisian gossips assume the father is Louis Viardot.

In this way, three years pass.

Furstadskaya Street,
Saint Petersburg, May 1856

N EARLY EVERY EVENING, IVAN TAKES REFUGE in Countess Lambert's little green sitting room, always finding her alone, surrounded by a host of candlelit icons and stacks of books. She is thirty-five years old, the same age as Pauline, but she is already gray-haired, a devoutly religious, unhappy woman who has lost her only son, and whose husband, the czar's aide-de-camp, neglects her.

She is sitting upright in her armchair, Ivan lounging on the divan, and for an hour or two, they have been communing, skirting subjects of inevitable discord. She has become a comfort to him in his loneliness. He knows that she disapproves of his lack of piety, his left-leaning political convictions, and sometimes he tires of defending himself, but they have a community of spirit and they share a penchant for luxuriating in melancholy. Now he wants her to help him obtain a passport.

Czar Nicholas has been gone for a year, dead of pneumonia at the age of fifty-eight. Some say he committed suicide or died of grief over the disastrous outcome of the Crimean War. His son, the more liberal Alexander II, is now Emperor and Autocrat of all the Russias, King of Poland, and Grand Duke of Finland. Ivan Sergeyevich can finally travel abroad.

Countess Lambert's pale eyes, shaded by the floppy brim of her white cap, are soft with affection, but her thin lips are pursed in irritation. He doesn't expect her to be pleased that he is leaving Russia, but he doesn't doubt that she will help him.

"I suppose you'll scurry off to Madame Viardot like a rabbit to its warren the moment you have a passport in your hand."

He leans back and smiles. He knows that his endless monologues on the extraordinary merits of Pauline Viardot irritate her.

"I should remind you, Yelizaveta Yigorovna, that I have a daughter in France whom I have not seen in more than five years."

"A daughter whom you could wait another five years to see without suffering unbearably. You are not fooling your friends, Ivan Sergeyevich."

"I am not trying to fool anyone. As for Madame Viardot, really, I have no idea how I will be received. I don't even know where to write to her. She may be in Vienna or Berlin. I have written to her in Paris to tell her that I hope to be at Courtavenel by the beginning of the hunting season on the first of September, but more than a month has passed and I am still awaiting her reply. I have also written to her mother, Madame Garcia. Perhaps she will send me an address."

He sits up now, and folds his hands between his open knees, leaning forward and latching his eyes onto Madame Lambert's.

"To be perfectly honest, I cannot help thinking it would be better for me not to leave. To go abroad at my age means resigning myself to the life of a gypsy, giving up my last hope of marrying and building a nest of my own. It means that I have abandoned all thoughts of happiness, you know, the breathless happiness of a young man. But what can I do? I wasn't fated for that sort of thing."

Countess Lambert works her lips as though she is chewing on his words.

"Fated! Are you such a victim of fate that you have no will of your own?"

"Yes, all right, weak characters like me love to invent a fate for themselves, relieving themselves of the responsibility of a free will. In any case, it's too late for me to retrace the steps that brought me to this point. As we say in Russia, once the wine has been uncorked it must be drunk."

His passport was issued in late June. Three weeks later, he left Russia. He would travel anywhere in the world on the faintest hope of seeing Pauline again.

Maida Vale, London, July 1856

Pauline travels less now, and when she does it is often without Louis. She has finally managed to convince him that she is perfectly capable of traveling with only Geneviève for company, and that he is needed at home to take care of their affairs and keep an eye on their little daughters. Away from her husband, she can remind herself of the great respect and affection she feels for him. When she is with him, his relentless adoration, which she is incapable of returning, claws at her.

Her life has fallen into a pattern. She spends the spring and fall at Courtavenel. In the winter, as there is no longer a place for her in the Paris opera houses, she tours Germany without Louis. In the summer, she is engaged for a few weeks in London, where the public still clamor for her, and where Louis has friends whose company he enjoys. This season, she is singing her most popular roles and, at the request of Giuseppe Verdi, the role of the gypsy Azucena in the London premiere of *Il trovatore*.

A week before her thirty-fifth birthday, and two days after her debut as Azucena, she is spending a lazy morning in her bedroom at the Maida Vale house, reading the mail that arrived with her breakfast tray. She holds the letter for a long time, not knowing what to do with it, presses the pages to her nose, hoping for some trace of lavender cologne. She waits until her breathing slows, until her hands stop trembling. Then she calls her husband.

"Papa! Turgenev has left Russia! He is in Paris!"

Louis Viardot enters the room and leans against the bedpost, his hands in the pockets of his silk dressing gown.

201

"You must be very glad. We will see him soon, then. We will have him at Courtavenel for the rest of the summer, I assume, and for the hunting season."

"Papa *chéri*, it will be good for us all. He will have a rest after his Russian imprisonment. The family will be delighted that he's back. You will have your shooting partner. Paulinette will have her father."

"And you?"

"And your wife will have the company of a dear friend."

COURTAVENEL, AUGUST 1856

EVERY MORNING AT COURTAVENEL, WHILE SHE dresses to go downstairs, Pauline reminds herself that he is nothing more than a friend. His hair has already gone gray, but at thirty-eight, it suits him. She finds him oddly more attractive than she remembered. He is almost another man, an older, less boyish, more substantial Jean. She struggles with conflicting impulses to touch him and to run away from him.

She is grateful for everything that creates space between them—the constant noise of the family, children, dogs; Maman who wants him to sit beside her, Tío Paolo who wants him to play chess. The two little girls, Claudie and Marianne, enchant him. He carries them around on his shoulders, tells them stories, threatens to devour them with kisses. The older girls are diffident—fifteen-year-old Louisette because she is jealous of the attention her mother lavishes on him, fourteen-year-old Paulinette because she is jealous of the attention her father lavishes on Pauline.

Even Louis seems cautiously happy to have him back in the fold. They have resumed their work together as though nothing interrupted it, translating into French Turgenev's novel, *Rudin*, and stories from his story collection *A Sportsman's Sketches*.

Now that the strangeness of the first days together have passed, Pauline has become used to having him nearby again. He found his old gray jacket in the closet of the room he has always occupied, and she smiled when she saw him wearing it, clothing himself in the past.

The breeze has set the leaves of the poplars fluttering in the sunlight. Ivan, who has been trailing Pauline since breakfast, catches her as she sets off for her favorite tree, carrying a book.

"Shall I walk with you?" he asks. She smiles and takes his arm.

"How happy we are!" he says.

"Are you so happy, Jean?"

"I am as happy as a trout in a stream with the sunlight bouncing on its waters. Each day seems like a gift. My heart is so calm and light."

In the shade of the elm, she spreads her skirts out without opening her book. He throws himself onto the ground.

"What a marvelous thing it is to lie on one's back, looking up! I feel I'm looking into a bottomless sea, which stretches out below me and that the trees, instead of rising up from the ground, are sinking like mighty plants, falling straight into the clear, glassy waves. Can you see how, when the wind ruffles the leaves, they are at one moment sparkling emeralds and the next a mass of golden green?"

She follows his eyes up toward the transparent blue sky and sees what he sees. She thinks he is poetry. *¡Ay! Pauline, he has reminded you of what you loved in him, shown you that forgotten sweetness you found impossible to resist.*

She falls onto her back beside him, blanketed by warmth that seems to spread from his body to hers, to penetrate the earth beneath them, to melt into the sunlight. She is grinning ridiculously, and she turns her head to see the same smile on his face. Without thinking, she takes his hand, his skin against hers.

"Yes, this is happiness," she says.

On the first of September, the hunting season opened, but the weather has been bad and the game scarce. The partridges all nested in the haystacks this year, and when the hay was collected, the birds scattered to who knows where.

It has been raining for days on end, so they have devised the usual country entertainments to occupy themselves. At the piano in the grand salon, Pauline has been playing through all of Beethoven's sonatas and symphonies with Louisette, making up names for each one.

In a makeshift theater in the attic, they entertain each other with theatricals. Paulinette always complains of feeling left out, so she has been allowed to star as Racine's Iphigénie, and to wear the elaborate costume Maria Malibran wore when she sang Rossini's Semiramide. Pauline plays Clytemnestre. Ivan takes the part of Agamemnon. Louisette, Ulisse. Maman is costume mistress. And Louis, who is much too dignified for play acting, confines himself to the audience, for which he is charged the ticket price of one potato, to be dug up from the garden with his own hands.

Ivan has invented a game, the *jeux de têtes*. At the top of a long sheet of paper, he draws a head, a portrait, just as it comes into his mind, of some sort of character. They sit around the big oak table by the fireplace in the grand salon. Each of them—including Paulinette, whose French is impossible—anonymously jots down a few quick lines describing the character in the drawing, then folds the paper over and passes it along.

A good comic actor, jealous of the success of others. Subtle, clever, but hard to get along with. Collects buttons. Attracted to distinguished people. Has tried, unsuccessfully, to write a vaudeville, but his literary talents help him to create roles. Observant. (Pauline)

Young, clever but extremely cold. Conceited but loves music and plays well. Likes to parade on the boulevards and criticize peeple. (Paulinette)

Well-born and bred, dry, vengeful, patient—adheres strictly to the rules of decorum—has a rather large fortune, politically to the right, has serious tastes in literature but lacks imagination; enjoys agricultural subjects, machines, etc. Will only marry for money and will be harsh with his children. (Ivan)

Ivan reads all of the comments aloud, and the winners of the "grand medal of honor" and the "most complete stupidity" are compelled to identify themselves with cries of "Author! Author!"

Ivan always seems to know where Pauline is. He finds her in the orchard, picking the first ripe apples. He finds her reading in the summer room. If she wanders into the billiards room alone, he appears there a few minutes later.

She has begun to invite him to her tower study, to play him the songs she is writing. He has begun to touch her, slightly, gently, his hand on her shoulder, his head bent against the top of hers, and she has begun to stand closer to him, to make the touching easier.

He stands beside her, leaning over her writing table, admiring a drawing of Louisette she made the day before, and when she turns her head to say something to him, he kisses her, and when he tells her how sorry he is for forgetting himself, she kisses him and somehow her arms are around his neck and his hands are on her hips, pulling her to him.

Rue de Rivoli 210, Paris, January 1857

I N THE LAST DAYS OF OCTOBER, when the hunting season was over and the old elm tree was a golden blaze, the Viardots returned to the house at Rue de Douai. Ivan found rooms on the Rue de Rivoli facing the Tuileries garden. Every day, if she can manage it, Pauline comes to his flat. Paulinette, fourteen years old now, living with her father and her governess, jealously complains that she treats him as though he were her husband. Ivan has no complaints.

He has no thought of returning to Russia. He has no thought of anything but Pauline. Rumors swirl through the salons of Saint Petersburg. Lev Tolstoy wrote to ask if it were true that he married Pauline immediately after the death of Louis Viardot. Ivan was astonished and a little pleased to hear of it, but he denied it. *What rumors you are hearing! Madame Viardot's husband is as well as he ever was, and I am no closer to getting married than you are.*

As fall turns to winter, Pauline stops appearing at his rooms. He is used to her absences. She often becomes so immersed in work she has no time for anything or anyone. But as the weeks pass, terrifying thoughts begin to plague him. He has to know that nothing has changed between them. He sends pleading messages. When can he see her? When can he talk to her? Where then, can they meet? He thinks only of what he might have done to turn her against him, examines and reexamines every word, every look, every touch they exchanged at their last meeting.

The holidays arrive. Louis, the ardent nonbeliever, disapproves of Christmas, but Pauline has long since persuaded him to make a tradition of celebrating the New Year with a festive dinner and an exchange of gifts. Ivan takes small comfort in her invitation. He is, after all, still part of the family. It would cause too much discussion if he and his daughter were not invited. Maman, Paolo and Mariquita, the children, even Louis would question their absence.

He arrives at the Rue de Douai as nervous as he was that first winter in Saint Petersburg when he barely hoped she would notice him. He has dressed with even greater care than usual, insisted that his barber visit him that morning, even on a holiday. He has doused his cheeks with the lavender water she loves.

They are all in the music room. Paulinette runs to Louis, who interrupts his conversation to kiss her cheeks. Ivan greets him, then scans the room for Pauline. He is called upon to return a dozen embraces, but he is barely able to smile. And then she enters the room, dressed in black silk glittering with jets. She stops to chat with Tía Mariquita. At first she appears not to see him, then makes a show of noticing. "Ah, here is our Jean! Is Paulinette with you?" Such studied warmth.

All evening, he watches her work at treating him no differently than any other family member. She neither ignores him nor looks at him too often. She addresses her conversation to everyone but him, then, as an afterthought, "Don't you agree, Jean?"

When all the others have left, he lingers, still hoping for a moment alone with her, for a smile, a meeting of eyes, some small acknowledgment of all that has passed between them. But she busies herself with anything that will take her away from him, attending to the children, consulting with the majordomo, leaving him sitting on a stuffed chair, conversing lamely with Louis, until Paulinette appears, pursing her lips, rubbing her eyes and whining that she wants to go home. He looks around for Pauline.

So, this is all there will be. Not a touch, not a shared smile, not even an instant when their eyes meet. At the door, as he shakes Louis's hand and accepts a friendly pat on the arm, she appears.

"Jean, Paulinette, you are going! It has been so lovely to see you again." And she offers chaste kisses on each cheek.

* * *

The next day is dismal, rainy, and cold. After breakfast, Pauline goes to the music room, as she always does, but when she tries to sing, her throat is tight. Her breath is shallow. Ivan has haunted her all night. It was horrid, horrid having him there in the house. She felt his eyes on her wherever she went. And Louis watched her incessantly. She was caught like a deer between two hunters. She would have liked to lunge at Turgenev, to hug him to her. She'd thought she would be able to share a look, a touch, some small gesture that he would understand. But even that had been impossible. She takes up her cloak and bonnet without saying a word to anyone and slips out of the house in search of a cab.

She cannot get to him quickly enough. She leaps from the carriage before the driver can help her down, presses a bill in his hand, runs to the gate, rushes past the concierge, up the stairs.

Turgenev answers the door himself, looks at her warily. She tries to return his gaze, but his eyes accuse her. They entreat her. Her eyes move about the room, settling on the mirror, the table, the rug, anywhere but on him. He steps toward her. She moves away. She has planned what she will say to him, rehearsed it silently in the cab. She will have to say it as quickly as she can. If she stays even a moment longer than absolutely necessary, she will lose the courage to say it at all.

"Jean, how are you?" She dismisses his servant. "I will keep my cloak, thank you. I cannot stay." She waits, staring at the floor, for the man to leave the room.

"I have been unfair," she says, still not looking up, "but I haven't known how to tell you. I cannot bear to cause Louis so much pain. Whatever has happened between us . . . I . . . My marriage is too precious, too important."

"You have come to tell me that after almost sixteen years of marriage you've fallen in love with your husband?"

"Yes, I know . . . I'm sorry . . . It's strange but . . .

"But?"

He goes to her, and she cannot move away. His hands are on her shoulders.

"Every part of my being is filled with you, and always will be. What has happened? Tell me. I beg you."

"Jean . . . It's not that at all. It's very difficult . . ."

"Pauline, there has been nothing we could not say to one another. Anything you have to tell me will be less painful than your silence."

"I haven't known how to tell you. I . . . you see . . . I am with child again."

"You . . . you are with child . . . and the father . . ."

She pulls away. "Jean, please. That question must not . . . I came to say goodbye. You know that in a few days I will leave for my season in Germany. I will write to you from time to time, of course. Louis and I, both of us, wish you every blessing. I am so sorry, really . . . I cannot stay here. Kiss Paulinette for me."

And she is running out the door, down the staircase before he can ask more, before she can say more.

She hears him running after her. She stops, turns, and looks up at him.

"Jean, you mustn't wonder if my love for you was real. It *is* real."

She hurries under the arcade of the Rue de Rivoli, crosses the wide street, and enters the Tuileries gardens. The sky, the trees, the ground—everything is gray. The wind blowing off the Seine carries the miserable, relentless drizzle of a Paris winter. She walks and she weeps until her knees give way, and she stumbles onto a bench. Pigeons scurry around her feet, picking at the stones and gravel. *Breathe, Pauline, breathe. What have you done? Where are you? Where are you going? Of course, Louis is the father. He must be the father.* He claimed her so often at Courtavenel. The more time she spent with Turgenev in the afternoon, the more attentive her husband became at night.

Run back to Jean, run now! Fall on the floor at his feet. Tell him you cannot do without him. You cannot. Jean. His face as she looked up at him. The grief.

Her head is in her hands; the soft leather of her gloves is wet. Her throat aches with swallowed screams. She will never be able to leave this bench. She will die, sitting there. They will find her at first light, her face encrusted with frozen tears.

But the chill drives her to her feet. *Go home, Pauline. You can do this. This is your life now. You will learn to live as a woman always lives, without passion. That sort of happiness is more than anyone has a right to expect. But you decided all this years ago. You merely lost your way for a time.*

At the Place de la Concorde she finds a carriage for hire and rides through the streets of Paris with a hand on her belly, silently talking to the child inside. "Who are you? Are you tall and rambling as a Russian bear, or slight and guarded as a French fox? Are your eyes as dark as mine and Louis's or as blue-gray as a Moscow winter? Who are you, my child?"

The house at Rue de Douai is warm and light. She hands her cloak and bonnet to the majordomo.

"Is Monsieur at home?"

"He is in his study, Madame."

The little girls, Claudie and Marianne, run to her, their governess smiling behind them.

She finds Louis sunk in his armchair, surrounded by his dogs. He looks up from his reading. A smile creeps out from under his mustache and wrinkles his eyes.

She leans over and kisses the corners of his mouth, left then right.

"These are my special kissing places, Papa *chéri*."

"How are you, *bonne maman*?"

"Have I become your *bonne maman?*"

"My dear, sweet *bonne maman.*"

Knowing that she has had the willpower to overcome her passion will bring her a kind of happiness. She will tell herself that although choosing the right path has nearly broken her, it has raised her up a step toward goodness. Her sacred art, her music, will save her.

* * *

Ivan has become physically ill. He has developed neuralgia of the bladder in such a virulent form, he feels the nerves in his groin are being twisted and pulled. At times, it seems that a lit candle is being held under his scrotum and the skin is beginning to melt. Piercing pains in his buttocks make sitting in a chair unbearable. He is unable to get out of bed, to dress. He gnashes his teeth all day in pain, and at night, he bashes his head against the wall.

The doctors have prescribed doses of quinine and strychnine, but his pains have only become worse. He has been diagnosed with *spermatorrhea*, the involuntary flow of semen, a condition known to affect not only the body but the moral condition of the soul. Its cause is attributed to excessive sexual activity, insufficient sexual activity, or masturbation of any frequency. A glass catheter was inserted into his penis, and, as he screamed in agony, silver nitrate was applied with a plunger to cauterize the afflicted area. For days afterward he was unable to walk, and urination was torture.

He thinks he has never been able to write, that he has no particular talent. He has squandered his life. There is nothing left of him but rubbish that ought to be swept away. He is a dead man, a living corpse, dumbly staring at his own coffin.

He wakes in the mornings in a state of dread, thinking of the years ahead, endless, useless, meaningless. And so the days creep along. He forces himself to stand up, to endure the burning pain when he uses the chamber pot. He allows himself to be dressed. He looks out the windows at the Tuileries gardens where he used to love to walk, where the children still play, bundled against the winter wind. His life goes on without him. Pillows are arranged so that he can sit, so that he can read. He escapes into Cicero, into Petronius, into the most distant past he can find.

In March, when Lev Nikoleyevich Tolstoy arrives in Paris, Ivan greets him from a well-cushioned armchair, swaddled in blankets, his pince-nez perched on his nose.

"My dear Lev, you are the sole hope of our Russian literature."

"I am nothing of the sort."

"Yet Annenkov writes me that in Petersburg your *Childhood, Boyhood, and Youth* is more fashionable than the crinoline."

"Does he, Vanishka? And Annenkov writes me that you are depressed and ill."

"So he does, I'm sure. I'm decomposing in this alien air, like a frozen fish when the thaw comes on. May God spare you the feeling that your life has passed by before it has begun. I don't know how you should act to avoid falling into such misfortune, so I cannot advise you. But you are ten years younger than I. You still have everything before you—an infinity of youth. As for me, in less than two years I will be forty, too old to be without a nest of my own. I will return to Russia in the fall, and when I go, I will say a final goodbye to my dreams of happiness."

Tolstoy throws himself into a chair and sits with his knees apart. He is stylish and elegant in slender trousers and a waistcoat, but he is not a handsome man. His small, deep-set eyes are shadowed by a prominent forehead and his nose hangs squat and flabby.

"Vanishka, I'm sorry. I see that La Viardot has quite broken you. I would never have believed that you could love like that."

"I love her more than ever and more than anything in the world. I would dance naked on the rooftops covered in yellow paint if she asked me to. You laugh, and I cannot blame you. I am undergoing a physical and spiritual crisis, Lev Nikoleyevich. If I emerge from it, I will be like one of those dilapidated Russian barns that are propped up with logs."

He glances at Tolstoy's stricken face and smiles. "But some of those old barns remain upright for a long time."

Two months later, Lev Tolstoy left for Geneva. He said that Paris was Sodom and Gomorrah, that he felt like a stone in a riverbed that was being progressively covered with slime. Ivan recovered enough to go out, to see friends. Alexander Herzen persuaded him to come to London for the annual literary dinner. Avdotya Panayeva, whom he barely tolerated, was there with her lover, Nikolay Nekrasov, a poet whom Ivan quite liked. He traveled with them to Berlin, where the German doctors advised him to take the waters at Sinzig.

He was there, at the spa city, when Louis Viardot's letter reached him. A son had been born. Paul Louis Joachim Viardot. Ivan over-tipped the postman, told him to use the money to drink to the baby's health. It was useless to wonder about the child's paternity, but he wondered. And he determined to behave flawlessly, despite wondering. He wrote to Louis. *I embrace you and congratulate you with all my heart, and I thank you for having thought of me.*

He wrote to Pauline. *What music is more beautiful than the sound of a newborn's cry? When you awoke to find this sweet creature, who was only yesterday a part of you, what must you have felt? Who does he look like? What color are his eyes?*

The waters at Sinzig were not helping him at all. He was advised to bathe his scrotum in the sea, so he set off for Boulogne-sur-Mer, where Pavel Annenkov was vacationing. In desperation, he submitted to a newly devised electrical treatment. But nothing relieved his pain for long, and wherever he traveled, his sorrow found him.

Vasily Botkin wrote from Moscow suggesting that they spend the winter together in Rome, and Turgenev, hoping to escape from the anguish that afflicted his body and mind, agreed. The son of a wealthy merchant, Vasily Petrovich could afford to indulge his taste for travel and luxury. They boarded a ship at Genoa that took them down the Italian coast to Livorno and then to the Roman port of Civitavecchia.

Rome was a great healer. In the face of its eternally green oaks and umbrella pines, its distant, pale-blue hills, and the clear light, which always seemed to be celebrating a holiday, Ivan's lingering melancholy began to disgust him.

Botkin was a good companion, an erudite man who devoted himself to writing essays and literary criticism. But Rome was made for solitude, and without solitude Ivan could not write. He and Botkin agreed to lodge separately, and he began to outline a novel, *A House of Gentlefolk*. When he tired of working, he wandered the city, consoled by the remains of ancient greatness.

* * *

In the spring of 1858, Ivan is back in Saint Petersburg, on the green velvet settee in Countess Lambert's upstairs drawing room. He feels like a man who has survived his own death, a creature who died long ago, while a version of his former self goes on existing. Yelizaveta Lambert, relentlessly pious, has become his mother confessor. She accuses him of the sin of self-pity, but she forgives him for it.

"Here I am," he says, "dead and yet alive. Not only my first and second youths have passed, but my third, as well. I am still neither a competent nor a reliable person, but I would like, at least, to become a person who knows where he is going and what he wants to accomplish. If the only thing I can be is a man of letters, then I ought to be more than a dilettante. There will be no more of that. Hard work will be my companion and my comfort. The most I can hope for now is to be nearly satisfied with near happiness."

He has exasperated her yet again. "Why is it that you persist in such maudlin protestations? You have lived for barely forty years. Your life is not over by half."

"The summer of my life has gone."

"But Ivan Sergeyevich, bright autumn days are the most beautiful of the year."

Théâtre Lyrique, Paris, November 1859

İT WAS A LAST CHANCE, A last great role. She expected a few performances, no more. The opera was old-fashioned, static. Who would want to see it? Gluck composed *Orphée* nearly a century before, when its simplicity was considered noble. Surely, Parisian audiences, accustomed to the excesses of grand opera, would find it dull.

Léon Carvalho, the new manager of the Théâtre Lyrique, had heard Pauline sing at his wife's *bénéfice*, and had persuaded Hector Berlioz to adapt the title role for her. When the opera premiered in Vienna, Orphée had been sung by a castrato. When it was performed in Paris, Gluck rewrote the role for a tenor. Berlioz would adjust the music for Pauline's mezzo-soprano.

He came to Courtavenel to consult with her. She had already sung some of his own work and admired it greatly. But the man who visited her château was broken, ill. He suffered from the combined torments of a miserable second marriage and persistent neuralgia, his spirit and body both crippled with pain. Nothing attracted Pauline more than the chance to alleviate suffering. She had nursed the bruised souls of Turgenev and Gounod. Now she ministered to Berlioz. She became his collaborator, his muse, his comfort, and for a time, he fell in love with her, putting her in the extremely uncomfortable position of having to sustain him without breaking his heart.

The premiere was a greater success than even Carvalho could have imagined. Gluck's sad music suited Pauline's weary voice, which had darkened into shades of inconsolable sorrow, of desperate longing.

On opening night, her throat was raw and painful. Yet she gave the performance of a lifetime. She sang of loss and the audience wept with her. George Sand wrote that it was "surely the purest and most perfect artistic expression that we have seen for half a century."

Eugène Delacroix designed the sets and the tunic she wore. A laurel wreath crowned her hair. She devised her movements so that the images on a Greek vase seemed to have come to life, yet the English critic Henry Chorley wrote that "there was not a single effect that might be called a *pose* or prepared gesture." She played the part of a man so well, young women fell in love with him.

J'ai perdu mon Eurydice. "I have lost my Eurydice." She sang it in amazement, unbelieving, dazed. "I have lost my Eurydice." She sang it again, wild with agony. "I have lost my Eurydice." She sang it a third time, swooning onto the corpse of her beloved, devastated. The audience, overcome with grief, broke into applause. They stamped their feet in anguish. They embraced one other and wept. They came from all over Europe to hear her. Charles Dickens arrived at her dressing room after the performance, his face disfigured by tears. The next day he sent a note: "Nothing can be more magnificent, more true, more tender, more beautiful, more profound!"

Every Monday, Wednesday, and Friday, she appeared at the theater, terrified that she would not be able to do it again, that the magic would fail her this time. It was not a thing she understood, not a thing she trusted. But night after night, the music, like the rushing river Styx, carried her into the depths of human misery, down into Hades and back.

It was a last chance. A last performance on one of the great stages of Paris, whose doors had been closed to her since the failure of Gounod's *Sapho*. And then it was over. A great singer knows when the final curtain has come down. In three years, she had sung *Orphée* one hundred and thirty-eight times, but it was *Orphée* that the public demanded for her farewell appearance.

She stands on the stage, head bowed as the applause thunders around her and the sound vibrates through her body. The audience has been on its feet crying her name for a full ten minutes. She lifts her head, pats her heart, waves goodbye. It is always dark in the wings, always her eyes, blinded by the spotlight, find it impossible to see. But this time, she falters, and Geneviève, who is waiting there for the last time, takes her elbow as she stumbles to her dressing room, ignoring every compliment, avoiding every eye.

PART FOUR

AN UNOFFICIAL MARRIAGE

You know those unofficial marriages—they sometimes turn out more poisonous than the more accepted form. I know a lot about the problem, and have thought deeply about it. If I have failed to deal with it up to now in my literary writings, it is simply because I have always avoided subjects that are too personal. I find them embarrassing. When it has all faded into the past, perhaps I will think about attempting something—that is if the desire to write has not disappeared.

I. S. Turgenev in a letter to the critic V. V. Stasov
December 10, 1871

BADEN-BADEN, PRUSSIA, OCTOBER 1863

———

THE AUTUMN BREEZE NUDGES TATTERED CLOUDS across a bright sky, coaxing leaves off the trees, rocking them as they flutter to the ground. October gentles Baden-Baden into winter. It is a season of last chances, of the last golden light, too precious to be wasted indoors. From her wicker chair on the balcony of the chalet, Pauline looks out at a flawlessly tended garden, at a lawn bordered with red and yellow stripes of chrysanthemum, dahlia, and helianthus. Under the boughs of a chestnut tree, shadows dance on the grass. She takes another sip of tea.

At forty-two, her face is still unlined, her hair still dark. She wears it in ringlets at the nape of her neck now, according to the fashion, and her gowns are adorned with ruching and lace panels. She leans back, resting her head against the chair, closes her heavy lids, and lifts her face to the October sun.

For decades, she was drenched in applause, now she bathes in silence. She was the most famous singer in Europe. Now she is a wife and mother, a singing teacher. She tells herself that she wanted this. She'd had no time to mother Louisette. She will, at least, be a proper mother to the little ones, pretty Claudie, Marianne, and dark-eyed Paul. She tells herself that she was wise to retire in triumph, that there had been no point in trying to continue. She has exhausted her voice, sung too much, sung everything.

In Paris, the gossips maintained that her little son Paul was Ivan Turgenev's child. They said that George Sand had been her lover before Ivan. Some even whispered that Madame Viardot, with her strange, strong face, was a hermaphrodite. She knew all this. She knew that she had been the subject of gossip since she first set foot on the opera stage.

France had become intolerable. Under the Second Empire, the musical taste of the Parisians, never of the highest order, deteriorated even further. While she tore at her soul in Gluck's *Orphée*, across town, Emperor Louis-Napoléon amused himself with Offenbach's comic *Orphée en enfers*, Orpheus in the Underworld.

She was no longer treated with the deference due a great artist. Most of the female singers now were courtesans whom any man might feel free to touch. It was time to find a new life. Louis had detested living in Paris for years. Louis-Napoléon's repressive regime sickened him.

They decided on Baden-Baden, the glittering green spa city in the Black Forest where the *beau monde* of Paris, Vienna, and Saint Petersburg paraded along shady paths in the afternoons and played roulette at gilded tables in the evenings. Louis could enjoy the hunting there. Berlioz directed the summer music festival where Pauline had performed for several years. Liszt is only a few hours away in Weimar. Pauline's childhood friend, the pianist Clara Wieck, now the widow of composer Robert Schumann, has a home in neighboring Lichtentaler. Maman can easily arrive by train from Ixelles. Pauline Viardot, the great tragedienne, has made an elegant retreat.

She sits on her porch, still resolutely regal, sipping her afternoon tea, wondering who she is now, who she will become. It has been decades since she thought of herself as a person separate from her voice. Her great ability to sing, to capture music and deliver it to an audience, has defined her worth. She is a virtuoso who has lost the only instrument she will ever own.

What can she sing now that her once-glorious voice has been reduced to splinters? Songs? Schubert, Schumann, Mendelssohn have written songs. She has written songs of her own and will write more. She will have to choose what she sings carefully, like a woman with an aging figure who dresses to disguise her flaws.

In those first days after her final performance at the Théâtre
Lyrique, she found it difficult to control her panic. She sat at her
piano, singing through the pages of her repertoire, weeping when
she reached for a spinning pianissimo and only a choked squeal
emerged. She tried again and again, but the voice she had com-
manded with such ease refused to obey her. She lifted her soft palate, opened her throat, relaxed her jaw, flattened her tongue, just
as Maman had taught her to do so long ago. But the sound, which
once poured from her body, rich and free, remained lodged somewhere in her memory.

The house on the Rue de Douai was filled with farewell gifts and
flowers. Letters of thanks had to be written. Her precious Cavallé-
Coll pipe organ and Pleyel piano had to be dismantled, packed and
shipped. Louis's art collection, the Vélasquez, the Dutch masters,
the marble busts and ancient relics, had to be prepared to follow
them to Baden-Baden.

In those final evenings in Paris, she had no idea what to do
with herself. She had gone to the theater three nights a week at
the very least, season after season. She wandered the corridors of
her home, up and down the curving staircase, deciding what to
sell, what to store, what to leave for the tenants, what to take to
Prussia.

It was impossible not to think of Ivan Turgenev. There were
not enough antidotes for longing. She told herself not to write to
him. He was too far away. Too much time had passed. Too much
sad fog lay between them. But she still talked to him silently, sharing her eagerness, confessing her fears. She picked up paper and
pen—how many times, a half dozen, more? She told herself she
knew better than to write him. It would be unfair to everyone. She
pushed her chair back from her writing table, stood up, walked
away, busied herself with one of the children, with one of the dogs,
found some other source of affection.

In five years, she had summoned Ivan only once. While the performances of *Orphée* went on month after month, she lived with

Louis at the Rue de Douai and the children stayed at Courtavenel with the governess and the nanny. When she could, she spent three days with them, leaving Paris on a Saturday morning and returning on a Monday afternoon in time for the evening performance. Perhaps she was a better singer than she was a mother, but she told herself that her children knew how much she loved them and excused herself for being absent.

Until she received word that three-year-old Paul was running a fever, that he coughed and cried without stopping. The doctors said it was bronchial pneumonia. She said she would cancel the remainder of her performances. The doctors said it was their job to cure her son, and that it was her job to sing. So she sang *J'ai perdu ma Eurydice*, expressing both the bottomless grief of loss, and the torment of guilt. And in a moment of great weakness, she summoned Turgenev.

That weekend, Paul's fever broke. He stood in his little bed, smiling, but Ivan was already racing across Europe. When he arrived, she hadn't known how to look at him. She was cordial, embarrassed, grateful, agonizingly cold. Ivan was meeting the dark-eyed boy for the first time, and she watched him examine the child, searching for some resemblance. And then he retreated to Paris on the excuse of visiting his daughter. Perhaps he would never forgive her, but her need for him was greater than her fear, and finally, she began to write.

"*Liebster Freund*, dearest friend . . ." The words streamed across page after page. The lamp had to be refilled with oil, and still she went on writing. She sealed the envelope and wrote his name. And why did she remember his Saint Petersburg address? But she did.

In Saint Petersburg, Ivan held the letter, thick as their long story folded onto itself. He stared at the way she had written his address, erratic as she was, some lines carefully, precisely formed, others hurriedly, impulsively scribbled. He held it in both hands, as though it were fragile, delicate. Then he tore at it. And then he felt sorry that he had nearly destroyed the precious envelope.

* * *

The Viardots are at the table in the breakfast room of their chalet in Baden-Baden. Crates of Pauline's Dresden china, her Bavarian crystal, her Belgian linens are stacked around them, waiting to be unpacked. The cook has prepared a real German *Frühstück* with ham and sausages, but Pauline has never been able to face much food in the morning. With the edge of a little silver spoon, she delicately cracks the top of a boiled egg in a porcelain cup.

"What do you think of inviting Turgenev to join us in Baden-Baden? It might be a chance to continue work on your translations of Pushkin."

Louis Viardot puts down his newspaper. His wife can make the most profound statements sound like idle chatter.

He looks at the woman he has always adored, the mother of his children, his friend. They decided together to leave France. The change brought with it a shared anticipation, but also an unease that has made them cautious with each other. Pauline's voice never betrays her, but he has always been able to read in her face what she attempts to hide with her words. There has been safety in that, in knowing what she feels, gauging his current position in the hierarchy of her thoughts.

He has never deceived himself by imagining that he is more to her than a safe harbor, a best friend. He realized she might turn to Turgenev, now that the music has ceased to consume her. He expected it.

"Shall we invite him to visit us then, *bonne maman?*" He supposes she has already done that, but he won't embarrass her by accusing her of it.

Her dark eyes sparkle at him as she refills his coffee cup. She has

been his wife for more than twenty years, but her look of affectionate approval still thrills him.

He gives her a wry smile in return. "Jean should really consider
settling in Baden-Baden," he says without a trace of irony. "Don't
you agree? What can he be doing in Saint Petersburg? He is such
a European, after all. He cannot possibly be content forever in
Russia. I will write to him myself, *bonne maman*. Leave it with me.
I can be very persuasive, you know."

In the drawing rooms, wags tell each other that the husband
loves Ivan Turgenev even more than the wife does. In truth, they
are like bark on an old tree, stuck together for so long there is no
separating them.

> *You know the place. It offers amenities of every kind. We see
> so many people here every day, just as we did in Paris, but one
> can step into the forest and find perfect peace and solitude. The
> availability of these two extremes pleases my wife and the chil-
> dren. As for me, I am sure to find hunting to fulfill my heart's
> desire. Already, for only 15 florins a year, I have managed to buy
> hunting rights in the forests surrounding Baden that are owned by
> the city—no less than 8000 hectares. It's possible to hunt here
> without being a citizen, and at no great expense.*
>
> *Why not imitate so many of your fellow Russians, who are
> here in large numbers, not just passing through, but established
> landowners? Really, you would not have to invest the greater part
> of your fortune to settle yourself in Baden.*
>
> *I will pass the pen to someone else. Little Didie wants to send
> you a drawing.*
>
> *Louis V*

* * *

Few of his friends are surprised that Ivan has decided to follow the
Viardots to Baden-Baden, but most are appalled. The worst of it is

having to explain himself to Yelizaveta Lambert, who is taking his departure as a personal defeat. She has spent years attempting to cure him of his obsession with Pauline.

He is on the settee in her green drawing room, attempting to exonerate himself. "Quite apart from the Viardot family," he protests, "Baden-Baden is a paradise. The town is nestled in a valley, like a child in the lap of its mother. The air is fresh, the woods are thick and full of game. Everywhere, there are gardens—and such fountains! The sound of running water is almost inescapable. If you were to see it for yourself, Yelizaveta Yigorovna . . ."

"So, Ivan Sergeyevich, you will perch precariously on the edge of another man's nest, where the slightest ill wind will send you spiraling into the abyss of a lonely old age."

"It is a risk I run. Madame Viardot has caused me pain. You have been witness to that. But she did it for the most noble reasons, and she suffered for it, as well."

He shifts his weight, stretches his legs out in front of him, folds his hands over his expanding belly. He lowers his head, then raises his shoulders in mock despair.

"Forgive me, Countess, but I have at last concluded that it is not a good thing for a writer to marry. He must be faithful to his muse. An unhappy marriage may do something for a man's talent, but a happy one is no good at all."

The flames of a dozen candles flicker over the icons that line the walls. The saints in their frames seem to shake their heads in disbelief.

"You are an unconvincing cynic, Ivan Sergeyevich. Perhaps you persist in your obsession with Madame Viardot because it protects you from the unthinkable tragedy of a happy marriage, but it will spell the end of your career as a writer. You, who write of nothing but Russia, have chosen to discard her like a bothersome mistress."

"I have not lost my love of Russia. It is she who has lost her love of me. The only service I can offer my country is as a writer, and that service, apparently, is no longer wanted. My *Home of the*

Gentry was very well received, was it not? And for a time, the younger generation applauded the sentiments I expressed in *On the Eve*, although I might add parenthetically that you, Countess, found nothing to admire in the book. Now I am universally reviled. Those who once praised me burn my effigy. *Fathers and Sons* is despised by every Russian who has read it, each for a different reason. Because I have attempted to describe the triumph of democracy over aristocracy, I have been called an ass, a spittoon, a poisonous toad.

"Why should I remain in Russia? It's not necessary that a writer live in his own country. At least there is no need to live there continuously. Why shouldn't I live in Baden-Baden? I don't know if it's because my expectations have diminished, but I have noticed that happiness comes much more easily to me now. I go to Prussia simply to build myself a solitary nest where I can await the inevitable end."

* * *

Baden-Baden is magnificent in November, flowers still blooming red and gold, the trees just beginning to lose their leaves. Ivan Turgenev has taken rooms on the second floor of a house in the Schillerstrasse. And he has fallen in love with Pauline Viardot all over again, with both the romantic passion of an eighteen-year-old and the profound gratitude of a man past forty. He loves her more than he loved her twenty years before, when he was too young to know that his love was a hopeless dream. He loves her more than he loved her when she first gave herself to him, when he first knew that his love was returned. He loves every part of her and everything about her. He keeps her portrait on his writing table and stares at it, as though seeing her for the first time. He finds her features fine, the darkness of her eyes and heavy brows enchanting. He worships her hands, her long, shapely fingers.

He loves her infectious laugh, the grace of her every movement. He loves her when she teases him, when she calls him "you awful man." When she catches his eye, complicit, suppressing a smile, he feels as though he has been singled out by the gods. His love for Pauline is so great it spills over onto everyone who is close to her. He is in love with her children, her brother, her mother, her students—even her husband.

In the afternoon, when he is ready to put down his pen, he rings for his servant who brings up a cutlet from the landlady's kitchen. Then he takes up his walking stick, his hat, and his gloves, and goes out into the sunshine. His dog, Pegasus, part black shepherd, part pointer, a descendant of his poor departed Diana, marches beside him, head lifted, nose twitching.

Ivan finds his usual bench under the trees, facing the clear little stream of the Oos, pulls his striped trousers up at the knees as he sits down, squeezes his spectacles onto the bridge of his nose, and takes a folded newspaper from his coat pocket. At that hour, the sun is at his back and the autumn light is soft. Leaves slide through the air like flecks of gold. Under the firs, fallen brown needles have been blown into little piles by the wind, reminding him of locks of hair on a barber's floor. Across the stream, flags fly from the roof of the Hotel Minerva, announcing the nationalities of the illustrious guests.

Baden-Baden, the summer capital of fashionable Europe, has not quite emptied out yet. His seat beside the gravelly trail of the Lichtenthaler Allée still offers him an agreeable balance of solitude and sociability. Boys run along rolling hoops with sticks. Young mothers walk arm in arm, beribboned hats tilted forward, faces veiled to the chin, while behind them, governesses try in vain to herd their children. Prince Menschkopff, wearing all his medals, rides by on his stallion, saluting every well-turned-out person on the path. As the prince approaches Ivan's bench, he pulls up and leans over in his saddle to share a word of greeting with the famous author. Cora Pearl, the English courtesan, waves a little golden fan as she passes, her carriage open so that no one can miss seeing her—her dress a violent shade of purple, her hair an ungodly shade of red. An ancient Russian duchess, with an elaborate confection of corkscrew curls pinned to her thin hair, shoots furious black glances from the ruins of her face as a liveried servant coaxes her wheelchair over the gravel and stones. A boy in a long apron and a small cap struggles to push a wheelbarrow laden with apples. A young woman in an embroidered cloak hurries down the path on her way home from the shops in the colonnades, trailed by a maid carrying her purchases. Washerwomen waddle slowly past, balancing baskets of dirty linen on their heads. Pegasus sniffs the posteriors of a pair of schnauzers who have come cavorting across the lawns, tongues dripping from their mouths.

Ivan, having decided that his meal has been sufficiently digested, folds his newspaper and replaces his pince-nez in his breast pocket. His bladder problems have disappeared. He has never felt so well. As he picks up his walking stick, Pegasus dashes to his side.

He has made it a habit to call on the Viardots in the afternoons, when he can slip in without intruding on their lives. It is a season of last chances. During those first months in Baden-Baden, he and Pauline were shy with each other. There were long looks, short conversations. Ivan took refuge in Louis's study, where they worked together translating Pushkin's *Dubrovsky*. When he emerged, the joyful expression on Pauline's face never failed to astound him, so that he hardly knew what to say to her. There were no discussions of the past, no demands for explanations.

Now as he climbs the Tiergartenstrasse, he can hear her at the piano, and he begins to hurry. The majordomo opens the door for him, nods, takes his hat and walking stick without saying a word. There is no need to announce him. He is a welcome guest who comes and goes as he likes. Pauline, hearing his footsteps, stops playing and reaches for him with both hands. She is smiling, and he feels like a child who has just been handed a wonderful gift.

"Tourguel!" she says.

He takes both her hands in his.

"Have you been in to see Louis?"

"Not yet, no."

"I'm not sure what he's doing. Possibly sleeping!"

Pauline has been filling her days teaching and writing music. She has little confidence in her abilities, although Liszt has called her the first woman composer of genius. Berlioz has praised her compositions. Adolphe Adam said he would have been proud to have written them himself. And Clara Schumann has called her the most gifted woman she has ever known. Ivan tells her that had her music been written by a man, she would be as famous a composer as she is a singer.

He worries that she will not be happy. What will she do with her great artistry for the rest of her life? She must be happy. Nothing must ruin this happiness.

"And you, Jean, have you brought something to read to me? Something you wrote this morning?" He has begun to submit all his work to her approbation, initialing the pages she approves with the letters S.I.P., for the Latin *sub invocatione paulinae*. But at the moment, he is writing very little, too happy to seek refuge in work.

"I will trade you a song for a story," she says. "What do you say? Or are you too lazy to hold up your end of the bargain?"

Hearing Ivan's voice, Louis calls from his study. "Turgenev! Come, I have something to show you!"

Pauline laughs. "Go on, you awful man! But come back. Come back to me later."

* * *

Louis Viardot has withdrawn gracefully. Always a pragmatist, he has resigned himself to a situation he no longer has the power to influence, protecting his position in his own family by forming an ever-tighter friendship with Turgenev. During the hunting season, they climb the mountain trails with their guns and their dogs and come down with packs full of slaughtered hares, foxes, and fowl. They have a bond of their own, a shared love of the chill air, the dirt and leaves underfoot, the patches of light and shadow, the victory of outsmarting the birds and animals they kill. They discuss politics, collaborate on French translations of Russian authors.

Viardot has little use now for most people. Turgenev has become one of the few whom he gladly tolerates. He has suffered enormous disappointments. He long since lost all hope of winning Pauline's love. His hopes for France and his republican ideals have been shattered by the megalomania of Louis-Napoléon. But he keeps himself busy.

He is working on a treatise, "Apology of an Unbeliever," dedicated to his wife, who constantly interrupts him when he tries to justify his agnosticism, which grows deeper with each passing year.

* * *

After supper, Pauline sits with her sketchbook and pencil, looking about her at her family, deciding on a subject to draw. By the fire, Louis is asleep in his chair, his white head nodding over his chest. Little Paul is on the floor in a corner by himself, reading. Claudie and Marianne are busy with their own drawings. Ivan is stretched out on the divan, nearly reclining, his eyes half closed.

She wonders what he can be thinking. His body is still long and strong, but his belly puffs out now. How she would love to rest her head on that dear old flesh! His gray hair is all in disarray where his head rolled back on the cushions, and his face is soft and warm with sleep.

She wants him to look at her, to see her. She wants to arouse that great mind. She needs to hear his voice, his stories, his humor. She needs the sound of their shared laughter, the look that so often passes between them.

"Tourguel! Tell us a story. Tell the children how you tried to run away from home."

He opens his eyes slowly. "Oh, Pauline! That's not a story for children! What are you sketching there? Is it me?"

The little girls rush at him, two little hands on each of his legs, little feet jumping up and down, little faces expectantly staring into his, little eyes wide. "Oh, please, Tourguel!"

"Oh, no!"

"Oh yes!" Little lips tightly pressed, eyebrows raised. "Yes, Tourguel! Yes, yes, yes, yes! Yes, or I'll pull your hair! Pull your hair! Pull your beard!"

He turns to Pauline, smiling helplessly, and she smiles back, nodding. Had their bodies grown together into one, they could not have been more closely connected.

It is assumed in Baden-Baden that Pauline Viardot is the mistress of Ivan Turgenev. Many assume that he is the father of her second and fourth children, Claudie and Paul. Ivan adores Claudie as though she were his own, and Paul's paternity is never discussed. If he is the father, to acknowledge it openly would destroy the comfortable life into which they have finally settled. It would destroy them all.

Frivolous Baden-Baden treasures its celebrities too much to sully them. The great prima donna is often escorted by both Turgenev and Viardot. They are an elegant trio, respectable by virtue of their accomplishments and their ages. The gray beards of the two gentlemen and the refinement of the lady render ludicrous all talk of passionate liaisons and doubtful paternity. Only the uppish Parisians who summer in Baden still find them a fruitful source of gossip. Maids in one of the great houses talk to maids in another, gardeners talk to gardeners, gardeners talk to maids, maids talk to their mistresses, and the story circulates that Pauline has been seen in her peignoir in the misty light of dawn, racing barefoot across the lawns between the Chalet Viardot and the Villa Turgenev.

* * *

Ivan Turgenev is a conscientious father, if not an attentive one. Even when he had little hope of any sort of intimacy with Pauline, he continued to spend some months each year in France with his daughter who was otherwise sent off to be educated at a *pensionnat*.

He is not particularly proud of her, but he is well-enough satisfied. She is a good girl, honest, nothing out of the ordinary. Now that she has begun to grow into a young woman, he finds her to be temperamental, vain, secretive, and stubborn, but these are all faults he recognizes in himself, and a tall man cannot complain that his daughter is not short.

When he moved to Baden-Baden, he considered that Paulinette might live with him there. He had spent years persuading her to be grateful, to love Pauline, who is, after all, the kindest, most generous woman on earth, yet his daughter has always resented her ersatz mother, and her antagonism only continued to grow.

Her visits had not gone well. During a particularly violent argument, he defended Pauline and rebuked his daughter as he always did. After that, Paulinette refused to have anything to do with the Viardots, and Ivan, striving to maintain the appearance of taking the upper hand, forbid her to appear in Baden-Baden again, settling her instead with a governess in the respectable Parisian suburb of Passy.

An old friend, Madame Valentine Delessert, née Comtess de Laborde, took it upon herself to find a husband for the daughter of the great author. Turgenev thought that Paulinette would make a fine wife, but he worried that her face, identical to his, although handsome on a man, lacked the delicacy of feminine beauty. And she cared little for music, for art, literature, all the expected niceties.

She rejected three suitors before she agreed to the proposal of Gaston Bruère, the twenty-nine-year-old son of a notary, who managed a glass factory in Rougemont owned by Madame Delessert's son-in-law. Ivan provided money for a trousseau, for a wedding luncheon at a restaurant in Passy, and, with some difficulty, a substantial dowry of 150,000 francs. He watched his daughter greet Bruère at the altar with a smile he had never seen on her face before.

Finally free to succumb to happiness, he has joined his life with Pauline's, their boats tied up side by side at the pier of old age. If he leaves Baden-Baden for business in Paris or Saint Petersburg, he is always terrified that something, anything, might happen to prevent his return to her. He thinks only of the moment when he will go mad with joy at the sight of her waiting for him at the Baden-Baden train station.

When they are apart, he writes to her every day. She wants to know everything he does, everything he thinks, everything he feels in her absence. She insists that he include every detail, no matter how small. "Really, I am a little ashamed of being loved so much," he writes. "I thank you a thousand times."

He was in Paris on March 6, 1861, when he received a telegram from Pavel Annenkov announcing that Czar Alexander II had issued a manifesto freeing the serfs. The Russian aristocracy, whose enormous incomes were threatened, were outraged. Turgenev, who had already freed his own serfs, rejoiced. Serfdom had been his sworn enemy. The czar once suggested that the portrayal of serfs in A Sportsman's Sketches influenced him to consider emancipation. It is the single event in Ivan's life that gives him a feeling of genuine accomplishment.

BERLIN, JANUARY 1867

IT WAS A LAST CHANCE. Ivan, on his way from Baden-Baden to check on his affairs in Russia, stopped in Berlin where Pauline has been engaged to perform. She no longer sings on the great opera stages, but the music is still inside her, boiling, steaming, demanding release. She chooses carefully now, confining her performances to smaller houses. This season she has scheduled concerts in Berlin, Leipzig, and Dresden. The power of her voice, which once effortlessly floated to the brilliant top notes of a soprano, then seamlessly descended to the lush, deep tones of a contralto, no longer dazzles audiences. The middle voice has become fragile, the top notes nearly gone, but the artistry remains. She understands the music more than ever before, but she struggles to express it.

Berlin is cold in late January, the streets wet with an icy slush that penetrates the thickest leather boots. Pauline doesn't dare risk walking about, especially not when she's expected to sing. She is still in demand at dinners and receptions, but she has turned down every invitation, refusing on the grounds of bad weather, her need to rest before a performance—all the usual excuses. She won't waste this chance to be alone with Ivan, away from the children, from Louis.

They have decided to spend the day in the warm refuge of the hotel's deserted common room, reading together by the fireplace. Now and then, she looks up from the comfort of her armchair to watch his hands holding a book, the finger that turns a page. She watches his belly rise and fall as he breathes, watches his pink tongue emerge to lick a lower lip, watches as he crosses and re-crosses his legs, imagining his thick thighs beneath the fabric of his trousers.

And when, noticing her watching, he raises a questioning eyebrow, she holds his eyes and smiles, then goes back to the page she was reading, trying to remember where she left off, only to look up again moments later. The hotel is quiet. They have not been so alone since that hurried, stolen night in Moscow long ago. She feels the fire, hot on her cheeks, wonders if their armchairs are too close to the hearth. From under her eyelashes she steals another look at his hands, allowing herself to remember them in her hair, on her breasts, between her legs. She tells herself to put those thoughts away, to put them away forever. And then she asks herself why.

They dine together at the hotel. She looks at him across the flame of the candle that flickers on the table. She watches the movement of his soft lips.

"All my life, I sacrificed myself at the altar of art," she says. "I had no other choice. Perhaps I was seduced by the applause, by the fame, the huge fees. But I denied myself the comforts any other woman would have demanded as a birthright. Is it too late now, to claim them? Is it too late for this happiness?"

He laughs. "Nothing is worse than a happiness that comes late. It deprives one of that most precious right to swear and curse at one's fate!" He leans across the table and takes her hands in his. She holds them against her cheek for an instant. And then they say good night. And that is how it should be.

In her room, restless and wakeful in her bed, she forces herself to conjure the music she will sing in two days' time. Some songs of Schumann. Some songs of Glinka. She hears the melodies, but she can feel Ivan's big soft hands on her body, feel his weight as though he were in the bed beside her, his breath, fast and hot in her ear, his beard brushing her neck, her legs entangled with his. She rolls onto her belly, covers her head with a pillow, but still she feels his body beneath hers where there is only a feather mattress.

She sits up in bed. It's a last chance. She throws back the comforter, begins to search for her slippers in the dark. *No, Pauline. What are you doing? What can you be thinking? You have come to an understanding. There are rules. You are together now, the three of you with the children, the family.* She lies back, covers herself again.

At sixty-six, Louis has become an old man. He has, in fact, decided to be old. She is forty-five, and she is alive. Just once. One last time, to lay her head on Ivan's chest, to feel his body naked against hers. Can it be so wrong?

She feels blindly on the dressing table for her hairpins. Her hands are shaking. The pins fall to the floor. Her hair tumbles down her back. She pins it up again, finds her cloak. If she should meet a stranger, she will appear to have just come in from outside.

A single gas lamp lights the corridor. She clings to the shadows as she searches for his door. She peers at the number to be sure, knocks softly, then waits, leaning her forehead against the wall. Perhaps he is asleep. Perhaps he won't hear her knocking. She knocks again. She knocks louder, confident now, imagining his joy. But when he opens the door, what she sees is shock and, she thinks, a kind of fear. He hesitates, confused.

"Jean?" she whispers. "Forgive me. I ought to leave you in peace." He has no answer for her. She hides her face in the collar of her cloak. His eyes are so soft. *Oh Pauline, how good he is, how much he loves you!* He has spent the day, the days, the years before, caring for her, never asking anything in return, eager, always, to do anything that might help her, cheer her, make her life easier. And here he stands, in his dressing gown, barefoot.

Oh, dear God! She had forgotten what it is to be wrapped in the arms of this big man. His hands are on her cheeks. And then they are both laughing, laughing. Her cloak has fallen to the ground. He lifts her onto the bed, covers her with his body. She is a closed blossom whose petals, constrained for so long, open again into bloom.

In the morning, he is on the train to Stettin, on his way to the boat that will take him to Saint Petersburg.

February 26, 1867

Liebste Freundin, adored creature,
   I have just begun to regain my senses, that is to say, I finally can keep my head above water. I cannot tell you how relentlessly sad I have been. Those days in Berlin, those unexpected, wonderful meetings, all of it, and then the cruel parting. It was more than I could bear. I was broken by the weight of those unforgettable events, more broken than I have ever been before. My feelings for you are too strong, too powerful. I can no longer live away from you. I must feel your nearness, delight in it. A day without your eyes shining on me is lost. But enough, enough, or I shall lose control of myself.
   I fall, with unspeakable tenderness at your beloved feet. Be a thousand times blessed.

                                                                 J. T.

I VAN TURGENEV STANDS BESIDE PAULINE ON the steps outside the entrance to his villa, waiting to receive their guests. He is too excited to be still and has been scolded for fidgeting, so he clasps his hands behind his back. She is dressed very simply, all in black, with no important jewelry. She does not want to draw attention to herself, but really, he thinks, she is the center of attention wherever she goes. He was so nervous dressing, he is afraid he must have driven his servant, Nikolai, a little mad, but he is flawlessly fitted and brushed and perfumed, and the gout, which attacked his foot in January, has disappeared at last.

He knows, now, that the sad fog that lingered so long between them has lifted, that she loves him finally, completely, that he will end his days as he is at this moment, beside her. Nor has he any doubt of his friendship with her husband. Louis himself suggested that he buy the plot of land that adjoins the Viardot chalet. Turgenev sold all his Russian property, with the exception of the Spasskoye estate, to raise the funds for this little castle. It has taken three years to build the house in the style of Louis XIII, and it has nearly drained his financial resources, but it is finished, the sanctuary where he can live out his days in peace and happiness. Five hundred trees and shrubs have already been planted on the grounds, although the rooms are still devoid of furnishings.

He is constantly encouraging Pauline—"coerce" is the word she uses—to compose. He wrote the text of an operetta in order to encourage her to set it to music. It's rather silly but, he hopes, amusing. This afternoon they are trying the work out with a family

243

performance, a rung or two above the plays they used to present in the attic at Courtavenel. There are parts for all the children. Even nine-year-old Paul has a comic speaking part. And Pauline's students—some quite good—will have the chance to perform before an audience.

Invitations to Pauline's Saturday afternoons are prized, even by the aristocracy, who are much too snobbish to consort with artists, certainly not theater people. But Pauline is a creature unto herself. And the great musicians of Europe, no matter how illustrious, consider it a pleasure and an honor to perform at the Chalet Viardot where they can admire Louis's art collection, which rivals any local museum. Ivan is something of an added attraction, certainly among the literary set. Editions of his work have been published in French, English, and German. And the Russian expatriates in Baden-Baden all want to meet him—especially those who find his novels reprehensible.

As the operetta *Le dernier sorcier*, *The Last Sorcerer*, requires more space than the Chalet Viardot can accommodate, thirty chairs and a piano have been carried across the wide lawns. It's a very simple production, but Ivan and Pauline are quite serious about the work. He believes it has the potential to be performed in important houses—in Weimar, for example, where they can count on Liszt's support, even Berlin, certainly some of the court theaters. Pauline's great genius should be recognized. He knows of no music more poetic, no love duet in any opera more beautiful than the one she has written for the sorcerer's daughter and the prince.

The sun has begun its descent behind the fir-covered slope of the Sauerberg, and as the earth cools, the breeze grows stronger, blowing a lock of gray hair across Ivan's forehead. Pauline is quiet beside him.

"You are so calm!" he says.

"And you are so nervous, foolish man! Ah, they're here."

At the curve of the Tiergartenstrasse, an open landau rolls into view, then comes to a stop under the villa's porte cochere and a pair of footmen jump down to open the doors. Augusta, queen of

Prussia, spills out of the carriage in a cascade of silk satin ruffles, followed by the voluminous skirts of her daughter, Louise, grand duchess of Baden. The queen is always the first to arrive. Ivan considers it proof of Pauline's incomparable goodness and intelligence that Augusta holds her close to her heart. They have been friends for twenty years—to the extent that a queen can be a friend to an opera singer.

Soon the Tiergartenstrasse is lined with carriages. Ivan stands at the back of the salon where he can signal the servants and observe the reactions of the audience. Louis is sitting in the front row of chairs near the piano, beside the queen and her daughter. Two sniffy Russian grand duchesses sit directly behind them. Pauline's brother, Manuel Patricio, who has come from London for the performance, is seated beside Clara Wieck Schumann, who has brought along her daughter, Marie. Ivan's French publisher Pierre-Jules Hetzel is seated beside his friend, the artist Ludwig Pietsch. Pauline's old nemesis, the soprano Giulia Grisi, is seated beside her lover, the tenor Mario, who is a prince of the kingdom of Sardinia. The conductor Hermann Levi has chosen a seat beside Charles-Wilfrid de Bériot, Pauline's nephew, a pianist and teacher, son of Maria Malibran.

Pauline takes her place at the piano. Ivan signals the servants to lower the gas in the chandelier and to light the little lamps along the proscenium. *The moment has arrived.* He takes a deep breath, covers his mouth with one hand, and hopes for the best. *Si Dios quiere,* he whispers. God be willing.

Ninety minutes later, thirty pairs of hands are united in applause. The ovation is really quite enthusiastic. Very enthusiastic, indeed. Pauline is standing beside the piano smiling, acknowledging the cast. How delighted with themselves Marianne and Didie seem. Even grumpy Louise, who sang the role of the prince, seems pleased.

Pauline is raising an arm in his direction. They are all applauding him! He supposes he should bow, or at least nod, but her eyes have latched on to his and he can hardly bear to look away.

The queen of Prussia congratulates him. "One must come to Baden-Baden to hear such perfection," she says. Clara Schumann catches his attention. "The work is so clever, so dainty, so light, so well-crafted and so full of humor. I'd like to embrace Pauline, but I have no hope of so much as exchanging a word with her. She is surrounded by admirers and besieged with compliments."

Louis reaches up to slap him on the back and tells him they are a great success.

"Yes, old man, it appears that we are!"

The majordomo announces supper and begins to lead the way to the Chalet Viardot, where cold beef and potato salad have been laid out on silver platters.

Louis Viardot offers his arm to the queen of Prussia.

"I'll just wait behind a moment," Ivan says. "I want to find the children." Standing with his hands in his pockets, he watches the guests file out. Then Pauline comes up behind him, surprising him with a hand on his arm, and joy surges through his body. "Shall we make our appearance?"

"Oh, shall we?" He laughs, looking at her, then looks away and laughs a little more. She pats his arm, and they walk along the torchlit path across the lawns.

CHALET VIARDOT, BADEN-BADEN, FEBRUARY 1868

PAULINE SITS BESIDE THE BED, HER hands folded in her lap, watching her poor Papa Loulou, who is nearly as white as the sheets on which he lies. She lost her father to pneumonia. She will not lose her husband. There will be no bleeding, no leeches, no cupping. She has permitted the German doctors to prescribe only a tincture of Peruvian bark with bitter orange peel to tame his fever and mustard plasters to soothe his chest, and has ordered that the room be kept warm to soften the air. The bronchitis has gone to his lungs and the exertion of breathing exhausts him. At night, she watches as he curls into himself, shivering with fever.

The relentless cough has reduced his usually gentle voice to a feeble growl. "Is it true that Turgenev has delayed his trip to Paris in order to stay with me? What can he do for me here? You must encourage him to go on with his plans."

She thinks that Ivan has become as married to her husband as she is herself.

"He refuses to leave Baden-Baden until you have recovered, Papa. You know he will not."

Louis turns his head away from her, gazes at the ceiling. "No, I don't suppose that he will." His breathing is labored, shallow. "And will you leave me, *bonne maman* . . . now that I am a sick old man?"

"I will never leave you, Papa. You ought to know that."

He reaches for her hand. "I have become a useless piece of furniture, something that has been in your possession for so long you no longer see it, but pass by it, day after day, without noticing it's there, where it has always been. So often, I'm excluded from your conversations, your music—even my place with the children has been occupied. How would you yourself feel if another woman, Madame Sand, for instance, were to replace you in the family, to take over your duties, to make you superfluous?" He gasps and coughs, shakes his hand free of hers, clutches his handkerchief to his mouth.

"Oh, Papa! Loulou!"

"My body is ill . . . but my heart is well and it is full of you . . . I love you . . . I adore you."

His words, his pleading eyes tear at her. Even after all these years, he hasn't understood. Has he been harboring this pained resentment, unable to express it until the illness weakened his resolve? Perhaps she has been selfish. *No, Pauline, you ought to admit it. You have been dreadful. You found it convenient to assume that your great contentment was shared by all those around you.*

"Papa . . . You are and always will be indispensable, to me, to the children, to . . . all of us. You have been my closest, dearest friend. If I have neglected you, forgive me. I will do better. But you must never doubt my loyalty. Never."

His dark eyes fall on her like a weight as she speaks. She hasn't said what he wants to hear, but she hasn't lied to him. She does the best she can for him, she always has. Watching his face, she sees how he clings to the slender threads of reassurance she offers him. That he should question her now, after so many years of marriage, frightens her. So long as Louis Viardot is her husband, she is safe, in the way that a bird is safe in its cage. There have been times when she nearly flew away, but she always came back.

A wan smile flutters over his lips. "What are we to do, then? Shall we work together to restore the peace and joy, the happiness and pride I have always known in calling you my wife and my friend?"

Oh, Loulou, always rational, always kind, always demanding what I can never give him. "Papa, whatever I have done, whatever I may do, I will always be your wife and your friend."

A blazing fire of wood and coke has been built up in the hearth. Batting has been stuffed around the windows to keep out drafts. The air has become too thick to breathe.

She stands up, leans over, and kisses his damp forehead. "You are still burning with fever. I will have a cup of linden flower tea sent in. You must promise to drink it. Jean will come to see you soon." She gets up, avoids looking at him, but her conscience stops her at the door.

"Papa *cheri*, your heart is so good."

* * *

In the study on the second floor of his villa, where French doors open onto a balcony overlooking the Viardot chalet, Ivan Turgenev works at his desk. Claudie Viardot, her easel a few feet away, paints quietly, the two of them bound in the sweetness of silent companionship. At sixteen, she has grown into a beautiful young woman, yet there is something in her that reminds him of her mother, who has never been beautiful. There are times when she laughs her mother's laugh, raising her shoulders and turning her head to one side, times when she uses her mother's gestures, when she turns her lovely hands over while making a point, or makes a certain clucking sound with her tongue in teasing disapproval.

Claudie may be the child of Louis Viardot's loins, but she is the child of Ivan Turgenev's heart, the sensitive and affectionate daughter with whom he can share his love of music, art, literature, his love of dogs. His Didie, his *Didelchen*, his little idol, his white angel, loves him even more than she loves her kind but distant father. She confides in her *parrain*, her "godfather," her Tourguel, always sure to find a consoling hand on her shoulder.

Since Louis took ill, Ivan has been in the habit of stopping to see him after breakfast, after dinner, before supper. He tries to distract his friend with conversation, and when Viardot is too weak even for that, he tries to amuse him by reading aloud.

This afternoon Ivan takes dinner in his study with Claudie, then walks with her through the garden to the Chalet Viardot. She runs off to find her sister, Marianne, and he enters the room where Louis Viardot lies.

"Well, old fellow, how are you?"

Viardot is sitting up in bed. Veins ridge the pale, wrinkled hands with which he clutches a shawl about his throat. "I remain among the living, just at the moment."

Turgenev eases himself into the chair that Pauline lately occupied. "Surely, Viardot, you are not planning on dying."

"Not this evening, if I can manage to avoid it, but soon enough. And then, in the words of the Buddhists, I shall need not paradise, but rest. My body shall be incinerated or rot in the ground, and, as I have faith in the existence of neither the soul nor the hereafter, nothing will remain of Louis Claude Viardot."

Ivan looks for a wry smile under the white mustache, but finds a grimace.

"Your memory will remain with all those who love you, my dear friend."

"Will you remember me, Turgenev?"

"I can only promise to do so if I should be so unfortunate as to outlive you."

"And as you are a much younger man, who will surely continue to live and thrive after my death, will you then marry my wife?"

Ivan busies himself opening his latest book, *Smoke*, slowly lifting the woven bookmark and placing it carefully down on the following page, as though performing a delicate operation that cannot be interrupted.

"My dear Viardot, the fever, I fear, has clouded your usually clear mind."

"Ah, Turgenev, I'm too old and too ill to pretend. Promise me that you will care for her and for the children."

Ivan raises his head. "You hardly need ask for such a promise."

Louis slides further under his blankets. "No, that was unfair of me. I daresay you care for them now, even while I live."

"And I shall care for you, as well. Now, will you please recover promptly, if only to ease my mind of worry?"

"Oh, enough! Read! At least I can comfort myself that I shall have died while listening to a good novel read by its author."

"You place yourself in the minority by finding it good, Viardot. I have managed, once again, to insult everybody. No author has ever been more vilified than I have for this book but I shall try, all the same, not to bore you too much.

"*Litvinov fell in love with Irina the moment he first saw her (he was only three years older than she was), but for a long time he failed to get a response, or even a hearing . . .*"

PART FIVE

AN END

CHALET VIARDOT, JULY 19, 1870

I T'S THE MORNING AFTER PAULINE'S FORTY-NINTH birthday celebration, and Louis Viardot has just read in the papers that the arrogant Louis-Napoléon, goaded by the bellicose Chancellor Bismarck, declared war on Prussia. The habitually mild-mannered Viardot is in a rage more passionate than any he has experienced in a life filled with provocation. He thunders into the music room to announce the news to Pauline and Ivan. The war, he says, will ruin Europe, and worse, it will disrupt the peaceful family life he has finally managed to arrange. Then he locks himself in his room, too infuriated to speak to anyone.

Pauline watches him slam the door and sits down at the piano again. "It will all be over by Christmas, Ivan," she says. "The whole of Europe expects the French to win, but Loulou is certain it will be the Prussians, and the Prussians themselves don't doubt it for an instant. The fighting will never reach Baden-Baden. If the French armies cross the Rhine, we should send the children east to Wildblad, but I cannot imagine they will get that far." She plays a little Mozart to calm herself.

On a morning two weeks later, Ivan is at his writing table when his gardener appears to tell him that heavy firing has been heard in the distance. The ground begins to shake under his feet as he rushes out to the porch. Behind his villa, the Schwarzwald rises green in the summer sun, and in the distance, he hears the echo of gunshots.

He drives his carriage up the winding road to Iburg Castle to see for himself, breathing harder and sweating more than the horse.

255

From the park outside the towering abbey he can see the whole of Alsace as far as Strasbourg on the other side of the French frontier. He closes his eyes to listen and hears nothing but the chatter of birds, the summer breeze ruffling the trees. But eyes open, he sees clouds of gray and red smoke rising across the Rhine, half-hiding the sun and casting a pall over the deep green of the dense forest. For a long time, he stands there, immobilized by sorrow, cursing the insanity of war until he is roused by the faint echo of cannon fire and drives slowly down to Baden-Baden.

In the hour he spent on the mountain, every wall has been plastered with notices announcing that the French have withdrawn from the battlefield. The roads have become choked with luggage-laden carriages. Outside the train station, frenzied Parisians crowd the doors, fleeing their summer homes.

The next day, the roulette tables are abandoned, the restaurants and theaters empty. Life in Baden-Baden changes so rapidly he hardly has time to comprehend his new situation before becoming bewildered again. The queen's carriage no longer appears at his porte cochere.

The Viardots are in a constant state of anxiety. French citizens are no longer welcome in Prussia. They rarely leave the chalet, receive no visitors, never venture into the town. Ivan runs errands for them. They play music. They read. They roll bandages for the wounded.

Ivan can still go out shooting with his dog Pegasus, but after supper, he sits silently with Pauline and the children, all the windows closed against the sound of the bombardment of Strasbourg. At night in his bed, he listens to dark rumblings, explosions muffled by distance.

On the twentieth of August at ten in the evening, when all the bells of Baden-Baden suddenly begin to ring, he runs into the Tiergartenstrasse to ask the neighbors what has happened. The Prussians have decisively defeated the French at Raisonville.

On the ninth of September, he stands in the entrance of the Chalet Viardot, shouting that Louis-Napoléon has been taken prisoner at Sedan. For the first time in nearly three weeks, Louis Viardot comes out of his room and stands on the landing. The fall of the French emperor, whom he has loathed for so long, is a great satisfaction to him, but he is not a happy man. "We no longer need fear for Europe," he calls down. "Now we must weep for poor France. The Prussian revenge will be brutal. They had no need to set fire to Strasbourg. What horrors will they wreak on Paris?"

Over the course of her career, Pauline earned enormous sums of money and Louis has invested it prudently, but the bond markets are in chaos, and their assets are blocked in France, leaving them close to financial ruin.

They have long discussions into the night.

Pauline insists that they ought to go to London, where she is still a marketable commodity. She knows that the audiences who once idolized her there now worship Adelina Patti, but she is sure that her name will still arouse fond memories in some, although others will barely recognize it. She will be engaged, if only to sing in small halls for small fees. And she can teach the children of the wealthy, talented or not, as Chopin had done.

Ivan, a Russian, has no reason to leave Baden-Baden, and no thought of remaining there without Pauline. His flesh and blood might be elsewhere at times, but his soul is always with her.

And so it is decided that in October, Ivan will escort Pauline and her daughters to the Belgian port of Ostend on the North Sea, avoiding France, which is still at war. They have been driven out of paradise.

They promise each other not to cry in front of the children, and in the carriage, Pauline keeps up a cheerful monologue, painting pretty pictures of what lies ahead. Her brother, Manuel Patricio, will be waiting for them when the ship docks. So many friends are already in London—the composer Camille Saint-Saëns. Clara Schumann will be there in a month or two. It will be a lovely adventure.

In the final moment before boarding the ship that will carry them to England, Pauline sends the girls away with their governess. And they face each other, Ivan's hands on her shoulders, her hands clutching the lapels of his coat. "I beg of you," she says, "do everything in your power to convince Louis to leave Baden-Baden quickly. Don't stay away a single day, a single hour more than is absolutely necessary."

In December, Ivan arrives in London with Louis and little Paul. Pauline has found dismal lodgings in a terrace house at 30 Devonshire Place, and Ivan has discreetly taken rooms nearby in Manchester Square. He is not fond of London, but he has a surfeit of English literary friends—George Eliot, Alfred Lord Tennyson, Charles Swinburne, young Henry James. In the mornings he goes to the library with Louis to read the war news in the French and German newspapers, whose stories are always in conflict, both sides claiming victory.

To raise funds for the Viardots, Ivan secretly publishes an album of Pauline's songs at his own expense, and helps Louis Viardot sell one of his treasured paintings, a Rembrandt, to the Russian grand duchess Elena Pavlovna. He builds a dowry for his beloved Claudie, arranges music lessons for Marianne, and enrolls Paul in an English day school at Regent's Park.

Pauline has always refused to be disheartened. She cannot survive without a measure of tranquility, and she maintains it at all costs. The London drawing room is dark and small, but she holds salons there, pretending not to care if the world finds her in such reduced circumstances, and she fills London's gray, foul air with music.

RUE DE DOUAI 48, 1871

SUMMER IN PARIS. THE FIGHTING IS over, but the buildings are pockmarked with scars from the shelling. Houses stand empty and silent, their outer walls blown away, while the furnishings inside remain in place, the floors stained with blood.

The house on the Rue de Douai is intact, but it has been closed up and abandoned, the garden overgrown. Pauline, Louis, and Ivan walk from room to room with handkerchiefs pressed to their noses.

She is fifty years old, too old to interest the Parisian gossips and past caring what anyone thinks. There is no point in pretending to live apart from Ivan any longer. He occupies four rooms on the third floor—a small study, a library, a sitting room, a bedroom. He covers the walls in silk brocade, installs an enormous Russian divan, a writing table, a cast of Pauline's hands, a bas-relief of her profile, a samovar. Under Louis Viardot's tutelage, he has accumulated a small art collection, works of Corot, Courbet, Rousseau, and lesser works bought on his own at auction for far more than they are worth. He pays the substantial sum of two hundred francs to have a listening tube inserted in the walls between Pauline's music room and his study so that he can hear her singing. His rooms are small, but he spends his days downstairs, living as one of the family.

He receives endless visitors—his young protégées Guy de Maupassant and Henry James, his friends Émile Zola and Gustave Flaubert. Russian expatriates come asking for favors he never refuses. Ivan is willing to help every Russian in Paris. He is an enthusiastic supporter of the artist Alexei Harlamoff, who was

259

born a serf, and commissions him to paint portraits of Pauline, Louis, and himself. He writes letters of introduction and circulates petitions on behalf of his countrymen, lends money without expectation of repayment, and is secretary of the circle of Russian artists in Paris. Pauline promotes Russian composers, arranges concerts.

When his compatriots call on him in his rooms, they are appalled. They blame Pauline for bewitching Russia's greatest living writer. They say his rooms are not even fit for servants. His bedroom is a shamble. Buttons are missing from his shirts.

His guests, the Viardots' guests, even the children's guests speculate on the relationship between the mistress of the house and her illustrious tenant. They see that Ivan's eyes never leave her. They watch her tease and flirt with him. They notice that she never smiles while he is melancholy, that he is cross when she is cross. And they wonder what might have been between them, until they understand that it must have been everything.

Flaubert is the only writer in France whom Ivan considers truly great, and he loves him more than any other man. One Sunday a month, he drags his gouty foot up three flights of stairs to Flaubert's spare, smoke-filled rooms on the Faubourg Saint-Honoré. Dressed in a silk pajamas and a red fez, Flaubert entertains a tight little circle of writers—Émile Zola, Edmond de Goncourt, Alphonse Daudet. And Ivan amuses them with stories, or reads aloud in his soft, high voice, translating at sight works of Tolstoy, Goethe, and Dickens.

Twice a month, the five writers meet for dinner at the Magny restaurant on the rue Contrescarpe-Dauphine. George Sand occasionally joins them, the only woman at the table, dressed in a fussy black silk gown, her delicate hands half-hidden by lace cuffs.

Pauline is no longer a great prima donna, but she has become a legend. Splendidly dressed in elaborate gowns, she moves through her music room on Thursday evenings, allowing her hand to be kissed as tea and cakes are served. She is revered, adored, and she is in her glory. Musicians passing through Paris on concert tours consider it a privilege to perform at her salon.

The writer Henry James stands at the back of the room beside the artist Gustave Doré, both of them bored. "Madame Viardot is as ugly as eyes in the sides of her head and an interminable upper lip can make her," James says. "But she is very handsome or, in the French sense, très-belle."

Plump, double-chinned, a dark wig covering her white hair, George Sand never moves from her place on a sofa, smoking incessantly, barely speaking. Ivan tells her that her approval of his work has been the greatest satisfaction of his life, and she smiles. It has not passed her notice that this giant of a man is bound to the will of the petite Pauline, but she knows that he has found his happiness in being governed, and as he is in good hands, she sees no harm in it.

The Viardot daughters, Marianne and Claudie, sing a duet written for them by Saint-Saëns. Paul plays a violin sonata written for him by his mother on a Stradivarius bought for him by Ivan Turgenev. Pauline always places herself at the end of the program. Tonight, she brings the evening to an end with a scene from Gluck's *Alceste*. As usual, Camille Saint-Saëns accompanies her at the piano. Her voice has had a long rest in the years since her farewell performance in Paris and has regained some of its luster. "She is superb," Henry James whispers. "That was the finest piece of musical declamation, of a grandly tragic sort, that I can conceive."

Louis Viardot, in his seventies, remains in his study. He almost never leaves the house, but he busies himself writing two volumes on the paintings and sculpture of Europe. Frail and bent, he shuffles through the last decade of his life in a voluminous dressing gown, avoiding company, rarely speaking when company is unavoidable. If there are guests at the dinner table, he prefers to take his meal alone. It is left to Ivan to escort his ladies, Pauline, Claudie, and Marianne, to concerts, the theater, the opera.

Ivan makes annual trips to Russia, where he still has business with his remaining estates and his publishers. And he retreats to Spasskoye to write, until separation from Pauline becomes unbearable. French skin begins to grow under his Russian hide, and he sloughs it off like a snake. Every day, he writes to her.

> *Time goes slowly without you. My feelings for you are so deep and unalterable that your absence upsets me physically. I feel I can hardly breathe. But when I am with you, I feel a calm joy. I am at home, and I wish for nothing. Oh, my friend, I have these past twenty-seven years to treasure. It will be with us as it was in Burns's poem, John Anderson, my Jo, and we will go down the hill together. May all the good angels watch over you.*

In February 1879, he is in Moscow to deal with the tedium of his finances when Maksim Kovalevsky, the editor of the *Critical Review*, arranges a dinner for him to which twenty writers and journalists are invited. Turgenev's works have been translated into French, Italian, Polish, German, even Serbian. He is well-respected in Europe, and the American publisher Henry Holt has issued his works in English translation with some success. But in his own Mother Russia, he has been reviled. He has not been forgiven for painting the men and women of his own class as superfluous, useless people, or for portraying thousands of faceless serfs as individuals with humor, intelligence, and emotions. His last novel, *Virgin Soil*, portrayed young revolutionaries in a light many found unflattering. He has succeeded in offending nearly all of literate Russia, and is hardly prepared to receive accolades.

So that night at dinner, when Kovalesky raises a glass to toast "the loving and tolerant teacher of our youth," Turgenev is astonished. A few nights later, when he appears at a reading of his work at the Society of Lovers of Russian Literature, he is greeted with thunderous applause and spontaneous speeches. Students mob him as he leaves the hall, nearly carrying him off on their shoulders.

The mood of Russia has changed, and a new generation embraces his liberal ideals. In March, when he arrives in St. Petersburg, his hotel is thronged with admirers. He is grateful, humbled, bewildered, shaken. His life has not been lived in vain. He has been given the highest reward a writer can hope for.

Dearest, most beloved Madame:

Imagine more than a thousand students in an immense hall. When I entered, the uproar was enough to bring the building down. Shouts of "hurrah." Hats tossed in the air. A student made a speech honoring me, in which he came so dangerously close to voicing the forbidden that the rector of the university, seated on the front row, was white with fear. I tried to reply without setting fire to the powder keg, while striving to avoid platitudes. And when I had finished reading, I was greeted with such—you will excuse the word—applause as I have never before experienced. I thought of you the entire time I was standing there, blushing and baffled, smiling blankly at the roaring crowd.

My dear, good Tourgline,

Your new triumphs will make you grow roots in Petersburg, which is fine as long as it does not make you homesick when you are in Paris. You will get bored here, without the fever of admiration around you—and there will be no more than the familiar faces, each a little older—or less young—who look at you happily but calmly, some eccentric friends, some good acquaintances, many dull ones, and always the same little routine, day after day. You won't abandon us, will you? God, what joy it will be to see you here again! But you will never have the strength to tear yourself away from all this youth, pawing you and leaping around you! In your letter, you don't talk at all of returning. I will be worried until you are back with us. Oh, you will have so many interesting things to tell me! You will tell

*me everything, won't you? <u>Everything!</u> I wish I were a little
bird. 100,000 caresses.*

                                          Your Pauline

They have grown old together, bound by all that has passed
between them. For a decade, their lives roll out like an exquisite
fabric, embellished with weddings and the birth of grandchildren.
Louisette marries a minor diplomat twenty years her senior and
moves with him to South Africa, but she soon returns to the Rue
de Douai with her little son "Loulou." Louis blames her willful,
stubborn behavior for the dissolution of the marriage. Pauline sur-
mises that Louisette has been reluctant to perform her conjugal
duties. "There is no reason why she should have been born female.
From childhood, she has been boyish, wearing trousers whenever
she could and going out shooting with her father." With Ivan's
help, Louisette takes up a teaching position at the conservatory
in Saint Petersburg, sings and composes music, cuts her hair short,
and lives independently, which suits her.

Paul has become an accomplished, ambitious violinist who
resents living in his mother's shadow and bristles when he is told
how fortunate he is to be her son. In Baden-Baden, when he was
a boy, it enraged him that Ivan tried to discipline him. One night,
when he was told to go to bed, he objected, "You can't tell me
that! You're not my father." And the look that passed between
Ivan and his mother silenced him. From that moment, he believed
that Ivan was his father, although no one could be persuaded to
discuss it with him. They are all in an untenable situation. Ivan
can never claim Paul without humiliating Pauline and Louis. And
Paul would be ruined, labeled a bastard. So the truth festers under
the unblemished skin of propriety.

Claudie marries a publisher, Georges Chamerot, whom
Turgenev adores. Gabriel Fauré, a protégé of Camille Saint-Säens,
falls desperately in love with Marianne. They become engaged,
but she is hesitant, and spends long hours conferring with her

Tourguel, tormented by doubts. In the end, she breaks poor Fauré's heart, marrying a less talented composer whom she loves more, Alphonse Duvernoy.

They have become a family, as contented as any.

* * *

And then it all begins to fall apart. In February 1882, Paulinette appears in Paris with her two children. In the economic chaos of the Franco-Prussian war, her husband, Gaston Bruère, lost his glass factory and has spent all her dowry and the money Turgenev set aside for his grandchildren. He has taken to drink and beaten her mercilessly, one day threatening to kill her, the next swearing he will commit suicide.

Turgenev's unhappy daughter has been a burden to him since he discovered her existence. Now it is his duty to rescue her, once again, to hide her from her husband. He is forced to sell his horses and carriage, and his most beloved painting, a Rousseau landscape, so that he can sustain her and the children at a hotel in an obscure Swiss village. But Paulinette is not satisfied. She complains of boredom, wants to travel, writes asking for more money.

> *My dear Paulinette,*
>
> *It is quite impossible for me to give you more than 400 francs a month. Live as quietly as you can. Your husband will hire investigators, and if he should find you, nothing will save you. He has already sent me a court summons and if he thinks I am involved he will proceed against me. He has the perfect right to sell everything you own, your jewelry, etc. Stay hidden and remain silent! I will try to send you something for a dress, and clothes for the children. But you must get used to the idea that you no longer have anything. May God grant that all goes well.*
>
> *I.T.*

In March, Louis, now in his eighty-second year, suffers a stroke that very nearly kills him. He can no longer walk, and considers it a triumph if he manages to move unassisted from the bed to the wheelchair. The doctors offer neither treatment nor hope, but demand complete bed rest. For years, Louis has chosen to confine himself to his study. He insists that the loss of his freedom will not be so great. But Pauline refuses to believe that the loss is permanent.

On a morning in April, when Ivan tries to get out of bed, his feet feel as if they have been pierced by pitchforks and he cannot stand. Pain tears at his chest and shoulder, and he has difficulty breathing. Pauline, already frantic with worry about Louis, leaves her husband's sick room to summon Jean-Martin Charcot, "the Napoléon of Neuroses."

The great doctor pronounces that Ivan is suffering from cardiac neuralgia. "There is nothing to be done about it," he says. "Medical science is virtually impotent in the case of this disease."

Madame Death has left one of her calling cards. Ivan has spent his life shuddering in the cold wind that blows in from the grave, expecting death with a terror that invaded his sleep. But now that death is finally staring him in the face, he refuses to recognize her. He tells himself that while his disease may be incurable, it is not fatal.

Pauline knows that she may lose them both, but she is determined to be optimistic. She tells herself that this, too, will pass, and that they will go on with their lives as they have before. On days when Ivan's pain diminishes or Louis feels well enough to get out of bed, she nearly manages to believe it.

She has had an upholstered armchair moved to the edge of Louis's bed, and a table placed in front of it, so that she can take her meals there. In the mornings, after the breakfast dishes have been cleared away, she reads the newspaper aloud. At times, she wonders if he is only feigning an interest or if the sound of her voice alone is enough to comfort him. She watches his eyes, waiting for them to close, waiting for his breathing to slow, and when she is certain that he is asleep, she quickly, quietly climbs the curving staircase to Ivan's apartment on the floor above.

Every morning she enters his room fearing what she will find there. A succession of new treatments has brought brief periods of relief, quickly followed by relapses into unendurable suffering. She stands before his closed door, gathers herself, breathes deeply before opening it.

Today, she finds him sitting up in bed, encased in an iron harness the doctors have devised, which is fitted to his shoulder so that it rests on his left collarbone. It eases his pain, but makes it impossible for him to lift his arm. When he smiles, she nearly weeps with relief.

"Are you better today, Tourguel?"

"Most adored Madame, I am perfectly well. You see before you a healthy man who can neither stand nor walk nor move in any direction without atrocious pain. Other hands must wash me and brush my hair, but I could live another twenty years this way, and so long as I am able to write a little on those rare occasions when the pain subsides, I shall complain no more than an oyster, who likewise cannot move."

It is a good day.

* * *

Together with Turgenev, the Viardots have bought a country estate at Bougival on the Seine, only an hour's train ride from Paris. They occupy the existing villa, and Turgenev has built a little dacha for himself just across the lawn. He has named the place "Les Frênes" after the ash trees that line the drive and surround the lawns. Bougival is a replacement of sorts for Baden-Baden, a resort popular with artists and intellectuals. The painters Monet, Renoir, Morisot, and Sisley summer there.

In May, Pauline decides that Paris will soon be too hot for two ailing old men, and she cannot continue running up and down stairs between two sick rooms. Ivan, constrained to his bed, chants "Bougival, Bougival, Bougival" like a small child. Pauline hires nurses, summons the children, the sons-in-law, and the grandchildren.

In the country air, Louis regains a little strength. Ivan, though still in pain, says that he has resolved to accept his situation with the cheerful despair of a man who is beyond hope, so safe from disappointment. "I will be sixty-five soon," he says. "I have lived too long and written too much."

Claudie has set up her easel in his bedroom. Her seven-year old daughter, Jeanne, his namesake, sits at his side, listening to his stories. It rains almost every day, but if the afternoon is sunny, he is moved onto the balcony where he lies motionless, watching the young people play croquet on the lawns. In the evenings, there is always music. When he feels well enough, he meticulously corrects the proofs to a new edition of his collected works. If he is to die, he says, he will at least leave a flawless legacy.

In November, they move back to Paris and Ivan's suffering increases. The doctors cauterize his shoulder in fifty places and prescribe a milk fast, with a little broth in the evenings. Pauline has learned to administer his injections of quinine and morphine. She has begun to feel that her own life has been snatched away from her, that she has had her fill of sick, old men.

By April, Ivan's cries can be heard in the neighboring houses. Relentless agony and nightly doses of morphine send him into delirium. At three in the morning, Pauline is awoken by a bell frantically ringing and runs to his room. When he sees her, he wrenches the knob from the bell pull and throws it at her, narrowly missing her head. "*Voilà Lady Macbeth!*" he screams. "That terrible woman is trying to poison me!"

The crisis passes, but he remembers it all and weeps, begging her forgiveness. "I imagined that I was at the bottom of the sea," he says. "I was surrounded by monsters so foul no one has ever described them because no one has ever survived the sight of them."

In the spring, he begs to be moved back to Bougival. Although he will not be able to see further than the foot of his bed, he will know that the lawns are sprinkled with wild daisies, that the tulip trees are in bloom. New life sprouts from the winter-weary boughs of the ash trees, while his own life is in its yellow leaf.

He would never say so, but he wants to relieve Pauline of the burden he has become and to allow Louis to spend his last days alone with his wife. He says that he is no more than a sick old man in a corner, no longer able to look ahead, trying not to see what is around him, his life occupied only in defending itself from death.

His emaciated body is wrapped in shawls and carried down the staircase by servants. When they reach the landing, Louis, gaunt and feeble, is waiting in a wheelchair. The two men have been rivals. They have become friends. Now they are together at the edge of the abyss. Louis takes Ivan's hands in both of his and they look at one another for a long, tearful moment. Then he signals the servants, and Ivan continues his precarious descent to the street, where he is loaded into the waiting carriage like a trunk.

Pauline watches from the landing as the door closes behind him, then returns to Louis, secluded in his bedroom. Ignoring the doctors, she keeps the window open at the end of his bed, so that he can feel the spring air, and she will feel a little less suffocated. He has fallen asleep again, and she sits silently, watching a pair of magpies settle on a branch of the Japanese maple in the garden below. She has had no time to think. The tidy spool of her life has unwound, and now she sees the threads heaped on the ground.

She has given up her Thursday-evening salons and Sunday-evening intimate gatherings. She no longer attends concerts or visits galleries. And she is tired. How she would love to have a long bath, to dress in a wonderful gown, never to enter another sickroom, never again to force a smile while the odors of urine and feces, alcohol, and vinegar assault her no matter where she turns her head.

Louis speaks rarely and always with difficulty, but he is never quiet. Even now, as he sleeps, his breathing is noisy and labored.

His flushed eyelids open, and his dark eyes stare without seeing. Then he grunts, struggles, and she leans over the bed, lifts his damp head to add another pillow, offers a sip of water from a spouted cup.

"*Bonne maman.*" His words are indistinct, slurred, but she understands and covers his cold hand with her warm palm.

"I cannot speak well . . . How trying it must be for you. . . . But tomorrow I may be . . . unable to speak at all, so I must beg you . . . to listen to me now."

His eyes close again. The effort of saying those few words has exhausted him.

"*Papa cheri*, we have said what must be said. Please, believe me."

He rolls his head a little in protest, and struggles to inhale enough breath to go on speaking. "I must . . . prepare myself . . . to be carried to unknown regions . . . but I do not go unwillingly. Remorse is the only real hell . . . and I have long ago relieved myself of that . . . Now my only hope is that Buddha was correct in preaching . . . that the purest form of happiness . . . lies in annihilation."

He raises a pale hand, as if to excuse himself, and his eyes close once more. Pauline turns back to the window. When she was born, her father was one of the most celebrated singers on earth. She can never remember a time without performances, receptions, galas, intimate suppers for which one must dress. But for more than a year, she has barely had time to wash her face or fix her hair. When Louis first fell ill, she immediately canceled all her students, but he was terrified that this meant he was close to death and begged her to tell him the truth. So she resumed teaching, just a few hours a week, somehow willing herself to pay attention during the lessons. And the wags began to whisper that Madame Viardot cares so little for her husband she continues to see pupils while he lies on his deathbed.

Louis is stirring now, gaining a little strength, struggling to make some sound. "Turgenev will not be . . . my replacement . . . no . . .

we have spoken of it . . . but you, *bonne maman* . . . you must . . . live . . . live in our stead."

Two weeks later, when he slips into the inescapable void, Paul, Marianne, and Claudie, their spouses, and their children are in the house. They hold each other and weep, and Pauline feels the rock on which she has stood for more than forty years give way. Louis-Claude Viardot, the old nonbeliever, is buried at the Cimetière de Montmartre without much ceremony.

When the news of Louis's death reaches Ivan at Bougival, he loses what little strength he has left. He thinks that Louis has shown him the path leading out of the forest, and he is ready to follow him without waiting any longer.

Pauline, exhausted and bereft, has no time to grieve her husband. After decades of longing and denial, she is alone with Ivan at last, but it no longer matters to either of them.

She last saw him only a few weeks before, but when she arrives at Bougival, she is aghast. He lies in his bed like a felled tree, his face flushed red against the white of his hair, of his beard and the pillows on which his head rests. His hands lay hideously knotted on the blankets that cover him even now, in summer.

"Touréfi!" At the sound of her voice, he turns his head, and she forces a smile. She takes her place by his bedside, and remains there, day after day, from seven in the morning until he dozes off, late into the night.

One morning she finds him with tears in his eyes. He has lain awake all night composing a story he wants desperately to write, but he is too weak to put pen to paper. "Tell it to me, and I will write it down for you," she says. "I write very slowly in Russian, but if you are patient, we will manage it."

"Oh, no! If I tell it to you in Russian, I will labor over every word, every phrase, searching for the right expression. I no longer have the strength for that. I will tell it to you in whatever language comes to mind, just as we do when we speak to each other, and you will translate it all into French."

In the story, the fallen head of a once noble Russian family, now ruined, resorts to horse thieving, and is finally murdered. Ivan calls it "An End." It is his last refrain, a wry obituary for the class to which he himself belongs.

Pavel Annenkov is summoned. When he sees his old friend, Ivan bursts into tears, and Annenkov, too, begins to weep. The great giant lies under the green velvet canopy of his bed, emaciated, his skin florid, his eyes sunken. "How can I survive," he asks, "when my legs are as thin as a grasshopper's?"

In July, he scribbles a last letter to Tolstoy, writing in stops and starts with a pencil on a scrap of paper. He worries that the younger writer, fixated now on spirituality and religion, has turned away from his proper path.

> *My dear and beloved friend,*
>
> *I haven't written you for a long time, but I was, and frankly still am, on my deathbed. I cannot get well. It's useless even to think of it. I write to tell you how happy I am to have been your contemporary and to make one last sincere appeal. My friend, return to literature! That gift comes to you from the same place as all the others. How happy I would be to think that my plea had influenced you. Russia's great writer, grant my request! As for myself, I am finished. I cannot write more. I am tired.*

When his pain becomes constant and unendurable, Pauline sends for a Russian specialist, Dr. Belogolovy. He tells her that the disease the great Charcot diagnosed as neuralgia was more probably a cancer that began in the clavicle and spread to the marrow of the spinal cord. There is no point, he says, in mentioning this to the patient. Ivan knows that he is dying. There is no need to tell him why.

When the doctor leaves, she comes back into his bedroom, and he searches her face, then turns away. "I am looking into the blackness of the tomb," he says, "not into a rose-colored tomorrow."

She knows that every day she spends with him might be the last and begins to sleep on a chaise at the foot of his bed, never leaving his side, watching him slowly dying.

After a lifetime of conversation, nothing of importance remains unsaid. They are reduced to discussing doctors and medication, constipation and broken syringes, whether he could be persuaded to take a little broth and whether he is well enough to receive a visitor this morning.

One day, he raises his head a little and asks, "Shouldn't we speak of death? I call to her a hundred times a day without the slightest fear of facing her. I see a tall, quiet woman, enveloped from head to toe in a white veil, her deep, pale eyes gazing at nothing, her pale, grim lips silent, and I watch you struggle to ignore her."

Pauline strokes his forehead. "You doubt the existence of anything beyond the grave, Jean. But I believe that the soul is immortal, that the great loves, whatever their nature might be, will all be reunited one day—provided that they have made themselves worthy of it."

"Dearest, most beloved woman, I have doubted everything, but now that my life is at an end, I have learned to doubt only myself, to believe in the existence of something else, and even to feel a need for it."

He has developed a howling hunger for death. The pain has become so atrocious that not even morphine brings much relief. He pleads with Pauline to throw him out the window. "Oh, but Jean," she said, "you are too heavy. And besides, I might hurt you." Even then, she can make him smile.

He entreats anyone who visits to bring him poison. When Guy de Maupassant comes to Bougival, he finds a pitiable creature. "If you are truly my friend," Ivan says, "you will find me a revolver. You will grant me this act of kindness."

Five days later, on the first of September, when roses still bloom against the villa wall and pale leaves flicker on the ash trees outside his window, he loses consciousness. The family arrives from Paris to say goodbye to their Tourguel. They insist that Pauline go to her own bed and take turns through the night so that Ivan is never alone.

The next day, when he opens his eyes a little, they are surrounding him. Pauline, numbed by exhaustion, leans her face close to his and whispers, "Touréfi, can you see us?"

"Ah, there is the Queen of Queens!" he whispers. "What good she has done!"

Her daughters begin to weep. Their husbands stare at the floor.

He looks at them through half-closed lids, one by one. "You must believe that I have loved you all sincerely and honestly. It's time now to say goodbye, the way the ancient czars did. You are not all here yet. Come closer. I want to see you all. Warm me with your bodies."

Claudie throws herself across his chest.

"My dear ones, my whitish ones," he says. And then he falls into a deep coma. His breathing becomes labored and red spots appear on his hands. At two in the afternoon, he tries to raise his head, his face contorted in pain. Pauline clutches his hand.

He twice utters a sigh, and then he floats away from his life on the sound of women weeping. Around his neck, he still wears a medallion containing Pauline's portrait, his initials engraved on its cover.

EPILOGUE

When I am no more, when everything that I was has scattered like dust, oh you, my only friend, whom I have loved so deeply and so tenderly, you, who will surely survive me, do not go to my grave, to my grave where there is nothing to be done . . .

But in the lonely hours, when that unexpected sorrow, so well-known to gentle hearts, comes upon you, take one of our favorite books and look for the pages, the lines, the words, which—you remember—brought soft and silent tears to both our eyes.

Read them, close your eyes and hold out your hand to me, to your absent friend. I will not be able to clasp it in mine. My motionless hand will be under the earth. But today it is sweet to think that then, perhaps, you will feel a light caress brush your hand. And you will see me, and tears will flow beneath your closed lids as they did in those days when we were both moved by Beauty. Oh, my only friend, whom I have loved so tenderly and so deeply.

Ivan Turgenev, *Poems in Prose*, 1878

For two days, Pauline remains at his side, alone or with Claudie, sometimes simply watching his face, sometimes sketching his dear, dead features. At first, his brows are still contracted by the last spasms of suffering, but on the second day, she sees that death's noble peace has made him beautiful again. His

275

face has regained its kindness and tenderness, and she half expects him to smile at any moment.

She is too devastated, too exhausted, to follow his coffin on the long journey to the grave, but Claudie, Marianne, and their husbands take the train to Saint Petersburg with the body of their Tourguel. Before they leave Paris, four hundred people attend the ceremony at the Gare du Nord.

Turgenev has become so celebrated in Russia that the authorities fear riots might break out at the gravesite. Permission to transport the coffin across the Russian border is delayed again and again. When the permit finally arrives, crowds gather at each station where the train stops. On October 9, 1883, a cortège more than two miles long follows the coffin to Volkovo cemetery, Saint Petersburg, where it is buried not far from those of Vissarion Belinsky and Nikolai Gogol.

Pauline is Turgenev's unofficial widow, but she is granted none of the sympathy accorded to a grieving wife. Apart from a stipend for his daughter and small sums for the Viardot children, he has left her everything. The Russians, who have always blamed her for his long exile, are outraged. She is besieged with claims for his paintings, his manuscripts, the seal ring that belonged to Pushkin. Distant cousins emerge to claim Spasskoye. Paulinette and her estranged husband Gaston Bruère, now temporarily reconciled, challenge the will. Bruère demands an inventory of Turgenev's dacha in Bougival and has the house at Rue de Douai sealed. Pauline comes home on a Saturday morning to find that police have barred her from entering her own home. Her son Paul refuses to defend her, siding with Bruère and Paulinette. Her sons-in-law intervene and Bruère is dealt with, but the blow staggers her.

Within two months, she has lost both the men whose love has always supported her. Her strong will finally bends under the crushing weight of grief, and her children keep the windows locked at the Rue de Douai for fear she will follow through on her threat to end her own life. After that, she tries to hide her sorrow from her children. They are kind and loving, but their cheerful young faces only irritate her, and she longs to be alone with her beloved dead, with the bitter comfort of memories.

For a long time, the sorrow is too much to bear. She tries to lose herself in a book, but cannot comprehend what she is reading. She can no longer compose, or draw or play the piano. Nothing interests her.

Then slowly, the enormous energy of her curious mind returns. She sells the estate at Bougival and the house on the Rue de Douai, and buys a fourth-floor apartment on the Boulevard de Saint Germain with a balcony overlooking the Seine and the Place de la Concorde. Her surroundings are new, but her books are still with her, her Pleyel grand piano, her favorite paintings and furnishings. Her most treasured possession, Mozart's original score to the opera *Don Giovanni*, is displayed in a cabinet.

The piano calls her, softly at first, then loudly, insistently, and she begins again. She teaches singing. She composes music. She works on a history of French song. The harsh lines of her face soften with age, and her dark hair becomes a white crown. She is no longer the ugly exotic. Dressed in the black and deep violet of perpetual mourning, she has become beautiful. She receives old friends who still remember her greatness and young musicians who know her only as a legend.

When Pyotr Tchaikovsky comes to see her, she speaks endlessly of Ivan Turgenev. There are fewer and fewer people with whom she can speak of him freely, fewer still who knew him. Maman is long gone. She has lost George Sand, Liszt, Gounod, Berlioz, Meyerbeer. Her brother, Manuel Patricio, lives to the great age of 101, but he is in London, and as they near the ends of their lives, neither he nor she are able to travel.

In her late eighties, cataracts begin to cloud her vision, and she begins to lose her hearing. Still, the music plays in her head. She remembers it all, every note.

Time moves rapidly, one year folding into the next. She no longer sleeps, yet the nights fly by, and the great clock at the Palais Bourbon seems to toll the hour every five minutes. On Sundays, she presides over family lunches, which now include seven grand-children and four great-grandchildren. In spite of her poor vision, she reads a lot. She writes a little. She thinks constantly.

On May 16, 1910, in her eighty-ninth year, she says, "I have two days more to live." And then she is silent, although she ges-tures and smiles at people no one else can see. Two days later, she dozes off in her armchair, and as the bell at the Palais Bourbon rings three in the morning, she dies smiling.

Pauline Viardot-Garcia is buried at the Cimetière de Montmartre beside the husband she never left, a continent away from the man she loved.

AFTERWORD

No one knows what the precise nature of the relationship between Pauline Viardot and Ivan Turgenev really was, and it is unlikely that anyone will ever know. In 1896, a provincial French veterinarian with literary ambitions informed the author Alphonse Daudet that he was in possession of a packet of letters from Ivan Turgenev to Pauline Viardot-Garcia, which he had discovered at a Berlin bookshop. Turgenev was already deceased, but Madame Viardot was still living, so an appeal was made to her for permission to publish the letters of the great author. She was appalled. Her son-in-law, George Chamerot, responded that as Madame Viardot had never released any correspondence from Monsieur Turgenev, she could only conclude that the letters must be forged or stolen. In either case, she would prevent their publication through every legal means available to her.

When she was confronted with the actual documents, she realized that in the rush to flee Baden-Baden, the letters had been left behind and had somehow found their way to the Berlin bookseller. Eventually, she was persuaded that a selection could be published, but only under her own editorial control, and provided that the original copies were to remain with her. She chose to "ink out" portions of the few letters she released, eliminating Turgenev's unflattering opinions of his contemporaries, as well as almost all references to his feelings for her, but the relationship insinuated in the letters was still enough to cause a minor uproar.

After the death of Pauline Viardot in 1910, the letters were published in full with the inked-out portions restored wherever possible, and additional letters were discovered.

Only a handful of letters from Madame Viardot to Turgenev have been uncovered, but it is obvious from his letters to her that he loved her passionately, and that his feelings were, at least in part, returned. Biographers disagree widely on the question of whether their love was ever consummated. Some argue convincingly that it must have been chaste; others, just as convincingly, that Turgenev was the father of at least one of Madame Viardot's children, and Paul Viardot never disputed the rumors that Turgenev was his father.

Pauline Viardot's compositions have endured. In addition to more than one hundred songs, many of which have been recorded, she wrote four operettas; an opera, *Cendrillon*; numerous piano works; and two volumes of violin music.